WINNING MISS WAKEFIELD

By Vivienne Lorret

Winning Miss Wakefield
Daring Miss Danvers
"Tempting Mr. Weatherstone" in
Five Golden Rings: A Christmas Collection

WINNING MISS WAKEFIELD

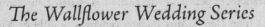

The Wallflower Wedding Series

VIVIENNE LORRET

AVONIMPULSE

An Imprint of HarperCollinsPublishers

Excerpt from *Daring Miss Danvers* copyright © 2014 by Vivienne Lorret.

Excerpt from *Finding Miss McFarland* copyright © 2014 by Vivienne Lorret.

EPub Edition JUNE 2014 ISBN: 9780062315762

Print Edition ISBN: 9780062315779

AM 10 9 8 7 6 5 4 3 2 1

For Michael

PROLOGUE

Hampshire, England, 1816

The manor looked much the same as he remembered it from his youth. Few windows graced the towering limestone façade, and those that did were shuttered and sunken. Barren yew trees flanked either side, resembling the gnarled hands of Death reaching up from hell to reap his grandfather's soul.

Satisfaction pulled Bane's lips into a tight grin. At last, he would reclaim what was rightfully his.

Without anyone to stop him, he strode up the weed-choked walk and through the door.

The grizzled old butler shuffled into the foyer. His one good eye narrowed, he huffed a sound of disgust. No doubt, Bane was the only man with gypsy blood in his veins who had dared cross the threshold.

"Don't worry, Mangus. I'm not here to set the place ablaze," he said as he whipped off his greatcoat and tossed it onto a bench. "At least, not yet."

The butler ignored him and altered his slow procession to head in the direction of the drawing room. "His lordship has been laid out in here, if that's the reason you came."

"It is indeed." Bane clapped his hands together and chafed them back and forth. "I must make sure he's good and dead. Tell me, Mangus, were his final moments terribly painful?"

Not missing a beat, the butler sneered. "You'll be pleased to know he passed peacefully in his sleep."

"You old codger," Bane said with a laugh and chucked him on the shoulder. "If the devil's own could sleep in peace—even for a single night—then there must be hope for us all."

Mangus grunted in response before he turned around and left Bane standing alone beneath the wide arch leading to the drawing room.

A table, covered in black silk, stood before him. The former Marquess of Knightswold had been dressed in all his finery. Wall sconces cast the corpse in eerie shadow, undulating in a way that gave the illusion of breath rising and falling in his grandfather's chest. For the first time since learning the news from the solicitor, a chill slithered down Bane's spine.

After all, if any man could possess enough evil and hatred to resurrect himself from the dead, Bane was staring at him now. His limbs felt full of porridge as he moved closer. However, it was his own pain and rage that propelled him, seeking confirmation.

Marked by spots of age, his grandfather's pallor resembled the ashy remains of a cold hearth. Beneath his paper-thin flesh, generations of aristocracy had formed the broad line of his brow, the bold curve of his nose, and the high set of his cheekbones. However, Bane was equally as certain that obstinacy was the reason for the rigid squareness of his jaw. Well, *that*, and the cloth tied around his chin and knotted at the top of his head to keep his mouth from gaping.

Yes, the Marquess of Knightswold was most assuredly dead.

Two gold sovereigns covered his eyes to pay the ferryman. "It still won't be enough to keep you from the gates of hell," he growled.

Bane expected to feel a sense of victory, of rightness, in knowing that the man who'd murdered his parents and driven his uncle to suicide had finally paid the ultimate price. But other than the anguish that had transformed into rage over the years, only emptiness filled him. Nothing could undo the damage his grandfather had done—and all because of a ruthless pursuit to keep the Fennecourt bloodlines pure.

Staring down at the monster, he fisted his hands and felt his one-quarter gypsy blood surge, boiling beneath his palms. His mother had been half gypsy and proud of her heritage. His father had loved her so dearly that he'd gladly accepted the terms that—should he marry her—he would be cut off completely and no longer recognized by the man who'd sired him.

However, stripping his eldest son of wealth and land hadn't been enough. Since Bane's father was legitimate by birth, the title would have passed to him, no matter what, and from him to Bane. This didn't sit well with the old marquess. He couldn't stand the thought of a mongrel inheriting the title and lands.

So around the time of Bane's thirteenth birthday—a year before his parents were killed—the marquess ordered the church records of marriage between his eldest son and gypsy wife destroyed, in addition to the ledger containing Bane's baptism.

Those acts effectively made Bane nothing more than a bastard in the eyes of society. Of course, there were those who knew what his grandfather had done, but if anyone had dared to speak out, they soon would have found themselves in dire financial straits, in debtors prison, or even in the grave.

The only one who'd stood up for Bane, even after his parents' murder had made the stakes much higher, had been his uncle Spencer. Yet soon, he too was attacked by the Fennecourt patriarch.

Financially crippled and facing the loss of everything he held dear—including the estate that had been in his wife's family for centuries—Spencer could see only one solution to end the tyrannical quest of his father. So on a clear night, three years past, his uncle had stolen into this very house, tied a rope around a beam of the vaulted ceiling in the old marquess's study, and hanged himself directly above the desk.

Undeterred, Bane's grandfather had gone about begetting another heir. Ultimately, a man so completely obsessed with pure bloodlines couldn't risk his title falling into the hands of a gypsy. His efforts, however, were in vain. His young wife and their child had died a mere year ago.

And now there was nothing to stop Bane from taking his revenge.

"Ah, so you *are* here," a familiar voice purred from the doorway. He turned to see his late uncle's wife standing there, bedecked in mourning garb. Absently, he wondered if her new husband, the elderly Lord Sterling, realized what expensive taste Eve had. "I'd wondered if you'd heard."

Bane inclined his head. "Mr. Shirham came to see me late last night with the news."

"Your grandfather's solicitor dropping by to see you? How crafty of him." She sauntered into the room as if she hadn't a care in the world. Yet her expression was cold and closed. She was always careful not to reveal herself, but he already knew it bothered her to be here in this house even more that it did him.

"I believe it's more of a matter of frugality," Bane added with his own degree of detachment. As a young man who'd made his fortune at the tables and track, he knew it never served to reveal too much. While he was fond of Eve— primarily because of how much his uncle had adored her—he never quite trusted her. Then again, he didn't trust anyone. "Without an employer, a solicitor's situation can be fairly bleak." And also, there was no reason to put a man in desperate circumstances if he could be useful.

"You would hire the man who'd conspired with *your grandfather*"—this time she said it with a trace of venom, a notable tell—"to destroy the lives of your parents and my husband?" After a quick intake of breath, she released a hollow laugh and turned her attention to the jewels at her wrist. "How unconventional."

He didn't put much stock in her rancor today or delve too deeply. They both had their reasons for despising the dead man in the room. "Oh, how did he put it?…Something to the effect *that not all who worked for the old marquess shared his beliefs on purity.*"

"And you believe him?" She looked at him as if he were a fool.

"He came bearing gifts." Bane lifted one shoulder in a careless shrug. "Apparently, he'd found a family register at the bottom of a desk drawer years ago and held on to it with this"—he gestured to the shell of the old marquess—"eventuality in mind. It bears the name of my father and the date of his marriage, albeit with a thick line of ink striking through them. Then my birth was listed below it, with another fat line through it. Yet the names remain legible beneath."

For once, Eve had nothing to say. Her eyes gleamed with an uncanny light, as if she were trying hard *not* to reveal the depths of her emotion. However, the oddest thing was, he could almost swear she was furious with *him* and not with his grandfather. Which, he knew, couldn't be the case since he'd done nothing to her.

In the end, he'd taken on the burden of her debt. Of course, he'd done so mostly out of guilt because he still felt partly responsible for the reason Uncle Spencer had taken his own life. Therefore, this reaction from her puzzled him.

Curious. His ability to read people was usually flawless. He counted on it.

"I'll never forgive you for any of it." Eve's quiet whisper drew his attention to where she now stood facing his grandfather's body.

"He doesn't deserve your forgiveness," he said quietly.

She made a sound, something shy of a laugh. After a subtle swipe of her fingers against her cheek, she turned to him, her features carefully in place. "Then it will be only a matter of time before the title is restored to you," Eve said, her lips pressed into a brittle smile as she toyed with the clasp of her diamond bracelet. "What a fine coup. Revenge at last."

At last? No. This was only the beginning.

CHAPTER ONE

London, 1823

Merribeth Wakefield closed the door and leaned against it as if marauders waited on the other side. A single bead of perspiration trickled down her temple.

"It's no use," she said to the only two other occupants of the retiring room. Thankfully, Lady Amherst's other guests in the ballroom below were now progressing to the outdoor amphitheater and wouldn't notice their absence. "The plan won't work."

Aunt Sophie released a slow breath and sank down onto the window seat in a rustle of lavender crepe. "The first hour of *mingling* went even worse than I imagined." Lifting away her brass-rimmed spectacles, she pinched the bridge of her nose.

Much worse. Merribeth expelled a puff of air that stirred the configuration of hot-ironed curls carefully situated over her forehead. The raven tresses threatened to frizz. Yet when she lifted her hand to her brow, she noted that beneath the lace edge of her fingerless gloves, her palms were damp as well. While she'd like to blame the weather, her nerves were the likely culprit, as it was only the first of June. Even so, the breeze from the open window felt divine.

Perhaps, if she locked the door and hid in here for the remainder of the night, no one would notice.

"Stuff and nonsense!" The exclamation came from Aunt Sophie's friend, who stood in front of a bank of mirrors. Lady Eve Sterling—or simply *Eve*, as she preferred not to be reminded of her late husband—gave her cheeks a pinch before drawing the tip of her finger over tawny eyebrows. Once satisfied with her reflection, she shifted her gaze and stared pointedly at Merribeth in the looking glass. "Tonight is your chance to prove you have nothing to hide. That your reputation is faultless, no matter what those wasps downstairs were whispering behind their fans," she needlessly pointed out. "Be brave."

"Brave?" Merribeth's heart had nearly frozen on the spot from the glacial stares she'd received the moment they'd crossed the threshold. "I felt as if I were standing in my shift and stockings and nothing more." *A spectacle on display at the Museum of Wallflower Specimens and Ghastly Occurrences.*

"That would certainly have made for a more interesting party." As it was, the only people invited to Lady Amherst's play were the scandalous—*her*—and the scandalmongers—*everyone else.* Or so it seemed.

"I'm so glad I could add my own turmoil to your list of this evening's entertainment." She should have known Eve wouldn't understand. The woman lived and breathed scandal and likely held a permanent place on Lady Amherst's invitation list.

"Oh, me too, darling," Eve responded with a wide grin, apparently not understanding sarcasm.

Sophie, however, did understand and cast Merribeth a disapproving glare. "Eve was kind enough to procure an invitation at a time when our other options have diminished."

It was true. She was ruined. News of Mr. Clairmore's betrayal, after five years of being *nearly* betrothed, had spread through every fiber of the *ton* like red wine on muslin. Now, for the past ten days, the only correspondences they'd received were apologies and rescinded invitations, as if Mr. Clairmore's leaving was *her* fault. That somehow she was lacking.

Perhaps she was.

She released a sigh. "You're right, Aunt Sophie. Forgive me, Eve. Apparently, my nerves have overrun my manners. I'm having trouble deciding which is worse: blending into the wallpaper as if every gown I wore were a damask print or these sideways glances of speculation."

"At least people notice you're not simply a wallpaper ornament," Eve said as she smoothed her hands down the front of a daringly cut plum-silk gown. Only weeks into mourning the loss of her second husband, no one would ever accuse Eve of blending in. In fact, most men said she rivaled her biblical namesake for Queen Temptress.

"Yes, I'm the piece peeling away from the crown molding," Merribeth muttered under her breath. Everyone noticed a flaw.

"Were we to live in a more primitive society, you could very well have been stoned for the rumors against you. Then again, I suppose this was the *ton*'s way of doing the same, just shy of the cut direct." Sophie retrieved a handkerchief from inside her glove and began to rub the lenses of her spectacles, mulling over them in contemplation.

It wasn't until her distinctive sense of logic was met with silence that she looked up. No doubt, she saw all the color drain from Merribeth's face when she replaced her spectacles. She cleared her throat. "Perhaps coming here was a mistake after all."

Merribeth cringed. Her aunt's more bookish nature didn't always provide her with the sense of comfort she craved. Not that she didn't appreciate all that her aunt had sacrificed over the years, but right at this moment, she wished her mother and father were still alive.

Eve spun around and shook her head. "Not attending would have been tantamount to confirming that Mr. Clairmore found her reputation lacking in some way. After all, he's declared his love for a vicar's daughter. Anyone would look sullied by comparison and, mind you"—she pointed the tip of her fan at Merribeth—"that was precisely the argument that helped procure your invitation."

The argument did nothing to bolster Merribeth's confidence or resume the blood flow to her cheeks. With her aunt and Eve, she need never worry about being coddled. In fact, part of her had always wondered if Eve had insisted on sponsoring her for a Season solely out of charity. Yet anyone who was acquainted with her above a week's time soon realized that Eve didn't possess altruistic intentions, no matter what Aunt Sophie might want to believe.

"Yet this entire scheme won't work if you continue to cower whenever your gaze is met. Stop looking like a stable puppy afraid of being kicked," Eve continued. "You must be confident. Head raised. Shoulders back. You must show them all that you have done nothing to lose Mr. Clairmore's good opinion and that he…merely had cold feet."

"Cold feet," Sophie mused, as if the two words were a cipher.

Merribeth looked from Eve to her aunt and felt like a puzzle missing several pieces. That day in the garden, when Mr. Clairmore had professed his overwhelming ardor for another woman, it hadn't seemed like cold feet to her. It had seemed more maniacal than anything else. He'd been positively possessed.

"It wasn't planned, you see. This violent feeling for Miss Codington has taken me by surprise," he said with a laugh as he looked up to the sky. Closing his eyes, an incandescent smile broke over his face, as if he were reciting a prayer of thanks.

She remembered staring at him, all the while wondering if she'd heard him correctly. Miss Codington, the vicar's daughter? Surely she'd been mistaken. The reason William had wanted to speak with her privately was because he was finally going to make their betrothal official, proposing in a grand romantic gesture. Any moment, he would have kneeled down. She'd been sure of it.

However, his words had disoriented her, forcing her to repeat them inside her mind. Even now, she tried to make sense of what he'd said. Why should feeling violent toward someone make him happy? And shouldn't he feel violently— *whatever that meant*—toward her and not Miss Codington?

Then, when he'd looked at her and his smile hadn't faltered for a single, solitary moment, she'd thought—*hoped*—he would tell her it was all a joke. A horribly cruel joke.

Instead, he'd laughed again and scratched the top of his head, mussing his golden locks in a way she'd never seen him do before. His eyes had been wild, his grin peculiarly lopsided. He'd looked a bit mad. Even more so when he'd reached out, snagged a cluster of lilacs from the overgrown shrub beside her, and buried his nose in the blossoms, inhaling the fragrance with obvious reverence.

"I never knew it could be like this…should be like this. Oh, Merr, I'm quite overcome with the rawness inside me. You would laugh to know how savage I feel when I'm near her, not at all the sedate, even stoic person I've always thought myself to be. Yet one simple kiss changed all that. Her lips…Great heavens! Her lips are like summer wine, and her skin is incredibly soft…soft like butter."

"But," Eve said with enough volume to pull Merribeth out of the memory. The scent of dying lilacs drifted through the open window, mocking her. "There is only one way to end all this speculation. You must get Mr. Clairmore back."

"I must…*what?*" Now, the remaining blood in her body turned as cold as seawater.

Eve held up a hand. "Even if you no longer want him, you must get him back. That is the *only* way to save your reputation."

"The only thing a renewal of Mr. Clairmore's affections could prove would be that he doesn't know his own mind," Sophie intervened. "Besides, you assured me that attending this ghastly event would be the start of restoring her reputation."

Merribeth was inclined to agree with her aunt. After all, that *had* been the plan.

It was like having opposing angels on either side of her. While Sophie and Eve had shared something of a friendship since their debuts nearly eighteen years ago, they couldn't be more different. One was patient and cerebral, while the other had a reputation for causing trouble solely for the sake of her own amusement. Merribeth hoped this new proposal would not fall under the latter's category.

"Precisely. The *ton* will see the alteration in his affections was merely the whim of a young man who didn't know better."

A whim for Mr. Clairmore, perhaps, but for Merribeth, it had been five years of waiting. Five years since William had made the comment about how easy it would be to marry her. Five years since she'd begun to see the future they could have together.

Yet in all those years, absolute certainty had remained elusive. While he'd spoken of marriage and children and a house in the village square, he'd never officially proposed. At least, not to her.

Now, she was no longer certain of anything.

Merribeth doubted Eve's latest plan could change that. "Mr. Clairmore was the one who decided he no longer wanted to marry me. What makes you think he'll change his mind?"

"We all *want* what we cannot have. So let him see that you've moved on without him and *make* him want you."

Ignoring the frisson of warning that slithered down her spine, Merribeth asked, "How?"

A triumphant smile lit Eve's face, rivaling the light emitted from the wall sconces. "Nothing unpleasant, I assure you. Simply spend a few moments in the company of a rake."

Merribeth went still. It certainly wasn't what she'd expected Eve to say. Then again, since when did Lady Eve Sterling say anything expected?

Sophie gasped. "I hardly think a seducer of young women is the answer to my niece's prayers."

"Perhaps she isn't saying the right ones, then." Eve laughed and then quickly pursed her lips. "Oh Sophie, it isn't as if I'm suggesting her ruination."

Her aunt settled her hands on her hips, her mouth a tight line. "Then what?"

"Merely a moment. A flirting glance. A whispered conversation. Perhaps even…a kiss." She held up her hand, as if she were giving a reprimand on decorum, not lecturing on the finer points of debauchery.

"Surely a few more parties and balls, dancing with handsome, *respectable* gentlemen would work just as well," Sophie coolly suggested. The only problem was, they weren't receiving new invitations to parties or balls. By the silence that followed, everyone in the room realized it too—which left only Eve's option.

"Kissing a rake will make her feel desirable. Confident. Every woman knows that when she feels a certain way, it shows. Men are drawn to that," Eve said simply, as if she held an apple in her hands and had asked them both to take a bite, whispering a promise that *it wouldn't hurt anything*.

Against her better judgment, Merribeth found her interest sparked. Was there a way to get Mr. Clairmore back, along with her future and her sense of certainty? While Eve's plan seemed far-fetched at best, her manner of delivery was persuasive. Eve exuded confidence in all aspects of her life. In turn, men were drawn to her like black threads to white cambric—

What was she thinking? She couldn't possibly be considering this. "We'll be attending your house party by the end of this week. Therefore, I won't even see Mr. Clairmore in time to make him jealous." Not to mention, she was more inclined to rail at him for the havoc he'd caused instead of attempting to lure him back.

"I'll invite Mr. Clairmore to the ball on the last night of the party and suggest in the invitation that it will be his chance to make amends." As if the matter were settled with Merribeth, Eve turned to Sophie and pressed her hands together in a gesture of supplication. "If that toad Mr. Clairmore had ever kissed our dear girl with any ounce of fervor, then she wouldn't be one step away from shriveling up like a grape left unattended on the vine. Just look at her, Soph. Doesn't she deserve a chance to experience what we both felt when we were younger, however fleeting it was?"

A shriveled grape, indeed! Merribeth's lips parted at the insult. She felt as if she were watching Lady Amherst's play after all. Any moment, the crowd would start to applaud, and the curtain would fall.

But then, to her surprise, her aunt's thoughtful gaze darted from Eve to her, as if the comment were a widely accepted fact, and the idea of kissing a rake held merit.

"It's the surest way to save her reputation and mend her broken heart," Eve said, pulling Sophie nearer to her way of thinking. Her aunt's pale brow furrowed for an instant.

Eve offered a small nod, as if an understanding passed between these friends.

That is enough! It was one thing to refer to her as an aging fruit but quite another to presume to know the inner workings of her heart, broken or otherwise. Lately, she'd been too confused and angry to decide exactly how she felt. At the very least, she should be allowed to decide for herself.

Merribeth released a frustrated breath that blew the curls from her forehead. "Forgive me for mentioning this, but I'm still in the room."

"Gracious!" Eve said with a laugh and snapped open her fan, half-hiding behind it. "With your Wakefield brow, you look positively mocking."

A fact that could hardly be helped. She was, after all, a Wakefield.

While her late mother had been touted as a pure beauty, with flaxen hair and soft beatific features, Merribeth had inherited her father's devilishly dark hair and sharp, angular eyebrows. During his life, he'd been famous for the severe arch. However, her feminine version of the same had only brought her censure. Those who did not take the time to know her assumed her mocking countenance meant she saw herself as superior.

As a gently bred woman with no dowry to speak of, that was hardly the case. Only her aunt and her closest friends in the needlework circle truly knew her. Oh, how she wished Penelope, Emma, and Delaney were here to help her through this evening.

Merribeth did her best to school her features and rearranged the fall of curls over her forehead for good measure, silently wishing that her Wakefield brow was the only flaw in her appearance.

Sophie didn't seem to notice and instead walked toward the door. "We should return. I'm certain we've missed the first act by now. Surely we can discuss this new plan to greater depth before your party."

"Of course," Eve said, closing her fan with a snap, a slow grin curling the corners her mouth as they started down the hall. When they neared the stairs, she stopped abruptly. "Devil take it! I've forgotten my lorgnette."

Sophie placed her hand on the polished rail. "I'm certain you'll see the play clearly enough. It is a very small amphitheater."

"The lorgnette isn't for the play, darling," Eve purred as she turned to Merribeth and glanced down the hallway. "How careless of me. I must have left my reticule in the study when I stole in there for a glass of port earlier. Merribeth, be a dear and fetch them for me. It's just at the end of this hall and around the corner."

Merribeth hesitated, suddenly suspicious of the *tragedy* of the missing reticule.

Turning her, Eve gave her a playful push. "But of course, I would never forgive you if you hid in the study all evening. So, hurry back. We'll save a place in the back row for you."

Even though the specter of suspicion loomed overhead, Merribeth had to admit that the idea of doing exactly what Eve suggested she *not* do was so appealing that she went without argument. After all, the likelihood of her aunt's friend introducing her to unscrupulous gentlemen when she returned was too high to ignore.

As she walked at a fine clip down the hall, the thought was enough to expose the raw edges of her irritation *and* her Wakefield brow again. *Heaven forbid.*

"If I feel like hiding in the study for the rest of the evening, I will. Or if I feel like handing over Eve's reticule to a footman and then hiring a hack to drive me home, I'll do that too," she said to herself with an admirable degree of conviction.

The latter held the most promise.

Finding the study, she pulled open the door, hoping to retrieve the reticule and then leaving Lady Amherst's immediately. However, the light inside the room was dim, with only the wall sconces behind her to aid her search.

In the center of the room, two leather wingback chairs and a tufted sofa faced an unlit hearth. A large desk sat against the far wall. No reticule in sight. Yet she soon realized that with the curtains drawn in the room, her trespass into the study could easily be discovered by any of the guests outside.

Not wanting any more attention this evening, Merribeth quietly closed the doors.

Now, the only illumination came from the parted curtains, where the glow of torchlight from the outdoor stage filtered in like strands of pale gold silk. The muffled voices of the actors and a spattering of laughter from the audience drifted in as well, pulling her across the room and toward the tall, narrow window.

From this vantage point, she could see everything of the play and the audience alike. Now *they* were the spectacles on display, and she had the best seat in the house.

At last, she felt her anxiety and irritation abate. The thought of leaving without anyone the wiser, returning to the small townhouse at the end of Danbury Lane and steeling into the kitchen for a hot cup of coffee put a smile on her lips. A genuine smile too, not the one she affected for society.

Here, in her solitude, she needn't worry about concealing the slight gap between her front teeth or the high arch of her brow.

From the corner of her eye, she spotted the glimmer of light reflecting off a series of cut crystal decanters atop a richly glossed cabinet. Reminded of how Eve had confessed to sneaking in here for a glass of port, she wondered if there might be brandy in addition to port. She'd always wanted to try brandy. However, Aunt Sophie didn't allow spirits, only wine.

Feeling daring, as if Eve's challenge for her to be brave had woven itself into the fiber of her soul, she quickly made up her mind. After all, this could be her only chance.

The only problem was, she wasn't sure which decanter was filled with brandy.

Lifting up the stoppers one by one, she sniffed. Each of the five had a different aroma, from fruity and floral to woodsy and oaken.

Not knowing which was which, she decided it was best to pour a splash from each decanter into the waiting tumbler. Then, as she'd seen gentlemen do, she picked up the glass and swirled the contents. All the better to mix it, she supposed.

She gave it a tentative whiff and wrinkled her nose. *Strange.* The combined fragrances weren't at all pleasant. Nevertheless, she was determined to try this concoction. Closing her eyes and holding her breath, she touched the rim of the glass to her lips—

A throat cleared. A decidedly low rumble of a sound. A very *male* sound.

Merribeth's eyes flew open on a gasp.

Turning, she suddenly realized she wasn't alone.

CHAPTER TWO

In the dim light, Merribeth could barely make out the silhouette sprawled atop the tufted sofa. What she'd discerned at first glance as a haphazard heap of cloaks was now stirring to life. The rumpled mass took form, rising languidly, like the first curls of smoke from a chimney.

Her pulse was anything but languid. It raced hard and fast beneath the flesh of her throat. A whispered voice in her head urged her to flee.

However, her feet weren't cooperating. It was as if she'd actually turned into the wallpaper she'd accused herself of being moments ago. Now, she felt trapped, forever pasted to this spot. She stared, unblinking, as the indistinct outline of a head atop a pair of expansive shoulders crested in front of the camelback sofa.

A man, then. She'd guessed as much from sound of his clearing his throat. Yet somehow, the confirmation escalated her riotous pulse.

The stranger remained in the shadows, his features obscured by the darkness. The spill of light from the window merely glanced across the toes of his boots. From their glossy points, she could see he wasn't a servant but likely a guest. She should have felt relieved. However, knowing the type of guests on Lady Amherst's list, this did not quiet her pulse a bit.

After all, his presence in a darkened room did not speak of someone looking for gossip but one escaping it. *Why?*

The more her eyes adjusted to the darkness, the more she took note of his shape, or more so his position. He remained carelessly sprawled, legs apart and bent at the knee, as if he were perfectly at home. Even in her limited experience with the opposite sex, she knew a gentleman would sit erect and cross his legs in the presence of an unmarried woman. He most certainly wouldn't sit so…so brazenly.

Perhaps he was no gentleman at all, then.

Instantly, she recalled Eve's adapted plan, which only made the coincidence of the "forgotten reticule" highly suspect. Most likely, she'd arranged the whole thing beforehand. Obviously, this man was part of a scheme. Meaning this man was, in fact, a rake.

Her pulse leaped higher in her throat, tripping at first and then sprinting like a rabbit from a fox. Only this fox—if Eve had her way of things—was set loose for the purpose of *kissing* the rabbit, not *killing* it. At the moment, Merribeth didn't know which unnerved her more: the prospect of the former or the latter.

With effort, she swallowed. "Why are you here, sir?"

"Apparently to watch a miserable attempt at suicide." With one arm draped over the back of the sofa, he lifted the other—which happened to be holding an empty tumbler—in a mock salute. "In vain, I tried to remain silent. For your sake. However, for mine, please do not drink that ghastly concoction. I should hate to be forced to explain your death to Lady Amherst."

She didn't know him, not from the sound of his voice at any rate. Certainly she would have remembered such a resonant baritone. Each enunciated word possessed a deep rumble, almost an echo, bringing to mind the sound of horses galloping in the distance. It was not a voice one could forget.

"Lady Amherst would relish the uproar of scandal from a death at one of her gatherings," she whispered, rambling out of a need to collect her bearings.

"Precisely why I should hate to be the one to tell her." He offered a dramatic sigh, as if pretending to be bored by their exchange. Yet she suspected he was grinning. "You'd leave me without a choice but to join the audience below, slip in unnoticed, and then feign surprise when one of the servants discovered your corpse."

She refused to laugh, even though the bizarre and inappropriate impulse was there all the same, tugging at the corners of her mouth. "I should hardly think this will kill me," she said with false bravado, lifting the glass once more. Only now did she notice that her fingers were damp. Most likely, she'd spilled some of her experimental blend when he'd startled her.

Strangely enough, it occurred to her that she was no longer startled. Her hands weren't shaking. Her pulse had slowed to a more sedate canter. The only thing she could attribute it to was the sound of his voice—deep, resonant…hypnotic.

"Perhaps not, but it wounds my sense of taste greatly."

He stood, moving unhurriedly as before, as if he did not want to frighten her. Or perhaps it was simply his way, not to rush. He didn't have the loose-limbed cockiness of a man her age, springing to attention with the desire to impress everyone with his agility and form. No, the stranger moved with a languorous arrogance of a man more settled into his skin. A sort of graceful conceit that suggested entitlement.

Now was certainly the time to flee, if ever there was one. She'd allowed his voice to lure her into a sense of calm. Still, she was aware of everything, watchful—nervous, certainly, but not as much as she should be—and more alert than alarmed.

For all she knew, he could be like one of those carnivorous flowers she'd read about in one of Sophie's scientific journals—lying in wait, luring in his prey, and then slowly seizing and devouring.

He chuckled, as if he'd read her thoughts. "Might I approach?"

"For what purpose, sir?" She swallowed, watching as his shadowy arm reach inside his tailcoat.

In the next instant, he withdrew a pristine white handkerchief. He held it out far enough for the light to fall upon it, making it shine like a beacon in the room. "An uncharacteristically chivalrous one, I assure you."

Merribeth stared, transfixed, as he took a step forward, allowing the light to fall on him too. She nearly gasped when she saw his face. She did know him. Or at least knew *of* him.

The Marquess of Knightswold, though everyone referred to him as Bane. He'd made his fortune in gambling. It was rumored that he'd bankrupted more than his share of gentle-men at the tables. Also, he was a rake of the first order, or so she'd heard. Positively unapologetic and irredeemable. He'd even tried to seduce one of her dearest friends, Emma Dan-vers, lately Emma Goswick, Viscountess Rathburn.

His hair was darker than hers, coal black and pushed away from his forehead in a careless, slightly mussed manner, as if a woman had recently run her fingers through it. Not that she would know what that looked like—though knowing he was a rake, she couldn't seem to keep her thoughts away from the scandalous possibilities.

Beneath a thick brow, he returned her appraisal. She'd recognized him by his eyes. No one could forget those. Like gray satin, they possessed an iridescent quality that made them appear as if they were lit from within and not reflecting the light around them. Looking at them now, she was nearly afraid of their intensity. If she were the superstitious sort, she might believe he could see directly through her clothes.

Right on cue, as if he'd heard her thoughts and found her struggle amusing, he chuckled. His full lips spread in a grin that was too gradual to be considered mocking. Yet she felt mocked all the same.

Uncharacteristically chivalrous, indeed. Her Wakefield brow arched, and she quickly brushed her hair out of the way so that he could see her disapproval and be warned. "Chivalry is not a purpose."

"True." He offered a nod. "I consider it more of a pursuit," he said, emphasizing the last word as he took another step toward her, forcing her to take a step back.

He was trying to be clever.

She narrowed her eyes, despising that she was the source of his amusement or anyone else's. Her irritation returned. "Of all the rumors circulating about you, a pursuit of chivalry is not among them."

He flashed his teeth in something of a grin. However, the even rows of perfectly white teeth were emphasized by four sharp canine points where the upper and lower met, making him look entirely too feral. This particular *grin* spoke more of danger than amusement. "Good. I was worried we'd have to go through the tedium of introductions."

Merribeth had manners enough to blush at her own rudeness. Glancing down, she readied an apology, only to find her attention fixed on his unexpected movement. In a slow sweep, he lifted his hand as he reached for her—no, not *her* exactly, but her *glass*.

She could have easily thwarted his advance or denied him access by moving out of his reach. He wasn't blocking her retreat. He was merely standing in front of her. Yet for reasons unknown to her, she didn't stop him.

Without asking permission, he slid his hand over the cut crystal, grazing the tips of her fingers. Even then, he pressed on.

He continued, sliding his fingers between hers, nudging them apart. It was like holding hands, only this felt *and looked* far more intimate. His hand was large, his skin much darker than her own. Blunt-tipped fingers spread hers wide enough that she felt the stretch and pull of the sensitive webbing beneath the lace edge of her gloves.

A staggered breath escaped her. Tingles began to dance over her skin to a strangely foreign tune, driven mainly by the percussive beat of her pulse. It was fast again, though not entirely from fear.

Of course, fear was part of it. Fear of the unknown. She didn't know him. Didn't know what he intended. All she knew was that Eve said kissing a rake would give her confidence and mend a broken heart. The idea seemed less absurd by the moment.

His fingertips nuzzled into her sensitive flesh and lingered. The tingles dancing along her skin followed her pulse like the Pied Piper, from her wrists, to her throat, to the warmth between her breasts. Further down, the piper abandoned his flute in favor of a drum. When she lifted her gaze to meet Lord Knightswold's, the light in his eyes shimmered, blazing with silver heat.

Suddenly, she imagined all those tingles taking the shape of pagans lit by moonlight. Wild and naked, they danced around this drum in a circle. A bead of perspiration trickled between her breasts.

"You're wet," he said in a voice that seemed to possess secret, intimate knowledge of things no gently bred woman dared think about.

She pulled back abruptly, leaving the tumbler in his hand. Only then did she remember the handkerchief he held in his other hand. Only then did it occur to her that he was commenting on the wetness of her fingers. *But of course he was.*

She blushed. Too late to recover from her embarrassment, she took the handkerchief and began to blot the dampness from her fingers.

"Now, what were you sneaking in here to try?" he mused, making it obvious with the way he turned his attention to the decanters that he wasn't looking for her to answer.

From the corner of her eye, she watched him tap the tip of his finger against his lip. She had the sense that he was allowing her a moment to recover. That was, until he slipped his fingertip into his mouth and tasted the remnants of the mixture that had been on her skin. Something inside her tightened in a way that forced her to close her eyes. She blew out a slow exhale.

"Let's see.… Were you after the port?" He made a show of sampling the flavor lingering on his tongue. Lifting one decanter, he inhaled and studied her with a sideways glance, as if he meant to read the answer in her expression.

She schooled her features into a perfectly neutral glower of disapproval.

He shook his head and set it down on the tray. "No. Far too bold and full bodied for a delicate palate." If he noticed how she bristled at his presumption, he gave nothing away and lifted a second decanter. "Perhaps the scotch? Hmm…" He sniffed and made a show of wrinkling his nose in distaste. "Smoky and dry. Most likely, aged in a room of cigar-smoking old men. There isn't an ounce of adventure in this spirit. And it's my guess that it was adventure you were after."

"You know nothing of me," she said, unable to hold her tongue a moment longer. She'd experienced a symphony of emotions in the past few minutes, but she never quite lost her undertone of anger. She was angry at Mr. Clairmore for betraying her. Angry at Lady Amherst for inviting her. Angry at Eve for putting her in this position. And especially angry at being the source of both speculation and amusement. "Rumors are not always founded in truth, I hope you realize."

He didn't look at her but kept to his task of sniffing decanters. His grin, however, spoke volumes.

Suddenly, she felt as if he'd herded her into that outburst solely to hear her admit that, perhaps, she knew nothing of him either. Nothing but rumor.

Touché, Lord Knightswold.

"Brandy," he said after a moment and turned to regard her. His gaze drifted to her mouth, as intimate as a caress. "You have brandy-sipping lips. Supple, with the slightest pout where their color changes from dusky pink to a deeper shade. No doubt, you even prefer coffee over tea." He *tsked* as if the heat blooming on her cheeks was from his uncovering a shocking preference for coffee instead of from his brazen compliment.

No man had ever said such things to her or about her. She wasn't sure how to respond. Not knowing bothered her. She was always sure of herself. Even when William had ended their five-year understanding, she'd known precisely what to say.

Yet now, her tongue was mute, and her head was filled with the sound of Knightswold's voice, as if her brain matter consisted of warm Christmas pudding, deeply spiced and velvety.

While she was thinking, he'd withdrawn a short tulip-shaped glass from the lower cabinet, poured in a splash of liquid amber, and began swirling it with the bowl resting in his hand. "Warming it improves the fragrance. The glass is shaped to better appreciate the subtle nuances."

Warmed by the heat of his hands. She had no idea why the thought made her breathless. Perhaps it was because she could still feel the tingles he'd created. Those moonlit pagans were sitting in a drum circle now, waiting for the music to begin, as if they sensed that another performance wasn't far off.

He lifted the glass, offering it to her, but she kept her hands by her sides. With a chuckle, he set the glass down. "It's for the best. Our hands were getting *far* too familiar."

She chose to ignore him and reached for the glass. As he'd done, she slipped the stem between the base of her fingers, resting the bowl in her palm. Tentatively, she swirled the golden liquid and lifted it to her nose. The sharp, fruity fragrance made the glands at the back of her jaw sting, but pleasantly, as if readying her tongue for a delight.

"Crisp, sweet apples," she said, marveling at this discovery. It hadn't smelled like this when she'd merely sniffed the decanter.

He smiled like a professor to his pupil. "Take a sip and let it linger on your tongue."

She didn't want to blush, but she couldn't help it. One moment she was fine and the next, she felt those pagans stand at attention. The drum beat in a slow, steady rhythm. A gentleman would not mention her tongue. A gentleman would pretend it didn't exist for the sake of propriety. Not Lord Knightswold, however. He spoke to her like she imagined men spoke to Eve. Like Mr. Clairmore had spoken of Miss Codington.

Normally, the only conversations she'd shared with men were more mundane talks about the weather or her needlepoint. Yet Lord Knightswold had commented on her tongue, as well as her dusky pink, brandy-sipping lips. While the things he said were shockingly bold, she didn't mind as much as she professed to. After all, tonight was about being brave and confident.

This could be her last night in society, aside from Eve's house party at the end of the week. Beyond that—if Eve's plan didn't work—she would be a spinster, and no man, well bred or otherwise, would speak to her, except out of censure and speculation. And after tonight, Merribeth had had her fill of speculation.

She would rather endure a dozen more blushes than return to Lady Amherst's guests.

Merribeth took a sip, letting the liquid slide over her tongue. The first taste was slightly sharp but quickly mellowed to a sweet hint of caramel. The more the brandy lingered, the more the caramel transformed, the flavor deepening to something rich and creamy yet smoky. When she swallowed, the finish was slightly nutty, and she widened her eyes in amazement.

"Astounding!" She smiled, forgetting the gap between her front teeth for a moment. However, she remembered quickly enough when his gaze drifted to her mouth. Out of habit, she lifted her hand to conceal it. "I never realized how complex a spirit could be. The flavors altered several times, each one more intriguing than the last."

He frowned, his brow lowering to cast his eyes in shadow. "Why did you do that—hide your mouth?"

To society at large, the flaw in her smile put her on the level with Chaucer's *Wife of Bath*—a woman who could not control her lust. The simple fact that her virtue had never been remotely in jeopardy had never mattered. The *ton* had judged by her appearance.

Her diastema, also known as the Sign of Venus, was considered too vulgar for polite conversation. So of course, Lord Knightswold would take notice. "Though no one has ever mentioned it to me directly"—she stared at him pointedly—"I've read *The Canterbury Tales*. I've borne the scrutiny."

"My, you are quite the scandalous creature." He grinned, brushing the pad of his thumb across his bottom lip in a way that made hers tingle. Likely, he'd done it on purpose to keep her unsettled. "Born with a smile that makes men and women alike think of dimly lit rooms, stolen moments, and endless hours of—"

"Why are you here?" she interrupted, though she was certain he had a dozen or more scandalous exploits to keep him on Lady Amherst's list indefinitely, thereby taking the focus off of her. She took another sip of brandy.

He watched her closely for a moment and then turned, heading toward the curtained window. "I lost a bet."

"You?" Merribeth took a longer sip, her breath fogging the glass. She enjoyed the way the nuances of the brandy kept her thoughts occupied.

He offered a negligent shrug. "I thought I would try it in an effort to free myself from monotony."

With his back to her, she decided to pour another splash into her glass and proceeded to warm it in her hand. "You lost on purpose, for the novelty?"

"Yes, and for the sake of keeping my friends. One cannot win all the time and still keep one's friends. Besides, I'd been accused of being a rustic. I lost to serve two purposes."

She laughed at that before she took another drink. This brandy was remarkable. Warming and smooth. She felt relaxed and…liquid. No longer rigid and inhibited. "Yet you are here, in a darkened room, where no one is likely to see you or even know you are present."

He cast a sardonic glance over his shoulder. "You found me."

"True. Much to my own embarrassment." She'd fallen right into Eve's trap. Although, she had to admit, when it came to men, perhaps Eve knew a thing or two.

Or three.

The idea made her giggle.

He turned and tsked at her in mock disapproval, like before. "You are, perhaps, the quickest drunkard I've ever witnessed."

"Hardly." She snorted. And because the sound was startling, foreign, and downright unmannerly, she giggled again. "I've had *barrels* more wine than this." Wine with dinner, at any rate—which brought to mind the fact that she hadn't eaten the dinner that evening. She'd been too nervous about attending the play.

"Most likely watered down."

She nodded absently in agreement. Aunt Sophie *would* water down the wine. Thinking that he might have a point about drinking too much too quickly, she set down the glass and released a little sigh of farewell to her first and possibly *last* taste of brandy.

"Now, give back my handkerchief," he said, holding out his hand as he returned to her side. "You're the sort to keep it as a memento. I cannot bear the thought of my handkerchief being worshipped by a forlorn *miss* by moonlight or tucked away with mawkish reverence beneath a pillow."

The portrait he painted was so laughable that she smiled, heedless of exposing her flaw. "You flatter yourself. Here." She dropped it into his hand as she swept past him, prepared to leave. "I have no desire to touch it a moment longer. I will leave you to your pretense of sociability."

"'Tis no pretense. I have kept good company this evening."

Either the brandy had gone to her head, impairing her hearing, or he'd actually sounded sincere. She paused, resting her hands on the carved rosewood filigree that edged the top of the sofa. "Much to my own folly. I never should have listened to Lady Eve Sterling. It was her lark that sent me here."

"Oh? How so?" He feigned believable surprise, but she knew better.

If it weren't for the brandy, she would have left by now. Merribeth rarely had patience for such games, and she knew his question was part of a game he must have concocted with Eve. "She claimed to have forgotten her reticule and sent me here to fetch it—no doubt wanting me to find you."

He looked at her as if confused. *But Bane and Eve must know each other*, she told herself. Why send her in search of a missing reticule when there was none to be found? Regardless, his company had turned out to be exactly the diversion she'd needed, and she was willing to linger. "I've no mind to explain it to you. After all, you were abetting her plot, lying in wait on this very sofa." She brushed her fingers over the smooth fabric, thinking of him lying there in the dark. "Not that I blame you. Lady Eve is a difficult person to whom to say no. However, I will conceal the truth from her, and we can carry on as if her plan came to fruition. It would hardly have served its purpose anyway."

He moved toward her, his broad shoulders outlined by the distant torchlight filtering in through the window behind him. "Refresh my memory then. What was I meant to do whilst in her employ?"

She blushed again. Was he going to make her say the words aloud? No gentleman would.

So, of course, *he* would. She decided to get it over with as quickly as possible. "She professed that a kiss from a rake could instill confidence and mend a broken heart."

He stopped, impeded by the sofa between them. His brow lifted in curiosity. "Have you a broken heart in need of mending?"

The deep murmur of his voice, the heated intensity in his gaze, and quite possibly the brandy all worked against her better sense and sent those tingles dancing again.

Oh, yes, she thought as she looked up at him. *Yes, Lord Knightswold. Mend my broken heart.*

However, her mouth intervened. "I don't believe so." She gasped at the realization. "I should, you know. After five years, my heart should be in shreds. Shouldn't it?"

He turned before she could read his expression and then sat down on the sofa, affording her a view of the top of his head. "I know nothing of broken hearts or their mending."

"Pity," she said, distracted by the dark silken locks that accidentally brushed her fingers. "Apparently, neither do I."

However accidental the touch of his hair had been, now her fingers threaded through the fine strands with untamed curiosity and blatant disregard for propriety.

Lord Knightswold let his head fall back, permitting—perhaps even encouraging—her to continue. She did, without thought to right, wrong, who he was, or who she was supposed to be. Running both hands through his hair, massaging his scalp, she watched his eyes drift closed.

Then, Merribeth Wakefield did something she never intended to do.

She kissed a rake.

CHAPTER THREE

The soft press of her lips wasn't entirely unexpected. She'd been gazing fixedly on his mouth, and a kiss seemed the obvious conclusion. But Bane would have put money against her going through with it. She wasn't the spontaneous, reckless sort, or else she wouldn't have waited all these years for her first taste of brandy.

Bane didn't know her name, anything about her background, or her circumstances. At the moment, it didn't matter.

Typically, he knew everyone—the result of spending most of his life waiting for another sharp knife to plunge into his back. One could never be too careful.

Yet within moments of their unexpected meeting, he'd gained a sense that she wasn't like the others. She didn't have an ulterior motive. None that he discerned, at any rate.

She'd merely found herself caught off guard by his presence and then lingered out of curiosity. He'd made sure of it. He'd wanted to make her curious. Wanted her to linger, which was…*odd* for him, although the reason it was odd escaped him at present.

He had been thoroughly distracted by Miss *No Name*, Miss *Sign of Venus*, as she ran her fingers through his hair. It felt heavenly. Wondrous. Divine. How long had it been since a woman had simply stroked his hair? Though he'd never admit it if asked, this was one of life's greatest pleasures.

Closing his eyes, he'd trusted this stranger more than he had anyone in years, and he couldn't put reason behind it, only the instinctive sense he'd come to rely upon. He was good at figuring people out, which was why he preferred the company of horses.

Then, a shadow had crossed over his face, accompanied by a hushed rustle of silk. Drowsily, he opened his eyes to see her gazing down at him. Her soft fingertips petted the shorter hair at his temples and followed the line of his whiskers to the lobes of his ears.

He'd opened his mouth to tell her that he'd willingly pay her five hundred pounds per annum if she'd never stop, but she shushed him with a shake of her head.

"Don't say a word…please," she'd whispered, leaning closer. "I only mean to borrow this for a moment and return it directly."

Then she'd lowered her mouth to his.

The kiss was sweet, filled with promises she had no notion of fulfilling. With her head tilted to the side, her dimpled chin rested against his cheek. He could feel the warm rush of her exhale fan beneath his jaw.

He fought the urge to return the kiss. He wasn't interested in tutoring virgins. He enjoyed women who were already broken in and saddle ready. He was no one's riding instructor. That was a job left for those sods who had to marry to produce a legitimate heir. He had more important things to do.

However, at the moment, he couldn't think of a single one.

The press of her mouth turned to small nibbles, tiny sips that pulled his flesh between hers. The swells of her modest bosom nestled the top of his head, providing him with simultaneous sensations.

Absently, he wondered if this was still the borrowed kiss or the one she meant to *return directly*. The more she continued, the more desperately he needed to know the answer. Because, surprisingly enough, he didn't want it to end.

Still, Bane controlled the impulse to guide her, to teach her to use her tongue to—

She opened her mouth, sliding the tip of her delicious brandy-flavored tongue along the seam of his lips, scraping the bottom one with her teeth. He gripped the cushion beneath him. Her fingers flitted about his throat—pausing at his pulse, tracing his Adam's apple—and then slipped beneath his cravat and collar. She pulled his upper lip into her mouth and suckled him for one mind-altering, devastating moment.

He was undone.

Unable to contain this unexpected desire a moment longer, he growled.

The sound startled her. She drew back abruptly.

He wished he could have held out longer.

Covering her mouth, she stared down at him, her eyes blinking slowly as if trying to understand what had happened. If she figured it out, he hoped she would enlighten him, because he was just as baffled.

"I—" he began, but before he could utter another syllable, his Venus turned on her heel and ran out the door.

It was for the best, he supposed. After all, he hadn't had a clue how to finish that sentence.

The following morning, Bane stared up at the sky blue coffered ceiling in his bedchamber and listened to the commotion in the hallway. His valet was doing his best to dissuade his unwanted guest from barging in, but it sounded as if he was losing the battle.

He grunted in mild annoyance. However, a man could not lie abed all day, staring at the ceiling, or else he might find himself comparing each shadow and highlight to the exact shade of a certain woman's eyes. Which, of course, he would never do.

The door opened, slamming against the wall. "Really, Bane! A guard at the door?"

"My lord, I—"

Without breaking his focus from the ceiling, Bane lifted a hand. "It's fine, Bitters. I am awake now." Who could sleep through all that caterwauling, if he'd managed to sleep at all? "Better luck next time."

When the door closed, Lady Eve Sterling let out a huff. "When Bitters told me you were still abed, I scarcely believed him. You never sleep late. Are you ill?"

"Ill of company, at the moment." He groaned and sat up, swinging his legs off the side of the bed as the counterpane pooled at his waist. Normally, he slept in the nude. Yet today, he was grateful to have already dressed when he'd set to prowling the house in the wee hours before dawn. "Were you concerned for my health, Auntie?"

Being a mere six years his senior, Eve loathed it when he called her *Auntie*, but it was the least she deserved. Instinct told him she was to blame for the reason he hadn't slept. Well, instinct and the fact that his Venus had used her name.

"Merely wanting to make certain I'm in your will." She breezed in and dropped her gloves and reticule on the cushion of a dark leather wingback chair near the hearth. "Without an heir, surely you would leave everything to me."

Most likely, she was here angling for one thing or another, wanting to see if the plan she'd cooked up last night had worked. However, whatever this new scheme entailed still remained a mystery.

Apparently looking to make herself comfortable, she moved toward the window and flung open the drapes. Sunlight streamed in, stinging his eyes. He winced and scrubbed a hand over his face. He hoped a pot of coffee would chase away the fog from his brain.

"You hang on my sleeve quite heavily. In fact, your yearly allowance, in addition to your staff's salaries, all comes out of my pocket. Therefore, it stands to reason you will be well provided for. Unless, of course, you exceed the generous stipend..." He paused mid-thought. There could be another reason for her unexpected visit. "Are you in deep again? Is that why you are here?"

He squinted in order to look at her. She wore her usual false smile and calculating stare above a green riding habit. Her pale hair was pinned beneath a high, feathered hat perched to one side. The ensemble was new, and he was sure to receive the bill by week's end. "If you have bet on the wrong horse again, I shall be very cross with you. How many times have I told you to bet only on mine?"

She lifted her eyes to the ceiling he'd been studying for hours, but the hue didn't hold her attention as it had his. "Is that what you think of me—that I only show up begging for money? You wound me, Bane. Truly."

He doubted it but held his tongue.

"Actually, I came to reprimand you for reneging on our bet, *Captain Sharp*."

Here it was. Eve always liked to renegotiate as she went along. He never reneged. "As agreed upon, when I *allowed* you to win at cards, I accepted Lady Amherst's invitation, and I attended the gathering."

"Holing yourself up in the study was hardly attending. No one even knew you were there."

Apparently, *she'd* known exactly where he was.

Standing, he pulled on a charcoal silk banyan and tied the sash around his waist. "As I recall, my acceptance and presence were the only two stipulations of our wager."

"Mingling was implied, as you well know," she said on the way to his dressing table.

"Then what are you after, hmm? Come to call me out? Will it be swords or pistols?" When she didn't respond—her focus was on rummaging through a flat walnut box filled with his medals and a few odds and ends—he made a comment sure to get her attention. "I imagine Lord Amberdeen would be more than happy to be your second."

She threw something at him. Expecting the mild retaliation, he caught the object squarely in his hand. It was his grandfather's signet ring. He remembered the pleasure he'd felt when he'd removed it from his cold, dead finger.

"Resorting to petty cruelty?" Eve asked. "My, you must be in a state. Tell me, what has you so ruffled this morning, or should I say *afternoon*?"

His thoughts quickly veered to a more pleasant memory. *Venus.* She was all he could think of. Her sky blue eyes, her blushes, her wit, *her kiss.* "I'm perfectly unruffled."

It seemed silly in the light of day. He hadn't lost sleep over a woman, let alone a virgin, in…well, frankly, never. If he wanted a woman, he had her. There had never been any need to lose sleep over one, even when he was a lad. That was, after all, how he'd earned his nickname. He'd had an afternoon tumble with a dairymaid just off school grounds. When he'd rejoined his party, he had a blossom of wolfsbane tangled in his hair. The name *Bane* had stuck ever since.

"Hmm…" she said, linking her hands before her and casually moving toward the window. "Perhaps a stint at my country manor will put you back in good humor."

Typically, the more he thwarted her, the more she revealed. "As you well know, my estate is a mere ten miles from yours. Besides with Gypsy coming in to foal in a matter of weeks, I'll be dropping by daily." Though the dark Arabian belonged to him, he kept her at Eve's stables for the time being, out of harm's way.

Unfortunately, the sire to her foal, Rhamnous, was unpredictable of late, crashing through the stalls, biting the groomsmen, and making the other horses nervous. Bane had seen it happen with former racing Thoroughbreds before. Some had a hard time letting go of the thrill of competition.

Yet sooner or later, they mellowed. Either that or broke one of their legs trying to escape and race one last time.

"True," she murmured, toying with the edge of the dark velvet drapes. "However, since I'll be hosting a party, it would be rude of you to simply pop over and not stay for the duration."

Bitters knocked on the door and brought in a tray of coffee and cakes, leaving it on the console by the door before disappearing without a word. That was precisely why he liked his valet. He didn't feel the need to speak for the sake of filling the air with the sound of his voice. A very admirable quality.

Bane picked at the cake, ensuring there weren't any currants hiding inside. His cook seemed to believe they were food of the gods. She put them in nearly every pastry. Since she was the same cook his father had once employed, he didn't have the heart to tell her he despised them. "*Your* guests. *Your* rude nephew. I don't see how this concerns me."

"Without another male, the party will be uneven."

"Again…" He let his words trail off, leaving his lack of concern hovering overhead as he chewed the rum-soaked cake appreciatively. He guzzled the first cup of coffee and then poured another without offering any to Eve. He wouldn't, not until she told him why she was really here.

"Then you leave me no choice but to force your hand," she said.

Ah. Here it was. He broke off another piece of cake. Finding a currant, he flicked it to the plate with the tip of his thumb. "This promises to entertain."

For years, she'd been trying—and failing—to get him to attend one social gathering or another. He'd given in twice this Season, and the only reason had been because he thought she'd finally stop needling him. Apparently, it had the opposite effect. She still wanted more, though he could not fathom the reason.

"I'm prepared to offer you something you've been wanting for the past seven years."

He turned and saw that she regarded him from across the room, expectant. "You've piqued my interest, I'll grant you that. What have I wanted from *you* these past seven years?"

"My silence on the matter of your plot for revenge and refusal to marry."

She was forever pestering him, so that was a wager indeed. *If* she could keep to her part of it.

The revenge against his grandfather wasn't finished. Even with the old man dead, Bane's title restored, and Ravencourt—his family's estate—now in his control, there were two final components. One, he had to find the man responsible for carrying out his grandfather's orders—of murdering his parents and then trying to wipe away all proof of Bane's existence—and make certain he paid the highest price for his crime. And two, the family name would die with Bane. There would be no heir—no direct bloodline to his grandfather, at any rate. Bane was determined to be the last of the Fennecourts.

With this ultimate revenge, he'd have the old man turning in his grave for all eternity.

"Your permanent silence on the matter *is* a prize worth seizing, and all for the price of my attendance?" He crossed his arms over his chest, unconvinced.

She smiled. "Well…not quite *all*."

"Ah, I thought not. Out with it. All of it, if you please. No altering the bargain once set in place." He considered her fortunate that he was bored enough—and empty enough, of late—to listen.

Eve held out her gloved hand and began by lifting her index finger. "Your attendance—which means that you will not leave the party or the grounds at any time unless we are having a shared outing. Your participation in all social events—cards, parlor games, and dinners, as well as dancing. And last, you must abstain from sexual congress for the duration of the party."

"The first two points are very well thought out, and I commend your thoroughness." He frowned. "However, the last one puzzles me. Why should my abstinence or lack thereof matter to you?"

She waggled those three fingers at him. "It matters because your charm and good looks won't last forever. There will come a day when you are lonely and too vile a creature to procure your own bed partner. Perhaps all this is because I want you to have a sample of your future life."

Or perhaps not.

"Nagging me even as you promise to nag no more," he said, *not* amused and *not* convinced. "You've managed to force your opinion of my life into this bargain. I have a feeling you will not be able to resist, even once I am declared the victor. No. Your reasoning is too flawed. We both know the only reason you pester me about marrying is because you believe your way of thinking far superior to mine." From the beginning, she thought a better revenge tactic would be to marry a gypsy girl and further taint the Fennecourt bloodline. The prejudice behind such an idea made him ill.

"All right," she said with a sigh. "Then the truth is, telling you that you can't do something almost always ensures my success."

That made more sense. Still, he would gain nothing from this bargain. "If my only prize for all I will suffer is relief from your nagging, then this proposition is highly one-sided."

"It would be, if not for one more coin I'm placing on the table." She smiled in a way that reminded him of a lethal wolf's trap. Something told him he was about to spot the bait. "I have the name of your grandfather's secret solicitor."

He stilled, the tip of his cup halting against his lower lip. His breath rushed against the dark elixir, causing ripples that nearly splashed over the rim.

Bane lowered the cup. "How did you discover his identity?" Shirham, the family solicitor, had known next to nothing of the late marquess's plot, neither had he known the name of the person who'd carried out his grandfather's diabolical orders. In all the years of searching through records, no evidence had been found concerning the secret solicitor's identity.

Eve grinned, dangling the bait directly over the trap. "A letter, which I have in my possession. It came to me by accident shortly after Mangus's death, little more than two years ago. You knew he died, didn't you?"

He'd heard. Shortly after Bane had proven his legitimacy and secured the title and all the lands warranted to the Marquess of Knightswold, he'd removed every servant who'd once been loyal to his grandfather. Unlike the monster his grandfather had been, however, Bane had settled them all with generous stipends and recommendations for other posts. Mangus, beyond the age for service, had gone to live with a widowed sister in Downend.

Bane thought they'd parted on decent terms, considering. Apparently, the old codger had still held a grudge against him. "Then he knew all this time?"

"No." Eve shook her head. "What he told us when we'd questioned him was true. He never knew of the plot, nor did he witness any clandestine meeting between your grandfather and the secret solicitor."

He was losing patience. "Then how?"

"I read his letters. Years ago, he wrote to his sister about a series of weekly visits to an obscure tavern in the next township." She flitted her fingers as if shooing an errant bee. "He made nothing of it at the time, but it sparked my interest enough to drive there and ask the old tavern keep if he remembered."

"And?"

"I was fortunate enough to speak with him. A good thing, too, because within days of our conversation, consumption claimed him." Her eyes gleamed, knowing she had Bane on the hook. "Which, in the end, leaves me the sole proprietor of the information you've sought for so long."

Her tone made it sound like a mere trifling thing. Yet she knew he would do anything to complete his own revenge.

The odds were suddenly in her favor. He didn't like it. Not one bit.

Bane's brow lifted, which reminded him of Venus and the way her expression had told him that she had little patience for games. *Ah, Venus, if only you were here in this room instead of my pesky aunt…*

"Then tell me, what's in it for you? What will you win if I choose to fail, because we both know I have never lost unless I've wanted to," he said, feeling the need to remind her.

"Gypsy," she said without hesitation. "Once the foal is weaned, she stays with me."

He felt as if she'd slapped him, and he reeled back reflexively. "Out of the question. She was never yours to keep or even to consider."

Undeterred, she shook her head. "Jester is quite fond of her, and I enjoy seeing them together."

In the short time Gypsy had been at Eve's estate, the mare had formed an attachment to a gelded skewbald pony they called Jester, which had been given to Eve by Bane's late uncle. Together, Gypsy and Jester made quite the odd-looking pair.

"I wanted to keep her safe. I never gave you any reason to believe anything else." Then it suddenly occurred to him. *This* was the reason she was here. "What is it you're not telling me?"

Eve drew in a deep breath, as if debating whether or not to continue her game or simply be done with it. She sighed. "Amberdeen won't end his pursuit of my land. You know how much it means to me, especially after your uncle…died for it."

Guilt rifled through him. After taking everything from his uncle, the old marquess had gone after Eve's land. Shortly afterward, Spencer killed himself, and Bane was partly to blame.

Of course, it didn't help that Eve would never let him forget it.

Nonetheless, he hated to mention the hitch in her plan. "Amberdeen's claim is sound. He has estate maps that clearly show his property markers." The markers revealed that 140 acres of what Eve had thought to be her land actually had been Amberdeen's all along. Considering the vast amount of acreage they shared between their two properties, 140 acres was a pittance. But family pride was on the line as well.

"I know. I've seen them," she said, her tone short and clipped. "That's why I asked him what it would take for him to leave things as they are now, as a sort of…a settlement."

Bane didn't like where this was going. "And?"

"He wants a foal from Gypsy."

He let out a bark of laughter. The idea was ludicrous. Not one single person of his acquaintance would even suggest a thing. Above all, she was more than just a prized broodmare. "That will never happen."

Eve swallowed. A clear indication she was hiding something else, but he didn't pursue it for the moment. There was no use trying to get the whole truth from Eve. It could take ages. He would have to investigate and find out on his own.

"Every time I've spoken with Amberdeen, he's come across as a reasonable man. I'm sure you can offer him something else he wants in return," he said with a smirk. They both knew that if the only thing Amberdeen wanted from Eve was the land, he easily could have taken the matter to the courts. Besides, Bane had suspected for quite some time that her neighbor wanted a far more *amicable* relationship with Eve.

He doubted it had anything to do with wanting a foal. "A man always has his price."

She gritted her teeth. "He isn't reasonable in the least. Which is precisely why you'll give Gypsy to me when you lose our bargain."

"It won't come to that," he said, determination setting his jaw. "Besides, you said yourself that Amberdeen only wants a foal."

"If a foal was all he wanted, then he would have gone to you," she said evenly, losing her patience. "Don't you see it won't end there? Therefore, once she is mine, I can dictate the terms with Amberdeen."

He watched her carefully. Why was she so desperate to have him attend this house party? Was it simply because she wanted him to lose the bet and claim her prize? Or was there still something he wasn't seeing? He didn't like not having the full picture. Then again, there were always ways to go around Eve and speak with Amberdeen himself.

She set her hands on her hips. "For the sake of our bargain, I must have an answer."

"First," he began, pausing to drain the last of his second cup, "tell me how you will know if I engage in *sexual congress*. Plan to have a footman follow me day and night?"

"I have eyes everywhere." She glanced pointedly toward his bed. "Inside your table drawer is a sheaf of *preventatives*. I doubt you're ever without them, as you would never take the risk of begetting a Fennecourt heir." She looked entirely too smug for his liking.

If her definition of sexual congress involved only activities where he donned a *preventative*, that left quite a bit of fun she'd overlooked. Then again, her recently deceased husband had been an old man. So perhaps she'd forgotten the fun parts.

Yet it was impossible to see past his need to complete his revenge. His task seemed simple enough.

Perhaps even too simple.

He knew there was a hidden trap, something she refused to divulge. Eve didn't truly care if he married or not. Pestering him was just another one of her games. Strangely, she found pleasure in reminding him of the tragic circumstances that had led him to vow against marrying or begetting an heir. More than anything, she seemed to delight in his hatred.

Yet when such a reward dangled before him, he'd be a fool not to play her game. Attend a house party and avoid tupping one of the guests for a fortnight? Done.

Surprisingly enough, it was the former that posed the most difficult task. The latter had grown tiresome of late. He never kept a mistress for long, finding it monotonous. Yet for some reason, even random encounters provided nothing more than a few hours of pleasure and were easily forgotten. In fact, the most extraordinary encounter he'd had in recent memory was being petted and kissed by a green girl who hadn't an inkling about pleasure. Though, she'd had a natural talent for it—that much was certain.

However, because of his skewed perspective and boredom, he'd already decided that a period of abstinence would set him back to rights. Though Eve didn't know it, she'd given him the perfect excuse.

"Very well. You shall have your bargain. However," he began, clarifying the terms, "I will draw up a contract stating the details. That way, if you decide they do not suit you and refuse to sign, then I will leave your party and be on my way." He waited a beat, letting her see the cold determination that had been bred into him. "If that happens, I will remove Gypsy from your stables, refuse to attend your party, and leave you to get out of Amberdeen's clutches all on your own from that point forward."

There was no way he could lose.

CHAPTER FOUR

Merribeth stared at the silver lamé behind the glass case. That length of ribbon must have been there before today. After all, she frequented Haversham's Draper Shoppe at least twice a week. This time, though, it felt like she'd never been here before. In fact, her entire world seemed equally foreign.

"Which one would you choose—the amaranthine or the chartreuse?" Delaney McFarland asked as she stepped forward, obscuring Merribeth's view of the silver lamé.

She blinked and suddenly Haversham's came into focus. Ribbon spools filled the far wall, trays of embroidery thread covered tables, and towers of perfectly creased handkerchiefs stood on either side of the counter. From behind copper-rimmed spectacles, the aproned clerk stared at her as he held a length of ribbon in each hand. His stance shifted, indicating he'd been waiting for her response for some time.

Her world was usually in color, some bright and vibrant, others in shades of pastels. Yet today, everything she saw was silver and gray, shadow and light. How many times had she noticed a coal black top hat or coat, or a silver pin winking from beneath the folds of a cravat? Everywhere she looked, her eyes sought comparisons to Lord Knightswold's hair and eyes, while all the colors she normally noticed went dim.

"Well? Which do you think?" Delaney exhaled her impatience, making Merribeth wonder how many times she'd repeated the question.

"The silver lamé..." The words at the forefront of her mind spilled out, unheeded. Too late, she realized that hadn't been one of the choices. "I mean, the chartreuse, of course."

Delaney turned her head, the motion setting free several wildly curling auburn tendrils from beneath her stylishly askew periwinkle hat. Her pale violet eyes squinted in disapproval. "For *my* coloring?"

It was Merribeth's turn to exhale her impatience. She felt her notorious brow lift. "The amaranthine, then."

"Ah. There you are," her friend whispered and tossed a cheeky wink. "I'd wondered where you'd gone."

Her comment drew Emma and Penelope's attention away from the selection of new threads. They both looked at Merribeth curiously, as if they'd also noticed her absence of mind on this afternoon's outing.

Since last night, Merribeth realized, her mind had gone on holiday. That could be the only explanation for what she'd done. She'd lain awake, replaying every aspect of her folly. She didn't know the woman who'd brazenly pressed her mouth to Lord Knightswold's, but she certainly wasn't the same woman standing here today.

She was changed. "I *am* out of sorts."

"Then we shall do our very best to put you back in," Emma said as she sidled up beside Merribeth and linked arms with her. She grinned in her usual friendly manner, yet there was a certain glow about her ever since she'd married Lord Rathburn only a month ago. It was obvious to anyone who saw her that she was quite splendidly happy.

A brief, unwelcome image of Mr. Clairmore flashed in Merribeth's mind, where she recalled his expression of supreme joy—*or* madness. She still wasn't certain which. Perhaps love was a combination of both. *Strange.* Although she'd been nearly engaged since she was eighteen, she didn't know the answer. Lately, her primary feeling was the bitterness over losing five years of plans.

Penelope joined their trio, holding three variations of blue embroidery thread, amusement lighting her eyes. "Back into sorts? I'm not certain anyone would want that either."

"Yes, I quite agree. Back into sorts sounds much worse than being out," Delaney said and then turned her attention back to the clerk. "This chartreuse is far too yellow green, as opposed to a greener yellow."

The clerk blinked at her logic and then looked past Delaney to their trio. After a mere glance to Emma and Merribeth, his gaze settled on Penelope as if seeking commiseration.

"Seems perfectly sensible to me," Penelope said with a slight shrug that caused her shawl to droop.

Grateful for the distraction her friends provided, ridiculous though the change in conversation may be, Merribeth felt relaxed for the first time all day.

From the moment they'd first met, they'd become the best of friends. It had all started here at Haversham's. A clerk had mixed up their orders, sending the wrong packages to each of their Danbury Lane addresses. By the time they'd set matters aright and discovered their common interests—needlework as well as their statuses as wallflowers—they'd become fast friends.

Merribeth knew she'd never have survived Mr. Clairmore's betrayal without them.

With a laugh at the clerk's discomfort, Delaney said, "Oh, go ahead and give me that horrid chartreuse as well. I'll give it to Miss Pursglove as a peace offering the next time I incur her wrath by acting like myself instead of a soldier of decorum."

Merribeth exchanged looks with Emma and Penelope. Delaney was impulsive to a fault, and there was no reining her in—not that they'd ever want to. To them, she was quite perfect just the way she was. However, to her decorum instructor, the dour Miss Pursglove…well, there was no hope to gain her good opinion. Not that Delaney wanted it. No, in fact, she was guaranteed permanent placement on Miss Pursglove's vexation list. New battle lines were drawn between the two of them daily.

"What length would you like in the silver, Merribeth?" Delaney asked, as the clerk set about wrapping the ribbon in brown paper and string.

"I am not interested in the silver," she lied.

Delaney made a passable attempt at intimidation with the lift of her brow. "I beg to differ. You were practically ogling the entire spool."

"*Ogling,*" Merribeth scoffed—which might have been convincing if not for a wave of heat rising to her cheeks. "If you'll recall, I'm going out of town and will have no need of it."

With Merribeth's meager allowance, she couldn't afford it anyway. Even though Delaney could, as a matter of personal pride, she didn't want her friend to buy it for her. Besides, her friend would want to see what she chose to create with it, and all Merribeth wanted to do was hold it in her hands and stare at it for hours, remembering the heated shimmer in a certain gentleman's gaze.

"Don't remind me," Delaney huffed, dropping her new purchase into her periwinkle reticule before cinching the silver cords. "I hope you know, you are leaving me to face the wolves alone."

"Oh dear," Merribeth said, with Emma and Penelope mirroring her concern. "I thought the backlash from last year's… incident…had died down."

The members of their needlework circle vowed never to speak of it. However, if her friend was suffering any of the societal injustice that had recently befallen her, then Merribeth was determined to speak of it and help in any way she could.

Delaney laughed. "I'm afraid *that* will never be forgotten. No doubt, they'll have it inscribed on my gravestone. *Here lies Delaney McFarland, the woman who*—Oh bother, what is *he* doing here?"

Merribeth looked up to see none other than Mr. Croft, the famed second party to *the incident*. Thankfully, he merely inclined his head in greeting but made no attempt to cross the store in order to speak with them. Besides that, he seemed quite busy acting as chaperone to three of his sisters. Merribeth knew of a fourth as well, but she was perhaps too young for an afternoon outing.

Since he's done them a service not long ago, she returned the greeting, keeping her society-approved smile in place.

However, Delaney did not. "That man seems to have no other purpose than to vex me. No matter where I go, he's there, in far too close proximity. And you know what happens when we are seen together, don't you?"

Merribeth knew. Seeing them together only reminded the entire *ton* of the infamous incident.

"I will never live it down so long as he frequents the same establishments." Delaney cinched the silver cords on her reticule tighter. "Though why he should step into *Haversham's* of all places when *Forester's* is far closer to his part of town, I shall never—" Her words stopped abruptly when Elena Mallory, gossip monger extraordinaire, sidled in and batted her sparse lashes up at him. "Of course. How lovely that my cousin should be here as well. No doubt she's behind this, hoping to create another scandal by luring him to a shop we're known to frequent."

"Surprisingly enough, she was not in attendance at Lady Amherst's last night. A fact for which I am ever grateful," Merribeth murmured. They'd ceased their acquaintance with Miss Mallory earlier in the Season when she'd tried to embroil Emma and Lord Rathburn in a scandal by spreading vicious gossip.

Her statement earned Delaney's interest. "Why, exactly, are you grateful Elena wasn't there? Strike that—the list is too endless. It's obvious why you wouldn't want her there. Both she and Lady Amherst are founding members of the *Scandalmonger Society,* I'm sure. Unless..." She drew in an excited breath. "You're telling me there was a *reason* she wasn't there. Or perhaps that something newsworthy happened, and you've yet to tell me? If it's the latter, I will forgive you only if you tell *all* this instant."

"Tell *all* of…what?" Emma asked as she rejoined them, holding the strings of her purchase.

Penelope flanked her other side and leaned in to whisper. "Did something happen at Lady Amherst's?"

Emma tsked. "That woman is notoriously cruel. I knew you shouldn't have gone. If she said anything to you, I'll…" She stopped and pulled on the corner of her mouth as if she were thinking. "I'll have the dowager give her the cut direct."

"If it was something truly dreadful, you don't have to speak of it," Penelope added, already acting like the perfect mother hen, even though the birth of her first child was still four months away. "You have our full support."

Delaney gasped. "Dreadful or not, she still has to tell us. After all, how can we support her fully without having the details?"

In unison, they turned their gazes on Delaney, who lowered her lashes in a pretense of shame. No one was fooled.

Merribeth lifted a hand to pinch the bridge of her nose the way Aunt Sophie did. *Drat!* How did she get herself into these conundrums? Her vow of not thinking, let alone speaking, of last night was pointless now. "Not here."

At least that was something upon which they could all agree. In the next few moments, they made their way through the door and to Penelope's carriage, which waited beside the pavement.

As the carriage drove them back to Danbury Lane, Merribeth took a deep breath, and focused on the bright side. The truth was, she didn't have to tell her friends, or anyone for that matter, *everything* that had happened last night. That stolen moment would forever be hers and hers alone. After all, she highly doubted someone like the infamous Lord Knightswold would remember her from amongst the hordes of other women he'd kissed.

As if summoned by her thoughts, a coal-black top hat caught the corner of her eye as they passed a gentleman on the pavement. The rumble of horses' hooves, plodding on the dusty streets, nearly sent her heart over the edge.

Unbidden, a memory swept over her. *You have brandy-sipping lips. Supple, with the slightest pout where their color changes from dusky pink to a deeper shade.*

Her cheeks grew warm.

At her very core, Merribeth was a romantic. However, losing Mr. Clairmore and her expectations of a future forced her to see things in a different light.

Merribeth decided that perhaps a different viewpoint was just the thing she needed to get through this crisis. From this point forward, she would adopt a bit of practicality and cynicism in order to keep her romantic notions in check.

"Now, tell us of Lady Amherst's."

Instantly, her mind returned to the darkened study, the sound of his voice, the feel of his fingers nudging hers apart. *No doubt, you even prefer coffee over tea.*

"You see…" Merribeth cleared her throat, wishing her mind would clear as well. "The thing is…I didn't exactly see the play." She was about to say that she wished she'd stayed home entirely but found the words blocked by her protesting lips. Indeed, her lips were very glad she'd gone.

She felt another rush of heat to her cheeks.

Delaney studied her. "We've already clarified you were present at Lady Amherst's, which leads me to believe this little tidbit you're sharing has nothing to do with Elena Mallory."

Merribeth swallowed, her gaze passing from Delaney to Emma.

"By the way you've been distracted today, I'd venture to guess that *something* happened last night." Emma blinked at her. "Though you don't have to talk about it…if you don't want to."

Something, indeed.

"Not really," Merribeth lied. "I made an appearance, bore the scrutiny, adjourned to the retiring room"—she left out the shameful bit about molesting Lord Knightswold—"and then returned home early to finish packing for the house party."

Penelope reached over to squeeze her fingers. "Then it was truly horrible. I worried for you."

"I know. You all warned me how it would be. Especially after Delaney went last year. However, I had to make an appearance in order to work my way back into the fold."

The trio scoffed at that.

"It isn't fair for you to be punished because Mr. Clairmore is an idiot."

"True," Merribeth agreed. Who was she to argue? "Lady Eve says that I should get him back and that it could be the only way to restore my reputation. Sophie agrees with her."

Delaney scowled and lifted a finger as if ready to rally the troops for battle. Then she shook her head and went still. Her hand lowered to her lap, her fingers drumming automatically, as if unable to hold still for too long. "It could work…*if* you could somehow lure him back."

"Eve claims that men are drawn to confident women and that I've been acting like a stable puppy, afraid of being kicked."

Their gazes fell away. "Well, lately…"

Ouch. She'd hoped they hadn't noticed how lost she felt. Yet they were her friends for a reason. Merribeth nodded. She hesitated but then said, "There was *another* part of her plan."

"Oh?"

"She claims that flirting instills confidence."

"Flirting? I suppose," Emma interjected, "with the right man, that is. As long as he's receptive. You wouldn't want to flirt with an overly shy gentleman and end up scaring him off. You both could end up scarred for life. Then again, you wouldn't want it to be the other way around either."

"Certainly not," Penelope agreed. "There are scores of men to avoid. Rakes, in particular. A sensible man would be the best for your task. While a sensible gentleman is occasionally a challenge to flirt with, he is worth the effort." No doubt she was referring to her own Mr. Weatherstone.

"I don't know, Penelope," Emma said, that glowing smile returning to her face. "A rake—at least a reformed rake—might be the perfect man for the task." No doubt she was thinking of her own husband.

"A rake?" Delaney asked, incredulous. "Even a reformed rake would bring her only more scandal. And I know better than each of you how easy it is to have your name on everyone's lips. I don't want that to happen to our Merribeth."

They were all trying to protect her, yet she was the one who'd already kissed a rake. And *not* the reformed type either.

If anyone needed to worry about taking flirting too far, it was she. "I'm certain Eve will employ the assistance of one of her friends to guarantee the latter doesn't happen."

The three of them exchanged a look of doubt, Eve's reputation having preceded her. However, no one said it aloud.

"Then, only one question remains," Penelope said. "Is the return of Mr. Clairmore's affections truly what you want?"

The question gave Merribeth pause. He'd hurt her when he confessed to such passionate feelings about Miss Codington. After last night, however, she could see how easily a simple kiss could addle one's brain.

Perhaps that's all it was for him—a temporary madness. If that were true, then Eve's plan was bound to work. Yet more distressingly, she couldn't help wondering why the idea didn't make her feel any better. After having her own indiscretion, could she forgive him his?

"What I want is…" *not to have my greatest fear come to fruition, not to face my future alone, not to live each day in uncertainty.* The words clogged her throat, and she had to clear them away. "Mr. Clairmore, of course."

"There is one way to know for sure," Emma said and reached over to place a small parcel on Merribeth's lap.

"What's this?"

"It's from all of us," Penelope said, and the others nodded. "We've noticed how you've lost interest in needlework."

Merribeth untied the string and unfolded the paper. Inside were a gentleman's handkerchief, a length of silver embroidery thread, and a shiny new needle. "Thank you, but I don't understand."

"Do you remember the handkerchiefs Penelope embroiders for Mr. Weatherstone each year?" Emma asked. "I did the same for Oliver for a wedding gift."

Merribeth looked to her friends, not quite understanding. "You think I should put Mr. Clairmore's initials on this?"

"No...well, only if Mr. Clairmore is the man you truly love. This is a way to be certain. *If* you love him, that is." Which, apparently, Delaney didn't believe for an instant.

Merribeth had to wonder—did she?

CHAPTER FIVE

Lady Eve Sterling's country manor was located in Suffolk, not far from the harbor. As Merribeth exited the carriage, a cool breeze rushed over the peony blossoms, and a sweetly scented caress stirred the raven locks escaping her bonnet. She stared in awe at the sprawling stone manor that would be her home for the next two weeks.

According to Sophie, the land and property had been in Eve's family since the sixteenth century, a gift once bestowed on a knight of the realm. The manor came complete with gatehouse, stables, chapel, and a pond that had been a moat centuries ago.

Ahead of her stood a wide oaken doorway. Recessed into the stone façade, narrow mullioned windows lined the first and second floors, catching the early afternoon light. The third story hosted dormers that resembled eyebrows arched in speculation.

Merribeth knew a thing or two about that. "How many guests did you say were attending?"

Sophie directed the footmen with their luggage and then turned to answer her. "I believe there will be twelve in total."

Only a dozen guests in a house this size would seem a paltry amount, although Merribeth was thankful the number was relatively small. "I imagine more of her friends have stayed in town, as it is not yet the end of the Season."

"Perhaps, though it will be her first house party in many years. She wanted to keep this party more intimate," her aunt said, gathering her knitting satchel from within the carriage. "She has rooms and servants aplenty to accommodate us all very well."

"To have such a home, I wonder why she does not have parties often," Merribeth mused.

"Likely due to the fact that her most-recent late husband did not care for the place. In fact, he did his part to ensure it was stripped from her, scoundrel that he was. He left her with a hillock of debts, abusing her abominably." She lowered her voice. "Although I try not to speak ill of the dead, I will say that I am glad he is no more."

Merribeth leaned in to whisper in her aunt's ear. "Then how is Eve able to keep such a fine house, in addition to the one in town and servants to fill them?" She knew from their own financial woes that people in dire straits were forced to make difficult decisions. Keeping a smaller house with only one or two servants was one of them. In fact, their home in Berkshire was little more than the size of Eve's gatehouse, and they could only afford to keep a cook. If it hadn't been for Eve's generosity, Merribeth never would have had a Season. So then, how could Eve afford any of it?

"Her nephew, from her first marriage to Mr. Fennecourt, keeps her in good standing. I daresay, he's had to come to her rescue on more than—*my dear*, we should not speak of such things. Not only is she our hostess but my friend as well. After losing touch with her for a dozen years, gossiping shows a severe lack of faith on my part." Sophie pressed her lips together, looking askance above the rims of her spectacles, though more so with affection than admonishment. She shook her head as they crossed the threshold. "No more. I believe I've told you enough to satisfy your curiosity."

"Never," Merribeth replied with a grin. In fact, she was more curious now than ever. When Eve had simply shown up at their house in Berkshire, little more than two years ago, she never questioned her aunt's unlikely friendship with Eve or even the reason why Sophie had never spoken of her. Instead, she'd been more excited at the prospect of having a London Season. Though it shamed her to admit, she'd been so busy with her friends, Mr. Clairmore, and embroidery that she'd taken her aunt for granted.

She opened her mouth to ask why she'd never heard mention of this nephew of Eve's until now, but the question disappeared from her tongue as they entered the foyer.

Merribeth was in awe.

Gleaming marble floors shone like mirrors beneath their feet. The far walls curved in, giving the space a semicircular feel, with rounded archways that led off to other rooms. Above them, the vaulted ceiling could put a church to shame, painted with a mural that made it appear as if one could glimpse heaven from this very spot. Ahead, a wide staircase, ornately decorated with a wrought-iron balustrade, curled like a serpent toward a minstrels' gallery.

"You're here," Eve called from the gallery, giving an uncharacteristic clap of glee.

As if she'd designed the house as an accessory to her wardrobe, flattering golden light followed her descent down the curved stairs, the train of her crimson gown trailing a step behind, as if flames licked the hem.

Sophie removed her straw bonnet and handed it to the maid, along with her knitting satchel. "Of course we are. We wouldn't have missed your first house party since..." Her words trailed off, leaving an obvious void in the room.

"I know," Eve said with a nod when she reached the bottom, her eyes going hard for an instant. Then she blinked and continued forward to embrace Sophie. "You are the first of my guests to arrive, not counting my nephew. Then again, he doesn't count."

Another mention of this mysterious nephew blared in Merribeth's ears like the blast of a horn at the start of a foxhunt.

Eve turned to Merribeth, took her by the shoulders, and startled her by pulling her in for a quick embrace. "I can't wait to introduce the two of you. He's nearly as sharp witted as you, and I just know you'll keep each other amused."

Why was it she never recalled hearing of him before? Surely, as Eve's benefactor, he would have been invited to dinner in the very least. Yet even more suspiciously, why was she hearing so much of him now?

"I'm not certain I want to amuse anyone."

"Don't worry, pet," Eve said with a laugh. "I wouldn't steer you in his direction. Why would I, if your main goal was to reclaim Mr. Clairmore? It would hardly be worth my effort anyway. My nephew is a confirmed bachelor and abhors the idea of marriage. I was merely suggesting that the two of you could make clever dinner conversation. That is all."

If that was all, then why didn't the instinct for caution wane?

Inwardly, Merribeth shook herself. Likely, she was on edge and overtired from the journey. There was no reason for her to imagine Eve was manipulating her—even if Eve was known for her infamous plots. "Then I'll have something to look forward to this evening," she said graciously.

Eve clucked her tongue. "Nonsense. You loathe the very idea, but I appreciate your effort of sincerity, nonetheless. Sophie, she has learned a trick or two from you, I daresay." She smiled again as if she had a surplus of amusement stored away in one of the many rooms. "Now, the two of you must want to settle in and refresh yourselves after your journey. Feel free to explore the house, if you are so inclined."

A maid in a frilled cap and apron appeared from an unseen doorway at Eve's words. "Right this way, if you please," the maid said with a curtsy before turning to lead them up the stairs.

The jangle of carriage rigging rang through the open doors. It announced the arrival of more guests, and Merribeth was grateful that neither the maid nor her aunt stopped to wait on an introduction. There would be plenty of time for those formalities later.

A new frisson of nervousness swept through her as she wondered if the next two weeks would be like the last two. Would she be caged in a house full of people who knew about her circumstances?

"One good thing about a party in a manor this size," Sophie said as they followed the maid down a series of halls, "is that there is always a place where one can catch a breath of fresh air." She reached over and squeezed Merribeth's hand briefly.

In other words, don't be nervous. She gave her aunt a nod of understanding. Now, if she could simply convince her stomach to stop churning, then all would be well.

They were led into a vast chamber with chintz wallpaper covered in violet blossoms. The immense bed was the size of a small sailing vessel, with diaphanous lavender curtains tied to each of the thick, richly carved posts. Overlapping lengths of velvet curtains adorned the arched window situated behind a tufted chair in the same hue. A marble-topped vanity sat in the corner with a vase of freshly cut irises.

"Begging your pardon, miss," another housemaid said from the doorway, her gaze on Merribeth. "Your chamber is this way."

Her own chamber? She looked to Sophie, who seemed not at all surprised by this. "Go. I have toured this house before. Now, I want to rest until dinner."

Not one to argue about such a pleasant surprise, Merribeth followed the maid down the corridor and around another series of maze-like corners. The journey gave her time to think on how strange it was for her room to be so far from Sophie's. After all, she was still an unmarried woman, and her aunt was her chaperone.

However, when her nervousness threatened to return, she reasoned it could be that the rooms in between theirs were uninhabitable for guests. If Eve's late husband had left her with a hillock of debts, it stood to reason she could not maintain *all* the rooms in a manor this size.

While she'd set her mind at ease by the time they reached her door, she wasn't at all prepared for the sight that greeted her.

Her chamber was as vast as Sophie's, perhaps even more so. Situated on a corner of the manor, her room was essentially inside a bartizan turret. Warm, golden sunlight filtered in through two banks of windows, adorned in draperies the shade of ripe peaches, with pale diaphanous sheers billowing in the breeze. Draped silk in the same hue fluttered against the rails of her colossal bed like a negligee. Painted peach blossoms decorated the walls, interspersed with hanging fruit so tempting that she wondered if the room was meant to resemble the Garden of Eden.

The footman carried in her luggage. At the window, she stared out at the vast rolling hills, dotted with the brown thatched roofs of the village houses, nestled together as the land gradually merged with the cliffs overlooking the harbor.

Looking out, her hand pressed against the churning sensation in her stomach. It was difficult to look out in the distance and not think of her parents or the terrible day they were swept out to sea.

While the nightmares had lessened in frequency over the years, they'd left a permanent mark on her. A need for certainty of her future. That was precisely why she was desperate that this plan of Eve's should work.

Anxiety made her feel flushed. Heat pricked at her scalp, threatening to make her perspire. Merribeth turned away from the view and focused on something else to keep her head straight. She stepped past the lush, cream-colored Turkish divan and over to the second window.

Unlike the other, this one did not host a far-off view of the sea but the length of the house instead. The corner of her room ended abruptly, jutting away from the main structure. Looking closer, she noticed a narrow balcony directly outside.

Unable to resist, she turned the small iron handle and opened the window. The air was cool and sweet, scented by the tall grasses and drooping willow branches beside the pond. She breathed in deeply. A sense of calm filled her. If her task was to spend the next two weeks in this place, she believed she could manage.

Before she left this view, she paid closer attention to the length of the house before her. Beneath the angle of the slate roof, windows dotted the expanse. Like hers, each room had a narrow balcony with a carved stone balustrade. The other views, however, were aimed toward the harbor and not the house. It seemed odd that this window should face the windows and balconies of other rooms. Stranger still, the window nearest hers was situated so closely that the balconies nearly touched.

Back inside her room, Merribeth found that the maid and footmen had gone, and she was at her leisure. She sank down onto the sumptuous pillows on the divan and smiled with pure delight. Automatically, she covered her mouth to hide her smile, but then remembered she was alone and could smile all she liked without ridicule.

And so she did.

Bane planned to hide in the east wing library for as long as he could. After all, it wasn't officially a party until all the guests arrived. The stipulation in his agreement with Eve regarding his participation, or lack thereof, didn't count. Not yet.

He knew his place in this wingback chair was only temporary. Far too soon, he would be forced to endure the company his aunt had chosen for his two-week stint in hell. His primary challenge would be avoiding a certain buxom widow that Eve had invited solely as a means to tempt him into losing their wager.

He'd flirted with Daniela Pearce at Tattersalls recently. While she knew nothing of horseflesh, her words suggested she knew quite a lot of another flesh. Enough to pique his interest, which was a true accomplishment these days.

The real pity was that he'd always enjoyed sex, the feel of a woman's flesh, the sounds of her ecstasy, the power he felt at knowing he could make her weep from the stroke of his fingers or the flick of his tongue. He had an appetite for it—a thirst that had gone unquenched for longer than he cared to admit. Seduction was more of a rote behavior anymore.

With any luck, after the wager with Eve concluded, Daniela Pearce could be the cure he sought.

Bane shook his head, stroking the pad of his thumb across his bottom lip. A cure? Or another diversion that would run its course? He was more prone to believe the latter. Besides, he already knew she wasn't worth the risk of losing Gypsy. He doubted any woman was.

He heard a series of raps on the door, one long and three short. It was the signal he'd worked out with Bitters when he spotted someone in the corridor. *Bugger.* It looked like his solitude and sanity would end sooner rather than later.

"Miss, I believe you'll find the other guests gathering in the Great Room before dinner," he heard his man say. Good old Bitters—he sounded every bit the snob.

"Yes, of course."

Bane listened, waiting for the sound of retreating footsteps.

"Shall I direct you, miss?" Bitters asked.

She—whoever she was—seemed to hesitate. "It's just that I want to explore a bit more of the house while the last shreds of my sanity are still intact."

Bane nearly laughed but kept his amusement to himself. It appeared as though he had a kindred spirit among the guests.

"Yes, but—" Bitters began.

He heard the handle of the door move.

"Don't say a word…please."

Bane went still. Those words. That voice. Surely, his ears must be deceiving him. *Don't say a word…please. I only mean to borrow this for a moment and return it directly.*

The door opened. He felt his heart sputter like a galloping horse suddenly stopped at the edge of a cliff. How many times had he replayed those words and that kiss? He didn't want to admit how they stirred him, even now. However, he was still unsure if this *miss* and his brandy-sipping *Venus* were one in the same.

Bitters didn't say another word, but he cleared his throat in disapproval before the door closed with a firm click of the latch. Then Bane heard her sigh.

His chair faced the unlit hearth, the door at his back. With windows on either side facing west and the days growing longer for summer, the room still possessed enough light for her to see him before he saw her. His heart began to gallop again, the sound rushing in his ears as if he were a lad waiting for his first glimpse of a dairymaid's bosom.

She sighed again, slightly louder this time. The whisper of her dress and muffled footfalls on the carpet told him she was in motion, likely gazing at the ancient texts on display. Since neither his aunt nor uncle had been great readers, he didn't believe the collection held anything printed in the past thirty years or more. Which was probably the reason this library was one of the smallest and least visited rooms in the manor. The exact reason he'd chosen it.

Impatient to end this mystery, he brushed his hand over the arm of the chair, hoping the movement would draw her gaze, a startled gasp, something—anything.

Nothing.

He exhaled, long and slow. Audibly.

She sighed in answer, sounding more impatient now and leaving him to wonder if she was waiting for him to notice her first. If this was Venus, he could imagine it very well. He shook his head, fighting a grin. Then he cleared his throat.

She cleared hers.

This time the grin won, but he still did not say anything. Instead, he coughed.

She released a tired exhale. "If our avoidance continues, I fear we will both grow hoarse before dinner. Although we are clearly strangers, as I know none of Lady Eve's guests, we must skip social formalities and introduce ourselves, else our dinner companions will think we are rude for not speaking, ailment or not."

It *was* she. The mistress of ghastly potions and stolen moments. The goddess of softly spoken words and borrowed kisses. *Venus*. Even without seeing her face, he knew. "You hold the opinions of others in high regard."

Now, at the sound of his voice, she did gasp. *Ah.* She knew him without sight too, then. He wondered if she would be embarrassed and bolt out the door, as she had during their previous encounter. Oddly enough, he found himself hoping she wouldn't.

Holding his breath, he waited. His fingers curled over the edge of the chair.

"I suppose," she began, her voice airy and winded, as if part of her *had* bolted out the door, leaving her body behind, "another solution would be for me to slip away, as if I'd stumbled into the library, noticed the fidgety hand of a gentlemen on the arm of the chair, realized I did not want to disturb a man who quite obviously had a nervous condition, and summarily left without a word."

He heard the door handle rattle and stood immediately, not wanting her to escape. But she'd duped him. A caustic brow arched and slender arms crossed over a frilly white concoction that, he supposed, was for the purpose of making her look demure. As if Venus could ever disguise her true nature.

Bane propped his arm along the back of the chair and crossed one boot in front of the other, pretending he hadn't been ready to dash across the room to keep her within it. "Perhaps it was less a nervous condition and more the idea of having his solitude disturbed that made him fidget."

"And now?"

Damn but she looked smug, daring to hide her grin from him. "A miracle cure."

She smiled then but all too briefly. "We have not been introduced."

"As you stated before, it would not be proper."

A lovely burst of color flushed her cheeks. He knew she'd blushed many times the other night, but the light had been too dim for him to admire its beauty. Now, she fairly glowed, the sunset captured in her cheeks, brightening the cerulean blue of her eyes.

"We seem to have abandoned propriety during our previous encounter," she said.

Wanting to tease her, he pulled a face of confusion. "Previous encounter? Are you suggesting we've met before?"

At first, she furrowed her brow and studied him closely. In that split second, he knew she was wondering if he was mocking her or seriously didn't remember. Then, as if she saw the truth stamped across his face, like a fool playing cards for the first time, her eyes narrowed.

"Forgive me, but with the light behind you, I could not make out your features." Up went that brow, more challenging than caustic. "I was mistaken. I do not know you, sir."

"Very few people do," he said, pleased without knowing why. He was pleased for the sake of being pleased, he supposed, even though the idea was ludicrous.

She pursed her lips. "And where does the fault lie in that?"

"With everyone else, I suppose." He shrugged. "I could hardly claim it."

"Not when you try *so* hard to be sociable."

He liked this game. A slow smile tugged at the corners of his mouth. "After all, you found me." *Again.*

Her gaze dipped to his mouth. The memory of the sweet press of her lips forced him to lift his hand and brush the tingles he felt on his bottom lip.

She blushed again and swallowed. "I should go to dinner."

"Why?" He wanted her to stay. Perhaps if they continued their senseless conversation until the light faded from the sky and room grew dark, she would be bold again.

"Because it is expected."

He chuckled and watched her stiffen. "All of society will fall if we do not do what is expected."

"Certain rules should be followed," she stated as fervently as a paddle-wielding governess. "Such as, the proper course for introductions."

Then, before he could cross the room to stop her, she opened the door and bolted.

Rushing after her, he watched her retreat down the hallway, relishing the indignation in her every step.

There was nothing finer than Venus in all her fury.

You will soon learn that the only rules Eve makes are the ones she expects to be broken.

And he was tempted to do just that.

Chapter Six

Merribeth waited outside the salon to catch her breath and cool her cheeks. Lord Knightswold was at Eve's party? She'd hoped never to see him again, never to be reminded of her rash behavior at Lady Amherst's. Yet she couldn't even seem to control her tongue in his presence.

What had possessed her to speak so brazenly, flirting with him? She was not so green as to believe it wasn't flirting. The instant she saw him, she felt the insistent beat of the drum that seemed to pulse only when he was near. However, she kept herself far from him. Best to avoid temptation.

Even though he professed not to remember, she highly suspected he was toying with her. His brand of flirting, no doubt. And yet...she wasn't entirely convinced he *did* remember her. After all, it was rumored he spent time with scores of women. How could one stand out from the rest? She knew from years of being a wallflower, in addition to recent events concerning Mr. Clairmore, she wasn't remarkable in the least.

That thought sobered her. The warmth from her cheeks vanished. She felt cold at the thought that something as altering for her as the night in Lady Amherst's study had been nothing memorable for him.

"There you are," Sophie said, peeking out the wide double doors of the Great Room. "Eve and I were ready to send out the hunting hounds."

Merribeth affected a grin. "I was exploring the house. It's quite lovely. I look forward to a tour of the grounds tomorrow." *Anything to keep me as far away from Lord Knightswold as possible.*

"If it does not rain," Sophie said, ever the voice of reason and sensibility. She linked arms with Merribeth and led her into the room. "For now, there are guests awaiting an introduction before we can begin dinner."

The Great Room—with vaulted ceilings; tall, imposing windows; and a fireplace so immense that it could fit a horse and carriage—was a very masculine space. The walls were bathed in a rich golden fawn, with a bank of windows swathed in midnight draperies from corner to corner, open to reveal the pond in the distance.

"Here she is," Eve said, walking toward them. "Now, this is Miss Wakefield's first house party, so I expect each of you to set an example of model behavior." Her words were met with snickers and sideways glances, though thankfully, none of them directed at Merribeth.

A gentleman with a square jaw and a generous salting of gray through his short brassy locks took a step forward and bowed. "I vow to keep my talk of battles to a minimum."

Before Eve could make an introduction, a curvaceous woman with an artful spray of feathers woven through honey brown ringlets sidled up to the man and slipped her arm into his. "Colonel Hamersley should sit beside me at dinner, for I do not mind heroic tales. The most conversation I get from my husband consists of flocks of our sheep and on which part of our land he'd last spotted them," she said with a laugh but cast a spurious look toward the slender, well-dressed gentleman standing near the hearth, holding a crystal cordial glass.

Eve directed her first introduction to that man, Sir Colin Whitworth, who had kind eyes and smiled warmly, despite his wife's waspish comment.

The Baron and Baroness Archer were next. Though they should have been introduced first by rank, no one seemed to mind Eve's rule flaunting.

Lord Archer swayed slightly on his feet and lifted his empty goblet in greeting. "The more the merrier!" He had the look of a man who'd been considered handsome at one time. Beneath the florid complexion and slightly rounded face, Merribeth could see the ghost of a rakish gleam in his gaze.

Beside him, his wife offered a small smile and patted his arm. Her frame and features were dainty, and she had an air about her that spoke of centuries and centuries of family money.

Daniela Pearce came forward, her reputation for being a hedonistic widow having preceded her. She held out her pink-gloved hand in greeting and then tugged Merribeth forward to kiss her on both cheeks. "I'm going to take you under my wing, darling, and together we're going to get him back," she whispered, pulling her closer. Her breath was scented with wine, and her ample bosom smothered Merribeth.

She looked to Eve, not for help but with accusation. *You told her?* Her aunt's friend offered a pout, pretending to beg forgiveness.

"I do hope Mrs. Pearce shares her secret with me," Colonel Hamersley said with a chuckle.

His remark earned an outraged giggle from the woman still in possession of his arm. "My dear Colonel, what a terrible flirt you are," Lady Cordelia said, batting her eyes and doing her best to arrange the tips of her feathers to draw attention to her own bosom.

Finally, Merribeth was set free, albeit a little deflated. "Thank you, Mrs. Pearce," she murmured. She didn't want to arouse suspicion of their conversation, in case there were still guests who had not heard of Mr. Clairmore's betrayal, which she doubted greatly.

"Unfortunately, our party is uneven," Eve announced. "Reverend Tiberon sent his regrets, and the last guest has been delayed. Ah, but here is the man of the hour—my nephew, the hermit."

Merribeth went still and gaped at Eve as she made the announcement. She knew of only one other person who hadn't been in the room before she'd arrived: Lord Knightswold.

Suddenly, her thoughts scattered like cinders on a breeze. *Nephew?*

"I'm certain someone would have discovered my hiding place, sooner or later," he said from behind Merribeth. His words rumbled through her body like a team of stampeding horses, lifting gooseflesh on her arms as well as the fine hairs at her nape. "One can never be a hermit for long at a house party."

"What's the use of being without the pleasure of another's company?" the widow Pearce asked. Apparently, her ample bosom meant she was deficient elsewhere.

"I can think of no reason at all," Archer replied as he tapped the rim of his glass for a footman to refill it.

Merribeth dared not turn. *Nephew?* Her previous assumptions were now riddled with doubt. She'd assumed that Eve had sent her to retrieve her reticule at Lady Amherst's for the purpose of a flirtation with a rake. Surely Eve wouldn't have sent her to flirt with her own nephew.

Oh dear. The weight of the world seemed to plummet to the bottom of her stomach. His presence in the room that night had likely been only a coincidence. If she had known Lord Knightswold was Eve's nephew, she never would have been so bold.

Her heart raced, and her palms were damp. Eve was about to introduce them. The question of whether or not he would reveal their previous acquaintance suddenly entered her mind. And why, of all the things she'd heard of Lord Knightswold, had she never heard he was related to Eve?

"Bane, you know nearly everyone here, so introductions are pointless. However, there are two people I'm certain you will love to meet. This is my dear friend, Sophie Leander."

From the corner of her eye, Merribeth watched her aunt bow her head and smile. "Lord Knightswold, I've heard so many good things about you from your aunt."

"A great pleasure, Mrs. Leander. I have heard equal praise of you."

When her vision went hazy, Merribeth realized she was holding her breath. Yet if she fainted, she'd draw more attention. *Better breathe, then.*

Then, even though it went against her instinct to flee, she slowly turned, keeping her eyes on the floor as if fascinated by the carpet. In truth, the Turkish weave was quite lovely.

She felt a hand on her shoulder. *Drat.*

"And this is Miss Wakefield," Eve said, emphasizing the *Miss*. In other words: *stay far, far away from this one.* "Sophie's niece."

When Merribeth lifted her gaze, she saw him grin but soon enough discovered his gaze was not on her but on the buxom widow past her shoulder. "Miss Makepeace, a pleasure," he said absently.

"Miss *Wakefield*, nephew." Eve clucked her tongue. "I can already see I'll need to rearrange the cards at dinner." She pulled Sophie aside and called the butler over, presumably to talk about the seating arrangement.

Bane met Merribeth's gaze for a brief, smoldering instant. "Forgive me, Miss Wakefield. It seems a few sips of brandy have gone to my head."

Her mouth opened in shock but then closed before anyone noticed. *How dare he say something to make her blush!*

Fortunately, her temper took care of any embarrassment. After all, he was just ogling Daniela Pearce. "Lord Knightswold, it's an honor to meet a gentleman who is unafraid of admitting favor for *temperance* in the company of his peers."

"Man can't hold his liquor," Lord Archer chuckled, draining another cup.

Bane grinned. "It's only brandy that affects me so, I fear. It has a tendency to stay with me. For days, in fact," he said, loud enough that it sounded as if he were making a joke for everyone's amusement. It gained him several more chuckles.

He stepped forward, as if to pass by Merribeth. Then he hesitated, his voice low. "I should probably abstain from it completely, but there's something indescribably tempting in the elixir."

Double drat. Her cheeks were aflame—she could feel it. He was bedeviling her on purpose. She feared her quick tendency to blush would reveal her secret and suddenly realized that her only method of combating his flirtation was to remove herself from his presence.

Then, as ever, Eve had perfect timing and announced that dinner was ready.

Merribeth breathed a sigh of relief, short lived though it may be.

Bane was never more grateful for a dinner to end.

Instead of gathering in the dining room, seated at the grand table that had once hosted a king, Eve decided that a more intimate dinner in the dimly lit conservatory was perfect for a smaller party. Because of it, they took their places at a round table, seated within elbow's reach of each other. The close proximity gave Daniela the notion of playing hide-the-napkin, as he frequently found her hand seeking the one in his lap.

On the other side of him, Cordelia Whitworth did not offer a reprieve. She was still cross with him for not accepting her advances a year ago. He'd tried to explain that, contrary to rumor, he did not dally with other men's wives, but she had taken his refusal as a slight.

Although his statement implied a moral quality that everyone knew he didn't possess, his reason for this had more to do with his ultimate revenge against his grandfather than anything else. Simply put, wives were not as careful as widows when it came to matters of begetting a child.

Because of his slight a year ago, Cordelia now focused all her attention on the colonel, who sat on her other side. Beside Daniela, Sir Colin would have been without conversation entirely, had it not been for the soft-spoken Lady Archer. Beyond her, Sophie and Eve kept to their conversation, which left Venus—or rather, Miss Wakefield—to the company of the leering Lord Archer. Her gaze had only strayed to Bane's once during the entire service, and that was only when she answered a question posed to her by the colonel on her other arm.

As for Archer, his clumsy, drunken hand had strayed to her arm so frequently, Bane was of a mind to believe that this drunkenness was a mere act to aid him in getting away with pawing other women in front of his own wife. Throughout dinner, the thought stayed with him. And more than once, his brooding gaze went to the opposite side of the table.

When dinner finally concluded, Eve suggested they all adjourn to the parlor for coffee and cake, instead of leaving the men to their cigars and port. For that, Bane was grateful. He wasn't sure he could hold his temper with Archer.

In the parlor, he remained standing to better deter Daniela from finding her hand in his lap again. She was busily making the rounds, flirting with Hamersley while Cordelia conversed with Eve. Archer lounged in the window seat, while his wife and Sir Colin puzzled over a game of chess in the corner. Miss Wakefield and her aunt occupied the floral settee.

Each time Venus took a sip of the dark brew, her eyes closed in obvious pleasure. He'd been right about her preferring coffee after all. Now he found himself thirsty.

Instead of motioning to the servant to refill his cup, he crossed the room to where the silver carafe waited on a table near Mrs. Leander and her niece.

Miss Wakefield's eyes widened and she went still as a rabbit on the green, her cup paused in midair, her lips parted for another sip. What he wouldn't give to have those lips parted for him once more.

He casually picked up the carafe and filled his cup, lingering long enough to make conversation an inevitability. "Mrs. Leander, my aunt informs me you are a superb knitter."

Miss Wakefield's aunt blinked and then smiled. "I can hardly respond without a show of either arrogance or self-derision, but I thank you nonetheless. Have you an interest in knitting?"

"My mother was quite exceptional in the art. As a boy, the quick work of her needles fascinated me, but I was unable to learn the skill," he said, keeping the conversation light. In reality, the true reason had been because she'd been murdered by his grandfather soon after she'd started to teach him.

He motioned to the pair of tufted chairs opposite the settee, and she inclined her head, welcoming him into their small circle.

"Knitting, or sewing for that matter, isn't a typical trade for a gentleman."

"No," he agreed, taking a seat. "My valet is skilled enough at mending, though I'm sure it's nothing compared to the fine embroidery I see on your shawl." The garment was draped over the arm of the settee beside her—intricate turquoise shells stitched along the edge above the flaxen fringe. He wasn't normally one to notice such things, but these caught his attention, and he didn't see any harm in paying a compliment when it was due. "Quite remarkable."

She smiled and looked to her seat companion. "My niece is an artist with needle and thread." Miss Wakefield's cheeks colored at the unexpected compliment, but she did not say anything before her aunt continued. "No doubt, the wife you choose will have knitting or sewing experience."

A startled laugh escaped him, nearly causing him to spill his coffee. "I see why you and Eve are friends. You are of a like mind."

"And you?"

"Am not." He was certain he said it with irrefutable conviction, closing the topic permanently, and yet…

"I'm sure you have your reasons," Mrs. Leander said, ignoring her niece's look of censure and her obvious plea to cease further communication. "Most likely this explains your lack of presence in society. A credit to your character is your firm resolve."

Strange, his *firm resolve* had always been considered *single-minded determination* by others and never spoken of favorably. Puzzled by the compliment, he offered a nod. "Thank you, and yes. Though my character is by no means unblemished, I would not add another mark against it by parading myself around the young debutantes, pretending I had any intention of marrying."

He expected to see Miss Wakefield bristle at this announcement. In the end, most young women were in society for the purpose of marriage, whether for a title or the fanciful ideal of love. He assumed Venus was no different. Her intelligent banter told him she was schooled in the art of husband-luring. However, instead of stiffening or taking offense, he saw her relax—not by any defect in her posture but simply an overall sense of calm that emanated from her.

"Some might rank that as the highest of character credits," Venus responded, her gaze thoughtful, as if she were considering a new philosophy. "Indeed, if a man has no intention of marrying, he should keep to his coterie."

"Or become a rustic," he said, hoping to see her smug amusement return. It did not. She did smile—a small smile more directed to her next sip than to him. Her quiet resolve made him curious. He found himself wanting to ask her to explain her comment. Yet when he opened his mouth to do just that, Daniela sidled up to their group.

"I could not help but overhear. I quite agree. A man who toys with a young woman's affections is the vilest of all creatures," she added with a pout and placed her hand on Bane's shoulder. "I am utterly heartbroken, Miss Wakefield, that you have firsthand experience in such horrible matters. A five-year attachment to one gentlemen, only to have him rush off in the opposite direction? You must be devastated. Why, of course you are. There is certainly no need for me to remind you of your loss."

Bane quickly put the pieces together. Abandoned after a five-year attachment? Now he understood why Venus had been invited to Lady Amherst's. That fact alone made a young woman a walking scandal, to say the least. Her reputation was likely in question. Yet his experience at reading people told him, *without a doubt*, she was an innocent. In fact, he wouldn't be surprised if kissing him had been the only bold thing she'd done in her life.

"A temporary loss only," Mrs. Leander interrupted, polite as a porcupine, quills at the ready. "He is simply too young to know his mind. A short duration apart will set it right again."

"Yes, of course. He will soon see what an angel he had in our precious Meriwether."

"Merribeth," Venus said, her voice low. "'Miss Wakefield,' if you please, Mrs. Pearce."

Though she attempted a polite smile as well, beneath the fall of curls over her forehead, he distinctly saw her brow arch. And what a fearsome brow it was. Bane felt his admiration of her charms grow exponentially.

"Oh, pish-posh. You must call me Daniela," she said as she took the remaining seat in their group. "After Eve explained the task she's put upon you, I eagerly volunteered to be your tutor. So, you see? We shall be bosom friends very soon, and in a fortnight, you will reclaim your wayward gentleman."

His Venus blushed furiously and cast a look of brimstone directly at Eve. "Our hostess is too kind."

"Task?" someone asked. When all eyes turned to him, Bane realized he must have been the one. Though he tried to pretend disinterest in the conversation, he found his curiosity growing by the moment.

"To gain back the affections of her beloved, of course."

Beloved? He highly doubted it. After all, he recalled asking her that night if she had a heart in need of mending. He recalled her surprising response as well. Now, when he glanced across the space between them, he would have placed a wager that she was remembering the same. "And Eve knows how to accomplish this?"

"Apparently, yes," Venus answered, doing an admirable job of schooling her features.

He tucked his smirk of doubt into his cup and drained the last of it.

"I find the plan inspired," Daniela said, finding it necessary to tap her hand against Bane's knee as she explained. "She is to flirt, be carefree, and enjoy herself immensely. Then, at the ball on the final night of the party, her beloved will see that she isn't devastated at all. This will spark not only his interest but a yearning to get her back."

And once her gentleman renewed his affections, her reputation would no longer be in tatters. Ah. Now he understood. "Impressive plan."

The man who'd cried off was quite obviously a simpleton if he thought his action would leave Miss Wakefield's reputation unscathed. Bane felt the dark mood he'd experienced at dinner descend upon him again. Before, he'd merely shrugged it off as an instant dislike of Archer. Now, he wondered if it was something else entirely.

"You must help our dear Meriwether, Bane. Flirt with her. We'll make a game of it as we would at *Forfeits*."

Although he didn't outwardly refuse, he didn't give Daniela the response she was hoping for either. The thing was, he never played a game unless the outcome was certain.

CHAPTER SEVEN

Merribeth didn't bother to correct Daniela this time, but set her coffee cup and saucer on the low oval table between them. "I fear exhaustion from the day's long journey has swept over me quite suddenly. Please forgive me, but I must retire."

"I am too tired for parlor games as well," Sophie said and made her excuses to retire early.

They both stood. So did Lord Knightswold and then Mrs. Pearce. Merribeth watched as the widow slipped her arm through his and sidled closer. A rise of temper churned in her veins like a tempest. It was so unexpected and overwhelming that she didn't trust herself to speak another word. Instead, she merely turned and walked through the doors beside her aunt.

"Do not take anything Mrs. Pearce said to heart and let her spoil your fun," Sophie said as they mounted the stairs. "She's merely the type who likes to put on a show with her claws. In this venue, her comments are harmless. Besides, it is the woman who sheaths her claws and waits for the perfect opportunity who ends up with the cream from the top of the pail."

Merribeth felt her nails dig into the tender flesh of her palms and thought how lovely it would be to scratch out Daniela's eyes. However, she would wait, as her aunt suggested. A grin curled up the corners of her mouth. She felt better instantly.

"You surprise me," Merribeth said once they reached Sophie's rooms. "I would have suspected a quote from one of your scientific journals. Instead, this sounds as if you have experience in the matter."

"Yes, well…I was a debutante once too." After a quick look over her shoulder toward the stairs, she pulled Merribeth into her room and closed the door. "Most likely, I should have mentioned this from the beginning, but our hostess and I have not always been the best of friends. Quite the opposite, in fact."

The revelation should have surprised her, she knew. After all, Eve had gone out of her way to ensure that Merribeth had a Season. Anyone would assume that only a true friend would act so selflessly. However, the fact that Eve had suddenly returned to Sophie's life little more than two years ago after a long absence had made her wonder. At the time, her aunt had said that sometimes friends find interests in things that pull them in different directions, and she'd spoken in her matter-of-fact way that effectively closed the topic.

Yet Merribeth couldn't help but remember the day Eve had offered to sponsor her, explaining that she couldn't refuse because it was her way of making amends.

"You do make an unlikely pair."

Sophie made a sound of agreement as she walked to the hearth to stir the low fire. "She was the premier beauty of the

Season. Every man was vying for her hand. Well…every man but one. Sir Herman Wrigglesworth, a bookish gentleman with a passion for Egyptian artifacts, actually preferred my company."

"Of course he would," Merribeth said with a smile, until she saw her aunt's solemn expression. "What happened to him?"

"Back then, Eve was fond of her schemes," Sophie said with sigh of resignation. "Of course, I don't blame her now. She couldn't help the way she was. Countless women have learned to use beauty to their advantage. Every woman possesses certain wiles or innate skills."

True. Although Merribeth would like to have thought that if she'd been born a beauty, manipulation wouldn't have been *her* skill. "And her scheme removed you from your gentleman?"

"Yes. Though I won't go into maudlin detail, I will say that by the end of my Season, I was through with the ways of the *beau monde* and fully prepared for a life as a governess."

Up until now, Sophie had told her that the reason she'd spent six years as a governess was because her Seasons had been unsuccessful. Merribeth now realized the truth, and her heart broke for the young woman her aunt once was.

"Were you terribly fond of Sir Herman?" she asked quietly.

"I didn't think I could ever love again. I told Captain Leander as much when he proposed a marriage of convenience." Sophie puffed out a breath and shook her head, as if the notion were preposterous. "But I'm very glad to have been wrong."

"You were happy, then?"

"Immeasurably. Just as you will be." She stepped forward and placed her hands on Merribeth's shoulders. Her expression abruptly turned serious. "Which is the *only* reason, mind you, I ever agreed to this scheme."

"Don't worry." Merribeth leaned in for a quick embrace. "This will work. I'll make certain of it."

Shortly thereafter, she left Sophie's room and headed toward her own.

It took a moment for her eyes to adjust to the dimly lit hall. The only sconces lit were in the corners, with nothing in between. The light faded into complete shadow midway down the first hall. Her gaze fixed to the pale flicker further down. Even though her mind was somewhat preoccupied with the conversation she'd had with her aunt, she still felt uneasy about passing all these darkened doorways, and so kept to the middle.

When she rounded the first corner, she heard the echo of heavy footsteps behind her. Instantly, her heart sped up, as did her own steps. This corridor was even longer and darker than the one before. She was certain the hall that led to her room was somewhere in between, but she could see no evidence of it.

"I thought I'd retire as well," the now familiar voice of Archer called out, although his voice no longer possessed a slur, as it had all throughout dinner. "The parlor seemed dull and lifeless without your presence."

She swallowed down a lump of fear at the thought of his following her.

"Archer?" another voice said. The husky tone belonged to none other than Daniela. "Oh, I must be turned around if your rooms are along this path. But my, you are the flatterer. I'd no idea you knew I was behind you."

Merribeth held her breath, wondering if Archer would admit to being in pursuit of someone else.

His footsteps abruptly stopped. "But of course," he stammered for a response. Thankfully, he didn't reveal his true target, which gave Merribeth the chance to escape. "I'd know the swish of your skirts anywhere."

Daniela offered an affected laugh. "What a teasing thing to say from a married man."

"Many rules are written solely for the sake of being bent... just a little," Archer said, affecting the slur once again.

Not wanting to risk another encounter with that horrible woman or the baron, Merribeth tiptoed down the hall and headed toward the pale flicker of a sconce not far off. She hoped it would provide enough light for her to find the path that led to her room.

Stepping quickly around the corner, she glanced over her shoulder, the worn soles of her slippers padding quietly over the runner. The sound of their conversation seemed to be closing in, along with Archer's heavy footsteps.

She hurried. Believing the hall to her room was nearby, she looked ahead—then stopped with a jolt as Bane emerged from the shadows.

With his gaze locked on hers, he motioned with an index finger against his lips. In the same instant, he glanced over her shoulder as if to indicate Archer and Daniela.

She nodded, both in understanding and in a request for his aid. Reaching up, he extinguished the sconce. Suddenly, she was immersed in darkness. The sconces behind her were too far away to offer anything but meager light, and it appeared as if the sconces behind Bane had all been extinguished. *By him.*

She barely heard him move toward her. Yet she could sense his nearness all the same. His hand snaked around hers, holding her captive. At the same time, he pressed his finger against her lips. "Don't make a sound, or you'll give us both away."

A shiver raced through her at his low whisper. His finger was warm and slightly rough against her flesh. The scent from his hand filled her nostrils, much the same way that the snifter of warm brandy had. The mélange of his unique fragrance began with the pleasing odor of freshly oiled leather, deep and rich. Underneath, was a combination of coffee and sandalwood. There were other fragrances too, but before she could identify them all, he lowered his finger, dragging it gently down her lips.

Apparently, he trusted her with their fate. Trusted her not to give them away. In all honesty, it went against her upbringing and every maidenly instinct not to step out of his grasp. Yet another instinct compelled her to go with him, allowing him to guide her in the dark.

He pulled her into a recessed doorway, turning so that she nestled into the corner while he remained closer to the outside, as if shielding her. He still held her hand too. And since she'd removed her gloves, her flesh was bare against his. *Bare and warm and secure.*

She shook her head, dislodging the errant thought before it took hold. Likely, the odd sense of safety she felt now happened because she saw him as less of a threat than Archer. Bane's actions spoke of a man keeping himself from being discovered more than looking out for *her* reputation. She was certain that only his love of solitude and tendency toward hermitage ruled his actions.

In a way, it was amusing. This rake—*the seducer*, the man every mama and well-intentioned aunt warned young women against—was hiding in a darkened hallway, hoping to be left alone.

Merribeth found it oddly endearing. She smiled to herself, wondering at the riddle of Bane.

"Bending rules? What fun is bending something when it could be more fun to shatter it to pieces?" Daniela's seductive drawl drew closer.

Startled, Merribeth squeezed Bane's hand. He squeezed back in reassurance.

The baron chuckled as his footfalls stopped. "I've a mind to break a few."

"Why, Archer," Daniela said with a muffled giggle. "What if your wife discovers us?"

"Are you saying you're not my dear Petunia? How could I have made such a mistake?"

Merribeth nearly groaned at the lie. At dinner, she'd wondered if his drunkenness was a pretense he used to flirt with other women without being called out for it. Now, she was sure of it. The despicable man.

"If she finds us, I'll let out a shriek and tell her you were saving me from a spider. I do detest them, you know."

"And if she doesn't believe me, I'll simply tell her you're all the same in the dark," Archer continued, panting slightly. "It's worked before."

All the same in the dark? Merribeth looked up, expecting to ask Bane. As if sensing it, he turned and placed his hand on her shoulder, though whether to quiet or reassure her, she couldn't tell.

Surely, it couldn't be the truth. Men had to have more sense than that. After all, she knew Bane by the sound of his voice. Even if he hadn't spoken, she would have recognized him by scent. Not to mention by the way he filled every space around him and seemed to take all the air for himself.

He was doing that now, especially with his hand on her shoulder, his thumb absently stroking the seam of her capped sleeve as if imbedding himself into every stitch. She could hardly catch her breath.

"Certainly your roaming hands ought to tell you the difference," Daniela said to Archer.

Merribeth had heard enough. How could she stand by and listen to this horrid adultery take place. Poor Lady Archer!

Bane shifted quickly and pressed his hand against her lips, as if he sensed she couldn't hold her tongue a moment longer. At the same time, he drew her out of the doorway and headed down the far hall, away from the loathsome Archer and Daniela. She was careful to keep to the runner, so that her steps were muffled. It surprised her that she could barely hear Bane's steps as well.

"Aye, and you don't mind either. In fact…" Archer's voice trailed off for a moment, the silence broken by Daniela's breathy moan before he continued. "I think you like it. And here I thought you were hoping to play a game of *seek and sigh* with Knightswold."

"What does it matter? *You're all the same in the dark,*" she mocked, her voice barely audible now that Bane and Merribeth had reached the end of the hall.

Bane opened a door and pulled Venus inside before he released her hand. His reluctance to do just that puzzled him. However, he needed both of his to make sure the latch wouldn't make a sound as it fell into place.

Pale, silvery moonlight filtered in through two narrow windows, casting the room in shades of gray. At least it was enough light to see the outline of furniture in the room. That way, neither of them was likely to stumble.

He went to the chest at the foot of the bed and reached inside. Pulling out whatever clothing or coat was on top, he quickly bundled the heavy fabric into a cylindrical shape and laid it at the bottom of the door. "So that our voices will not be heard," he whispered, sensing her unspoken question.

"Where are we?" she asked, her voice more curious than wary. He wished it were the other way around.

"My bedchamber." The hushed words filled the room, charging the air. He shook his head, warding off errant thoughts. "You needn't worry. Unmarried maidens with marital designs are not to my taste. So if you have any for me, abandon them quickly."

To her credit, she didn't gasp or start. Instead, he caught a glimpse of a smirk before she turned and crossed the room toward the far window. It was open just enough to create a breeze, drawing in the cool sweetness of dewy midnight. Or perhaps that was her scent, drawing out an emerging poet within him.

Again, Bane shook his head as he propped one shoulder against the corner post of the bed and watched her silhouette.

"Yes, I'm already aware you are not one to take advantage when presented with an opportunity in a darkened room. Yet apparently, the same cannot be said of me. Oh, wait. We are pretending we've never met before, are we not?" She leaned forward, her face out the window, and breathed in. "Yes, I prefer that."

Moonlight on her dark hair, weaving paths of starlight… His thoughts trailed off as he realized she was doing it again— turning him into a horrid poet.

"As do I," he said, wanting to bait her into an argument, though he knew not why.

Any other woman would have bristled but not her. She laughed instead, the sound teasing the inner canals of his ears, forcing him to swallow down each trill, making them a part of him.

"You think rather highly of yourself. Holing up away from society because you fear every unattached maiden is vying for your hand. You needn't worry," she said, tossing his own words back to him over her shoulder. "My marital designs are already engaged."

Though he'd meant to rile her, somehow she'd turned the tables. For reasons beyond him, *he* felt irked. "What about his? Is he free to accept *your* suit?"

When he saw her shoulders stiffen, instead of feeling triumphant at achieving his goal, he instantly felt like ass.

"Eve assures me that he will renew his affections of his own accord."

Still, her response chafed him, and his next words were out before he knew what he was saying. "You have put your faith in my aunt? My, what a lambkin you are." Even though he tried to sound amused, there was a distinct edge of bitterness.

"Believe me, I would have nothing to do with her scheme if I were left with another option." She breathed out and turned back to the window. "Even if I were to find another man willing to marry a penniless woman with few connections, my sullied reputation would carry on with me. My husband would lose respect. Our children would be outcasts by association. In addition, the alternative option is spending the rest of my days with Sophie and tainting her reputation instead. So, you see, I am at a crossroads."

"This gentleman, this *man*"—for he was no gentleman—"who jilted you, is he a simpleton or did he know what he was doing to your reputation?"

"Ours was not an official engagement but more of an understanding," she said with an exhausted sigh, as if she'd spent far too many hours in contemplation over this topic. "We'd known each other since I was ten years old and first moved to Berkshire with my aunt and her new husband. William was our neighbor, his father a wealthy solicitor. We played together, partnered at country dances. As we grew older, many commented on what a fine pair we made. So when he told me how easy it would be to marry me and began speaking of children, I took that as his way of professing his intentions." Her voice grew quieter. "Instead, I only recently discovered, he merely believed he was speaking with a friend about *his* future. Not *ours*."

Bane held back the impulse to cross the room and offer... *what*, he didn't know. Comfort, perhaps? Although the only method of comfort he could imagine would be in his arms and in the nearby bed, and *that* he would not do. "He should have made it clear from the beginning."

"Perhaps. And then, perhaps I should have asked him to clarify instead of spending the past five years planning our life together." She shrugged and absently ran her fingers down the edge of the curtain. After a moment, she said, "My dress was beautiful."

"Pardon?" He was distracted by the movement of her fingers over the fabric, remembering how they'd felt in his hair. How they might feel on his flesh.

"My wedding gown. I spent the past five years embroidering every inch of the muslin. At first, I only meant to add a curling ivy border to the hem, but as time went on, the gown became more elaborate." She sniffed and tried to hide the swipe of her hand against her cheek. "It's really quite lovely."

This time, Bane grabbed hold of the post to keep from crossing the room to her. Bringing her here was a mistake, he could see that now. Too much was at stake—the wager, his revenge, Gypsy.

He thought he'd have more control over his response to her than this. The most ludicrous part of it was that this conversation wasn't the least bit arousing. Quite the opposite, in fact. She was talking about wedding gowns and confessing a need to plan out every detail of her future, which was another reason why he avoided debutantes and balls.

However, he found himself wanting her in a way that he'd never experienced. This wasn't about idle curiosity or an escape from the mundane. This wasn't about desire either, although that was always present when she was in the room. This was about *her*.

Likely, this strange feeling had everything to do with the bargain he'd made with Eve. The simple fact that he *couldn't* make love to Merribeth, or kiss the tears from her cheeks, or comfort her with endless hours of pleasure must be the sole reason he felt desperate to do so.

The overwhelming impulse startled him. He had to get her out of his room. Out of his thoughts. Out of his reach. While there were countless ways of bringing her pleasure that did not require him to don a preventative or steal her virginity, for the first time he didn't trust himself with the strength to hold back.

He'd never been this tempted before. Widows and courtesans tempted him, *not* virgins. Not married women either, for that matter. *Then help her marry*, a voice whispered. It was the only solution.

"I'll help you." The words came out in a frantic rush.

She turned her back on the window and stared at him. "Help me with what?"

"This task Eve has put upon you." He made a stirring motion with his hands, impatient. "I'll teach you to flirt. I'll help you win back your Mr. Clairmore."

Merribeth didn't know whether to be offended by Bane's offer or grateful. Her first instinct was to take offense. After all, she'd endured Mrs. Pearce's pitying words and uncalled-for-boldness on a private matter.

It had been humiliating to have her problems announced to Bane. Once again, she was the museum spectacle, the curious specimen of the *Desperate Wallflower in Dire Straits*.

She drew in a breath, forcing herself to look on the bright side. For reasons unknown to her, Bane seemed eager to help her, not humiliate her. That alone helped chase off embarrassment. He had a way of making her feel comfortable about saying what she wanted to say, without risk of censure. So in the end, it was easy to feel grateful.

Of course, there was a different feeling that *didn't* sit well with her and that caused the twinge of pain.

It was silly, she knew, to be hurt that he was eager to help her get Mr. Clairmore back. As if the offer clearly stated that he didn't want her for himself—which of course she already knew. So why should hearing him say it directly wound her?

"Very well," she said, her tone formal and stiff, even to her own ears.

"*Very well?*" He made a sound in his throat. His gray eyes caught a shred of moonlight, seeming to absorb it until those two intense points were all she could see. "With my help, you are assured success in your scheme. Besides, I never embark on a task or wager unless I'm certain of victory. Perhaps a little gratitude is in order."

It wasn't her scheme, but she didn't bother to correct him. She actually found his bristly behavior amusing. "I am a quick study, Lord Knightswold. And the first thing I learned from you was not to assume that the rumors about you were true. So far, in our short acquaintance, I've seen no evidence that you can assure my success. You've displayed no particular prowess for flirting. However, if it will please you to hear it, before you've even put forth the smallest effort to assist me, then here it is: thank you. I am *ever* grateful for your assistance."

He stared at her for a long moment. His gaze speared through her like a silver needle through silk. Even though he stood perfectly still, waves of energy flowed from him, stinging her flesh with tiny pinpricks of awareness.

He released the post and regarded her for a moment longer. Only now did she realize he'd been gripping it the entire time. She wondered at the reason for that but even more at his reason for letting go. Now that she'd challenged him, would he cross the room to her to prove himself worthy of rumor?

She held her breath, waiting. Hoping. A breeze blew in behind her, stirring the fine hairs at her nape, making her shiver.

Then he shook his head and chuckled. "Keep your thanks for a fortnight, Miss Wakefield." He moved to the door, his steps not as unhurried and languid as usual. Obviously, he was ready to see her go. "I imagine the task will not be a simple one. For either of us."

"I imagine not," she said, already hearing regret in his tone and trying not to take offense. Head high, she crossed the room, prepared to walk out the door.

Bane held up a hand as if to ward her off. Now, she did take offense. He acted as if she carried an infectious disease. *Wallfloweritus* or something equally ghastly.

"Let me make certain the path is clear before I escort you."

She glared at his retreating form, waited a breath, and then stepped over the threshold.

He returned at once, blocking her way. "Neither of us can risk having you seen leaving my room. Or walking this hall, for that matter."

"It is highly unlikely that I would endure censure for the sake of being on this path."

He crossed his arms over his chest. "Apparently, you still have much to learn about holding on to the shreds of your reputation."

"Perhaps," she hissed through her teeth, wishing she could raise her voice above a whisper. "Though I would warrant that no one could find fault with me for walking to my own room, which happens to be there." She pointed to the end of the hall.

She'd recognized her window when she'd looked out of Bane's. Why Eve had put them in such close proximity puzzled her. She reasoned it was likely due to the fact that only a certain number of rooms had been prepared for guests. Compared to the other guests with whom she might have been neighbors, she decided to be grateful.

"Your room"—He swallowed, causing his jaw muscle to twitch—"is next to mine?"

When he said it like that, she couldn't help but swallow as well. It *was* rather scandalous. "Apparently so."

"I'll have it changed at once."

Irritation at his eagerness swept over her. Now it was her turn to cross her arms. "Yes, and when you tell your aunt that you'd like a different room, be sure to tell her the reason. I'm certain she would love to hear how you found out."

Right at the moment when she was certain that steam was rising from her head, he chuckled.

"Miss Wakefield, this might be the longest fortnight of our lives."

Of that, she had no doubt.

Naming the Roses 111

kept a firm grip on her sleeve to remind him not to
shake loose her hold on the field.

"Yes. Well." She studied the hedges bordering the
...

Or was she too shell-...

CHAPTER EIGHT

"...the perfect morning for a walk," Aunt Sophie concluded.

The first part of her statement had gone unheard beneath Merribeth's yawn. However, the last part left Merribeth enough of a clue for the appropriate response. Not only that, but she could identify uncalled-for-cheerfulness when she heard it.

She squinted against the sunlight cresting over the rolling hills to the east. "If it were the perfect morning, I'd still be asleep." Instead, she'd lain awake most of the night, thinking about Bane and his sudden desire to help her win back Mr. Clairmore. What had prompted him to aid her in something that he must view as trivial? He gave every indication of loathing the institution of marriage. Why had he seemed so adamant—nearly desperate—to ensure hers?

Her aunt cast an entirely too smug grin. "We turned in early last evening."

Merribeth grumbled.

"I warned you about having more than one cup of coffee last night."

Coffee. Her entire body whimpered with longing at the mere mention of the word. "A better warning would have been, 'My dear niece, I plan to barge into your room before sunrise and pester you until you agree to walk the grounds with me.'"

"And aren't you glad you indulged your poor, aging aunt? We have seen so much of the lands this morning. Did you know that the ruins of a ninth-century leper hospital are nearby as well? I even heard talk of relics from pagan Danes who once sought refuge here. Can you imagine? I think tomorrow—"

"Absolutely not. Tomorrow, I already have firm plans to avoid the sunrise."

Sophie frowned and reached up to remove her glasses. Once they walked into the shadows of the tree-lined path, the temperature cooled and fogged her lenses. However, not having perfect vision didn't prevent her aunt from casting a look of disapproval. "The whole purpose of our attending this party is to enjoy ourselves. I've seen what the past few weeks have done to you. The merriment has left your eyes. I want you to have fun and to—"

"*Be brave.*" If nothing else came of this house party, at least these lessons would cease in less than two weeks.

"Precisely," Sophie said with a nod. She rubbed her lenses with the corner of her shawl.

"Still, I cannot guarantee my attendance tomorrow morning," Merribeth said in all seriousness. "I distinctly heard my coverlet and pillow conspiring to hold me captive until luncheon. I fear no amount of bravery will save me."

Apparently, her aunt's sense of humor had yet to awaken. "We only have this fortnight. After that..."

Merribeth drew in a deep breath, prepared to tell Sophie that she would take her task of regaining Mr. Clairmore's affections more seriously, but in the same moment, she caught the scent of something delicious on the breeze. "Do you smell coffee?"

She turned, sniffing the air for another whiff. *Yes, coffee!* Up ahead, a host of angels directed a beam of heavenly light to a thatched roof and the long fieldstone structure of the stables. The scent grew stronger. Her mouth watered as her feet propelled her across the dewy lawn. The promise of the dark elixir was close now.

In the stable yard stood an Arabian with a glossy black coat and an exceedingly round belly. The mare nuzzled the nose of skewbald pony with cream-colored markings and which stood at least three hands shorter. Long, fringed lashes swept down as the mare's eyes closed, as if with pure affection. The pony responded in kind, pressing his muzzle to her neck.

The sight stole Merribeth's attention for a moment. Then the fragrant breeze hit her again, and her focus returned to her main goal. With a slight shift of her gaze, she spotted the object of her obsession—though whether it was the coffee or the man holding it, she couldn't be entirely sure.

Sitting on the wide top rail of the fence, with his back against a tall corner post, was none other than Lord Knightswold. In his grasp, he held an earthenware tankard, with a hinged pewter lid propped open over the handle. Ribbons of steam curled upward, and by the rich fragrance drifting toward her, she knew it wasn't ale he drank this early in the morning but something far more pleasing.

Beside her, Sophie kept pace. "My, what a surprise. He appears quite comfortable there, does he not?"

As he drew the tankard to his lips, she couldn't help but admire his profile. That easy, languid grace he carried with him was patently evident now. Even though he scarcely moved, there was something in the way he watched the horses that spoke of contentment. She felt as if she were seeing a man perfectly at home in his surroundings.

Yet as she drew closer, she noticed something else that puzzled her. He looked different somehow. There was an unguarded quality to him this morning, here with these horses. She had the strange suspicion that this was the only time she'd witness such an expression. At the thought, an unfamiliar yearning to understand more about him unfurled inside her.

She pressed her fist to her breast, where she felt it stir.

"Are you unwell?" Sophie asked, slowing her steps.

Realizing what she'd done, and disliking that she wasn't allowed an unguarded moment, she dropped her hand to her side. Keeping her gaze straight ahead, Merribeth said, "I could say 'perfectly well,' if you were only now waking me."

Although he made no observable motion that gave his awareness away, she saw the change in Bane instantly. One moment, he was content to be alone with the horses and the next, he was aware and guarded. It was as if the morning light over the paddock suddenly dimmed and the air around him darkened.

Slowly, he turned his gaze, a carefully crafted smile of greeting in place. Yet when he saw who approached, his smiled altered into the smirk she knew better. Unbidden, a blush warmed her cheeks, even before she had the presence of mind to know what embarrassed her.

"Forgive our trespass on your solitude, Lord Knight-swold," her aunt said. "We were drawn in by the quaint image of these two affectionate friends."

Merribeth turned with a start, only to realize Sophie was referring to the horses. *But of course she was.* Thankfully, her aunt didn't notice the look of dismay that must have been on her face.

Bane chuckled. Of course, *he* wouldn't miss a thing. "There is nothing to forgive, Mrs. Leander. They enjoy the attention."

Merribeth didn't have to look at him to know his amusement was directed at her, but she lifted her gaze all the same.

She was right. He was looking at her and rather intently too. Though nothing had happened last night in his bed-chamber, she felt changed all the same, as if a bond had been forged between them. They were connected now. He'd vowed to help her in her quest. And without knowing very much about him at all, she knew he was not a man who made promises lightly.

"Good morning," she said, her voice insubstantial, as if every remnant of breath had left her body.

He lifted his tankard in salute. "And to you." Then he took a sip, and suddenly she was reliving the feel of his lips beneath hers and tasting the flavors that mingled on his tongue. Just as suddenly, a heated shimmer flared in his gaze, as if they were of like mind.

She heard a small sound, like the mew of a cat, and realized with embarrassment that the noise had come from her.

Reaching up, she placed her hand to her throat. "Forgive me, I—" She broke off, not knowing what to say. After all, she couldn't very well announce that she'd been reliving the kiss they'd shared. Or rather, the one she'd borrowed and then returned.

"I'm certain Lord Knightswold wouldn't be shocked by your secret"—Sophie began, startling Merribeth for a beat—"fondness for coffee."

"Very little shocks me anymore," Bane said, sounding like the jaded man everyone knew him to be. Everyone except for Merribeth. She didn't know why, but she knew there was much more to him than he let on.

And she had the strange urge to discover it all.

"Would you care for a sip, Miss Wakefield?" He held the tankard out in offering.

"Thank you," she said without considering how it looked. It only occurred to her after that if anyone else had made the offer, she would have politely declined. *Too late now*. She already had her hands on the ornately carved earthenware.

Sophie let out a gasp. Knowing that her aunt wasn't usually prudish when it came to matters of propriety, Merribeth turned her curious gaze on her.

"Is that a depiction of the Knights Templar on your cup?" Sophie asked.

"It is," Bane answered. "One of Eve's ancestors discovered a collection of relics in the caves beneath the priory ruins. The cook, Mrs. Carwin, keeps them locked in her cupboard but allows me to use this one for my coffee when I visit. She claims it's better to fill this once than to risk her fine crockery in the stables."

"A collection. Do you think she would allow me to…" Sophie's eyes went round. Then, as if she remembered her place as chaperone, she turned to Merribeth. "You wouldn't mind if I abandoned you for a moment, would you?"

Merribeth lifted the tankard and took a sip. "I am content to be right here. Besides, we are in full view of the house"— though no one else was likely awake at this hour—"and there are at least a dozen groomsmen and gardeners milling about," though she had yet to see one.

Apparently, it was all the excuse her aunt needed. With a wide grin that made her look ten years younger, Sophie patted her shoulder and left in the direction of the kitchen.

"I'm quite put out," Bane said, feigning insult. "One woman abandons my company in favor of some dusty relics, and the other only wants me for my coffee."

Merribeth smiled, greedily breathing in the dark aroma. "I'm certain my aunt would have remained if she were fond of coffee as well. There is plenty to share."

"Somehow, I doubt she would want to sip from the same tankard."

She took another sip. "Mmm…perhaps."

"Though you are not bothered by it," he said, his voice low, evoking a memory of a darkened study. "In fact, you turned it so the rim touched your lips where it had touched mine."

She lifted her gaze to his, waiting for embarrassment to come at the truth of his statement. She'd done it on purpose, knowing full well that he was watching her. However, no sudden flame burst in her cheeks. "Perhaps I was claiming the rest of it for my own."

To make her point, she took another long draw of the deliciously dark elixir. She closed her eyes but not before she saw another flare of heat in his.

"You need no help in flirting," he said with a wry chuckle that nearly sounded like a groan. "I've a mind to take lessons from you instead."

Panicked, her gaze flew to his. "But I do need your help. I am never like this with anyone else. You're the one who makes it easy to…"—*be myself*, she nearly said and wondered where the thought had come from—"to flirt." She took a breath. "I need you to teach me how to be this way with other gentlemen."

His gaze darkened. He lifted a leg from the opposite side of the fence and jumped down to the ground with ease, though perhaps landing too close to her. Yet, he didn't move apart—to keep a proper distance—and neither did she. "If I were any other man, a statement like that might make me jealous."

How her pulse could go from something of which she barely took notice to something that practically burst through her skin, from one moment to the next, she did not know. Right now, it was all she could feel. Her whole being was one violently pounding pulse point. "But you are not just any other man, are you?"

He shook his head, and his gaze drifted to her mouth. In the next instant, his hand was beneath her jaw, pressing against her wild pulse. The pad of his thumb swept over her bottom lip, spreading the dewy remains of the coffee like a balm.

Without thinking, her tongue darted out for one last taste, only to come into contact with his thumb. Driven by impulse, she closed her lips over the tip and flicked her tongue across his flesh. He tasted salty and smelled like leather, pine, and coffee. She closed her eyes and swirled her tongue over him again.

Bane's low growl shocked her out of her temporary insanity. She took a step back, discontinuing the contact. What had she been thinking?

This is all part of flirting, she tried to tell herself. Yet a small voice inside her whispered that *this* was quite different, at least for her.

Clearly, she hadn't been thinking at all.

Not knowing how to explain her actions, she abruptly thrust the tankard at him. The lid fell closed with an audible clap. "Perhaps my aunt is right. I should limit the amount of coffee I consume."

"Or perhaps you should be wary of the company you keep." He smirked at her, his thumb absently stroking the lip of the tankard.

A laugh of self-mockery bubbled out of her throat. "I'm beginning to think it is the other way around."

Bane found himself distracted all morning and through luncheon.

The crux of his problem lay in the fact that he'd made a bargain with Eve to be sociable. In other words, he couldn't escape.

Eve thought it would be a grand idea to picnic on fringed blankets overlooking the pond. Luncheon baskets were packed to serve two, which forced an intimacy within the group. Bane had the unfortunate *pleasure* of Daniela's company.

They sat beneath the veils of willow branches on the far side of the party. Most everyone chatted amiably. With the party situated on a slight hill that sloped down to the water, it made for easy conversation, acting almost like an amphitheater. They didn't have to raise their voices, even when conversing with those upon other blankets. This observation, however, went unnoticed by the exuberant widow.

"You have not touched your cake. Have you no taste for sweets, or are your *appetites* more of the savory variety?"

Several pairs of eyes flashed in their direction, including Miss Wakefield's. "Though I'm certain the cake is divine, I simply do not care for currants," he said, ignoring her efforts at flirtation.

She gave a laugh and reached forward to pinch off a corner of his cake, displaying her bosom to greatest advantage. "How very singular, my lord. Perhaps you could use more variety in your life."

How she'd ever managed to pique his interest, he couldn't fathom. Her inane bawdy talk was tiresome. He was of a mind to thank Eve for their bargain. It had saved him from making an enormous error.

"I do not believe I am alone in my aversion. It appears Miss Wakefield doesn't like her cake either." The truth of his statement was in a mass of crumbs spread out over her napkin, with a pile of currants off to the side. Why the sight stirred him, he had no idea.

Well, perhaps he had *some* idea. He just didn't want to think about it at the moment.

"Oh?" Daniela cast an appraising look over her shoulder and then returned the full force of her attention to him. "It appears our dear Meriwether doesn't care for carrots either, whereas I enjoy carrots a great deal."

"My aunt and I are saving the carrots for the horses," Merribeth commented innocently, apparently not noticing that Mrs. Leander and several others cringed at the widow's thinly veiled innuendo.

When Archer let out a chuckle, and her gaze slipped to her aunt's, Venus's eyes went round. Quick learner that she was, a wave of understanding dawned and with it, a fresh flood of color to her cheeks.

In the next instant, she narrowed her eyes, and the breeze blew the dark, curling tendrils from her forehead to reveal her wickedly arched brow. A peculiar thrill shot through him.

"Oh gracious, Sophie," she said with a convincing pretense of alarm, pointing up to the branches. "Is that a nest of spiders over Lord Knightswold's head?"

Her comment was met with instant shrieking. Daniela leapt to her feet and flew out from beneath the canopy. In fact, she was so quick that if she had been a horse up for auction, he would have paid a monkey for her.

"I believe those are silkworms. Perfectly harmless," Mrs. Leander commented calmly, as if there weren't a woman dancing around and shrieking a few steps away. She gave her niece a small smile of approval.

Eve took this opportunity to stand and redirect the party's focus. "Whether spiders or silkworms, it's clear that our luncheon is over." She smoothed her hands down the front of another perfectly tailored dress, which likely had cost Bane a pretty penny. "I propose to take our party round the bend to where I spy a trail of goslings. If we take our crumbs, we could feed them."

Surprisingly, no one offered resistance but readily gathered crusts of bread into napkins and followed the path to the opposite end of the pond. Archer went behind the hill where Daniela had disappeared.

Bane was in no hurry to join the party, partly because he longed to enjoy a few moments of quiet solitude and partly because he saw that Venus had forgotten her shawl. Any moment, she would return for it.

Preoccupied by the idea, he made his way to the shore and began tossing bits of crust into the water. It bothered him that he'd found himself distracted by her since they'd met. He couldn't even sleep without thoughts of her interfering. Now, knowing that she was staying in the next room only made it worse. He couldn't wait for the party to end, for this... *obsession* of his to cease.

Then why was he waiting for her to return for her shawl?

He shook his head. This wasn't like him.

In the early morning hours, he'd come up with a likely conclusion to explain his unusual behavior. His bargain with Eve. Apparently, declaring abstinence for a fortnight kept him constantly imagining the opposite. Though why his mind only entertained the idea with Miss Wakefield was another puzzle. After all, he never dallied with virgins. What would be the point? Virgins knew nothing about pleasure...

His thoughts drifted back to this morning and to the way her warm, soft mouth had closed over the tip of his thumb and to the feel of her tongue swirling over his flesh.

He shuddered.

All right. So perhaps this particular virgin knew a little about pleasure, albeit accidentally. Certainly enough to pique the interest of an engorged part of his anatomy. Venus possessed a natural instinct for pleasure that could easily be guided by the right instructor…

Damn! He must stop these thoughts at once!

He looked down at the erection, straining into an unmistakable tent beneath the fall of his breeches. It actually caused him pain, a deep, clenching ache. He wanted nothing more than to grab the next available female, seduce her right here on the lush bed of grass, and hear her whisper his name over and over again. *Bane. Bane…*

"Lord Knightswold?" a familiar voice asked, just as a hand touched his shoulder.

He jerked, startled away from his erotic thoughts, only to find the object of them before him. "Miss Wakefield."

"I apologize for startling you. I spoke your name several times."

He didn't have a ready response and so let his gaze drift over her features—the sooty lashes that framed her blue eyes, berry-stained lips, elegant throat with a wildly thrumming pulse beneath her jaw, and back to the berry-stained lips again. He knew their texture. Their warmth. Their flavor.

She blushed as if she'd read his thoughts.

"I see no reason to delay your instruction," he said, grasping at the first non-erotic thought he could pinpoint. Then again, part of him was imagining another type of instruction, especially when he saw the tip of her tongue dart out to wet her lips.

"My instruction? Oh, yes. The flirting, of course," she stammered, as if her own thoughts were as muddled as his. "I don't know. I really shouldn't tarry. It would make people suspicious."

"We'll walk together," he said without analyzing how quickly he came up with a reason to keep her company. However, as he moved forward and felt a twinge in his groin, he knew that he'd need a moment before he could walk without making his condition obvious. Then again, all Merribeth had to do was look down.

He moved to stand behind her and settled his hands at her shoulders. "You look flushed, overly warm. Allow me to carry your shawl." Before she could consent, he slipped it from her shoulders and held it in front of him. However, the motion caused the soft pear-blossom scent of her hair and skin to rise. Drawing in a breath caused another jolt of pain through him.

"Thank you," she breathed, unaware of his agony. "It is rather warm. I believe the goslings have the right of it by keeping to the water."

Venus in the water was the last image he needed at the moment. He nearly groaned. "As for your instruction, we'll begin with the most rudimentary." Somehow, he soldiered on and started down the narrow path. Since he chose a meandering pace to conceal any oddness in his gait, she easily kept up with him. "The key to flirting is all in the look. You have to look at a man as if you know a secret about him."

"A secret," she mused, a playful smirk drawing out a tiny dimple in the corner of her mouth. "Like filching the silver?"

Grateful for the distraction, he chuckled and shook his head. "An intimate secret, my dear." It was strange how the endearment slipped out naturally. Since he was certain she would merely believe it was his way of flirting, he refused to think too much of it. "Try Sir Colin, there."

Up ahead, the man in question was warding off an attack of feathers. Each time his wife nodded or turned her head in conversation with Eve, the plumage sticking out from her turban would slap him in the face, causing him to scratch his nose. No doubt, Eve was completely aware of this and delighted in holding Cordelia in conversation for the sole reason of torturing one of her guests.

"But I know nothing of Sir Colin."

He shrugged. "It doesn't matter. Think of something scandalous…*wicked*…and then, imagine him loving every minute."

Though blushing profusely, Miss Wakefield took his first challenge seriously. She closed her eyes and drew in a deep breath. By the time she exhaled, her color returned to normal. Steadily, she turned her gaze to Sir Colin, her brow puckered in deep concentration as if he'd set a puzzle before her.

"I have it," she announced, her voice ecstatic with triumph.

Her face was bright. Her eyes captivating. Her mouth curved in a full smile that radiated something straight to him—only this time, not in the vicinity of his groin. No, this sensation was decidedly north, in the center of his chest, like bullet burning a deadly path through him.

Struck by the force of it, he nearly staggered back and looked down, expecting to see a smoking flintlock in her grasp.

"All right, let's hear it," he rasped, feeling strangely out of breath. He had to get hold of himself.

Her smile faltered and the rosy glow in her cheeks paled by degree. "You never said I'd have to *tell* you."

Damn, but he wanted to kiss her. Right here, in front of everyone. How she could make him want her in his bed one moment, want to run away the next, and now want to laugh, he didn't know. He refused to think about it. All he knew was that in a fortnight, he would finally have relief.

Curiosity piqued, he slowed his steps so they wouldn't return to the rest of the party too soon. "I have to know whether or not you've gained an understanding, especially since your first response was 'filching the silver.'"

She reached out her hand and brushed her fingers through the tall grass by the bank, but he knew it was only a pretense. She wanted an excuse not to look at him when she told him. "I imagined his secret was that he enjoys it when feathers brush against him, only he pretends not to."

"Ah." She was more observant than he'd given her credit for, and he'd given her a great deal already. "You are a quick study, Miss Wakefield." Of course, she couldn't know how feathers could sometimes play a part in bed sport, so her guess only proved her inventive mind and offered another image to keep him awake tonight.

She pulled off the top portion of one frond and resumed her pace beside him. Brushing the tip against the palm of her hand, she made his mouth water. "Then do I pass the first lesson?"

He cleared his throat. "I don't know, try it on me now." He let out a breath and wondered why he was tormenting himself. "Only this time, you must look at me while the secret is in your mind."

Without hesitation, she glanced sideways at him. A slow smile curved her lips. Her sharp brow arched in challenge. "Far too simple. I already know one of your secrets."

The way she looked at him made his blood heat to a painful degree. He situated her shawl in front of him. "Rumors do not count. You must use your imagination."

"Oh, but I don't have to, do I?" she said coyly. Her gaze shifted to his hair, all the while stroking the blade of grass between her fingers.

His scalp tingled and his tumid erection throbbed. "The point of the exercise is to imagine something you don't know."

She licked her lips and pressed them together. "There are so many things I don't know. How could I possibly choose a single one? Besides, I rather like *remembering*, as opposed to imagining." Her gaze traveled down the length of him.

He stumbled a half step. The toe of his boot must have caught on small hill. Either that, or he couldn't lift his leg anymore. How was it that this woman—this innocent *miss*—managed to keep him off balance?

Her smile widened. Then, as if she sensed they were too near to the others, she lifted her fingers to hide it, even as her eyes danced with amusement. "High marks for the day?"

This day's lessons aren't over yet, an urgent voice in the back of his mind said. "You must prove your high marks at dinner this evening. Since Sir Colin is shy and easily unnerved, we'll consider him the elementary level of your schooling."

From the corner of his eye, he saw Eve making her way to them. "Did I hear mention of dinner this evening? I'm glad, because I have a special surprise for Merribeth."

An uneasy suspicion cooled his blood.

"Of course you know one of my guests was detained. Some urgent matter." She flitted her fingers and directed her next comment to Merribeth. "I believe Lord Lucan Montwood will be perfect for our little project. He is the second son of the Marquess of Camdonbury. He recently sold his commission and is now a man about town, in a manner of speaking."

Venus's smile fell and the brightness vanished from her eyes. "I don't see how that makes him perfect."

"He's quite destitute and needs to marry an heiress. Rumor has it that his father refuses to pay any more of his debts. Therefore, you'll have the freedom to flirt openly with him without anyone getting an idea that he's genuinely pursuing you. It's wonderful practice." She took a step closer and pointedly looked from one to the other. "Far more suitable than my nephew's company."

"Please do not mince words, Aunt."

She gave another flippant gesture, but her gaze was oddly serious. "A jealous woman holds poison on her tongue, Nephew." Then, she looked over to Daniela and Cordelia, who both happened to be staring in their direction. "Have a care for our ingénue."

It bothered him that he hadn't realized how his actions had drawn speculation. Apparently, he'd managed to fool himself into believing no one would pay mind to an insignificant walk beside a pond, in full view of the entire party.

He should have known better.

It wasn't his typical behavior to spend time with an innocent. Or to forget himself, for that matter, to the point where Eve—of all people—felt the need to remind him of his place.

He should've been relieved to have his eyes opened once again. Instead, he felt irked. He didn't like the sense that he was a puppet, and Eve pulled the strings.

"Not to worry, *Auntie*," he growled, his mood darkening. "Miss Wakefield would no more forget her ultimate pursuit than I would mine." He would never risk losing the one thing that meant the world to him.

CHAPTER NINE

Lord Lucan Montwood was attentive and attractive—two qualities one should always have in a dinner partner, if at all possible—with dark hair, and eyes the color of brandy by firelight. His manners were impeccable. He was clever and quick with compliments.

In fact, Merribeth felt no pressure to say much of anything. Because he was skilled at wording his questions and comments, she could be an active member of the conversation with a simple grin or a nod of her head.

Although he was a master of charm, everything about him seemed calculated to her. There was something that spoke of rawness beneath it all that made her keep her guard up. A second son with no profession, limited funds, and little chance of inheriting much of anything must do what he can, she supposed.

The thought made her uneasy.

Not because she imagined for any moment that he was interested in a wallflower with a questionable reputation. More so, because she felt as if she were doing the same—pleasing those around her in an effort to secure her future.

She glanced toward Bane, several times in fact, but each time he was too distracted in conversation with Lady Archer and Aunt Sophie. Though Montwood and Sir Colin were attentive, she found herself feeling adrift, without a mooring line to shore.

Then something sparked her memory. "I believe we have an acquaintance in common," she said to Montwood. "You might recall dancing with her at the Dorset Ball. Miss McFarland?"

He flashed a smile that gave the impression of being genuine. It even revealed a dimple. "Ah, yes. Now that you mention it, I do recall spying the two of you together in the gallery at one point. What a happy coincidence." He touched the rim of his wine goblet to hers and leaned closer, lowering his voice. "I must say, I hold your friend in very high esteem, though I wish she and I had met under different circumstances."

Merribeth thought of Delaney and the burden she'd kept with her since the incident at her debut. She frowned.

"Please do not misunderstand me," Montwood said quickly. "I was referring to my own circumstances. Surely you are aware—as is the whole of humanity—that I am without a farthing to my name."

She felt her cheeks color. "I do not let circumstance direct me to one's character."

"Then I hope we can be friends as well." His grin widened at her nod. "Lately, I've come to believe that the only thing worse than being penniless and without option is having riches thrust upon you to the point where you cannot trust anyone. Your friend is very brave."

Merribeth hadn't thought of Delaney's circumstances in that regard before and appreciated this new acquaintance with Montwood for that very reason.

After dinner, they gathered in the parlor. Again, her gaze automatically sought Bane. She found him leaning against the mantle, with his legs crossed at the ankle and his hand curled around a white porcelain cup. The widow Pearce stood beside him, her fingers flitting over his sleeve.

Merribeth's mood turned decidedly darker. It was silly, she knew. After all, Bane was not *hers*—nor could he be, even if she wanted him. Which of course she didn't. He belonged to no one but himself. And as such, he could do whatever he pleased with whomever he pleased. So then, why did seeing it bother her so much?

Looking for her aunt in the hope of retiring early, she spotted her conversing with Lady Archer and Sir Colin—*Sir Colin!* Her task. She was supposed to flirt with him at dinner. Oh, how could she have forgotten? It was her sole reason for being here. Not to mention, Bane's sole reason for helping her.

She felt a painful twinge in the vicinity of her heart, as if someone had reached inside and pinched her. A wake-up pinch, saying, *You foolish girl! You're wasting your time daydreaming about a rake who has no interest in you, other than to see you married to another man!*

Lively piano music brought her back to reality, clearing her head. It didn't surprise her to see Montwood at the piano. Charm was his profession, after all. With a waggle of his eyebrows, he invited her to sit beside him.

Although she'd never received a request like this before, her natural impulse was to decline and retreat into a corner. She disliked being the center of attention. However, since she needed to change in order for Mr. Clairmore to see her in a new and intriguing light, she put on a brave face and acquiesced.

Montwood's agile movements caused his arm to brush against hers more than once. At first, she thought it was an accident, but when she saw him grin, she realized he was flirting. *Flirting!* With her? Before the notion went to her head, it occurred to her that Eve likely had told him of her plight, more or less explaining how pathetic she was. Just as she had done with the widow Pearce. This time, however, Merribeth refused get angry. She had a purpose here, after all.

Since her task was to flirt and convince everyone she was a confident woman instead of a *kicked puppy*, she was determined to make a convincing go of it. She needed all the practice she could get before William arrived.

Merribeth took her first lesson from Daniela and reached up to brush a speck of lint from Montwood's shoulder. Then she took a lesson from Bane and held Montwood's gaze, imagining she possessed an intimate secret about him.

Unfortunately, the only thought she could muster was the memory of what it was like to run her fingers through Bane's coal black hair.

Montwood's notes went sharp. "My apologies, Miss Wakefield," he said and then cleared his throat and resumed playing. "I was distracted by the...er...color of your eyes."

Pleased, she smiled but then hastily covered the gap with her fingertips. "Blue eyes are hardly remarkable. More than half the guests in attendance have blue eyes."

His grin altered from a generic friendliness she'd seen him use with everyone to something more playful. This time when he met her gaze, he looked as if…as if *he* knew an intimate secret about *her*. "None like yours."

Feeling decidedly restricted, she let out a breath. This was how the game was played, she told herself. Yet she was unprepared to be successful, even if it was all for show.

She tried to figure out her next course of action. A compliment might offer a distraction until she could study Daniela again or even Lady Cordelia. "Your skill with the piano is quite adept. I imagine that having long fingers assists you."

Montwood gave her a wink and added an extra trill of the keys. "In many ways, Miss Wakefield."

Of course she hadn't intended her compliment to be flirtatious, but apparently, from the knowing look Montwood gave her, he'd taken it that way.

She felt her cheeks color. "That is to say…I know nothing of…I wouldn't want you to think…" *Drat*. She didn't know what she could possibly say, and her momentary bravery had all but abandoned her. "I believe my aunt is calling me," she said quickly and rose from the bench. However, instead of crossing the room to sit beside her aunt, she left the parlor entirely.

In the hall, her sudden appearance surprised three maids and a footman, who were all lingering near the staircase, no doubt listening to the music. Everyone jerked to attention, including her. She tried to think of a request that would explain her exit from the parlor, but she was too afraid of what she might say by accident.

Feeling out of her depth, she merely nodded and proceeded to walk briskly down the hall, as if she'd been sent on
a mission of the highest priority.

Bane wondered if murdering Montwood would alter his
agreement with Eve.

It wasn't as if he wouldn't be participating in the various
activities at the party. He'd commit the murder on his own
time. Perhaps invite Montwood on an outing where the lad
would have a riding mishap near the edge of the cliffs. Of
course, there was always the possibility of a hunting accident.
Or drowning…

"I hope that wicked grin has to do with our plans for later,"
Daniela said, gripping his sleeve and rubbing her breasts
against his arm. "Daphne Broadmore claims you've learned
quite a few tricks from a French countess."

The vision of Montwood's lifeless body floating in the
murky depths of the pond faded when he looked up from his
cup of coffee. His grin faded as well when Montwood began
another ribald tune.

Merribeth had not returned. While he was glad he didn't
have to endure watching her adhere so…thoroughly to the
task he put upon her so, he also didn't like wondering where
she was. He'd assumed she'd merely stepped out into the hall
for a breath of fresh air because she'd been unprepared for her
flirtations to be so successful.

He could tell she had no idea what a temptation she created.

A quarter hour had passed since then. He made sure to
keep an eye on Archer and Montwood. Both were still in

the parlor. Only now, he needed to extricate himself without inciting curiosity.

He knew that any random excuse would draw suspicion. However, if he could force Daniela into causing a scene…He was ashamed at the idea that came to mind. Or at least, he *should* have been ashamed. And that was enough for him. "I was imagining something much more diverting."

Her breath escaped her in a laugh, her gaze drifting down to his mouth, where he purposely flicked his tongue over the tip of his canine. "*More* diverting, even than what you did to…Daphne?" Her breasts heaved against him, her eyes glittering as if she'd stumbled upon buried treasure.

He nodded. "Though, I must warn you, years of being jaded have twisted my interests. I've abandoned the French method. The way I see it, the Corsairs had the right of it—whips, bondage, and a certain amount of force to gain total submission."

He waited for her to gasp and withdraw. Instead, Daniela wet her lips. Apparently, he had her on the hook.

He tried another tactic. "Of course, I haven't mastered the art of not leaving marks…but I'm sure they'll heal in time. My previous lover—*not, the widow Broadmore*, though it would be ungentlemanly of me to divulge her identity—is recovering well. At least, that was the last accounting I heard since she removed herself from society. I'm sure she'll be able to stop wearing veils…someday."

Absorbing this, Daniela swallowed, her face going pale. "She was left with…scars?"

"Not too many." He shrugged. "I'm certain she'll find another lover who won't mind them…eventually."

Eyes wide, she took a step back.

He advanced, keeping his voice low. "I'd assumed that by your obvious displays, you were equally jaded. I'd convinced myself that with such a reputation preceding you that your methods of seduction, which offer no real distinction between you and, say, a common chambermaid, were all to hide your true perversions. I thought we were of like mind."

She swallowed. "We are not."

"Pity." He pursed his lips. "At the present time, I've no interest in a mild diversion. However, once we've returned to town...*perhaps*." After all, he didn't want to burn a bridge entirely when he didn't have to. All he needed was an excuse to leave the parlor.

He saw the war within her, one part insulted, the other mortified. The former won the moment, and she narrowed her eyes. The outer edges of her rouged lips turned white. Yet even in her fury, she still didn't hold a candle to a single arched brow from Miss Wakefield.

"How is this for a *mild* diversion?" She shoved his arm, effectively spilling coffee over his sleeve and waistcoat.

He gave her a smile and a nod. "Thank you, Mrs. Pearce," he said, meaning it thoroughly.

Chapter Ten

Seeing a faint trace of light glowing beneath the library door, Bane turned the knob. "I knew I would find you in here."

Startled, Miss Wakefield jumped and nearly dropped the open lamp she held. The taper wobbled, the flame sputtering. Drawing the candle closer, she shielded it behind the cup of her hand.

The flame grew brighter instantly, illuminating her narrowed eyes. "You shouldn't be here."

"And you should be thankful it's only me and not Montwood." Thinking about what he'd witnessed, his jaw hardened, a muscle ticking when he gritted his teeth.

She scoffed. "*Only* you?"

Even though they both knew he was equally as dangerous, or more so, to her reputation, he didn't concede the point to her. "After the way you teased and flirted with him, I'd be surprised to hear him knocking at your bedchamber later, expecting recompense for the state you put him in."

"Montwood is charming, but anyone who spent more than five minutes with him would know his tastes run to more ample pockets. However, the same cannot be said of your tastes. It seems you prefer feminine endowments that are all flesh and no substance." Now, she cupped her hand around her ear. "Strange, I wonder if I'll hear the scratch of the widow Pearce's fingernails on your door?"

He grinned. "You're jealous."

Merribeth bristled. "I would no more be jealous of her than you would be of Montwood."

"Jealous of Montwood? That over-pandering peacock?" The idea appalled him. He'd never been jealous a day in his life. Though the notion that he could be experiencing it for the first time left him unsettled. As it wasn't true in the least, he didn't know why he let it bother him.

"*Jealous*, indeed," she said with a huff, mirroring his thoughts. With a withering glance, she turned back to study the shelves. "And furthermore, I came in here for the sole purpose of finding a book. I wasn't running from anything."

"Or making a hermit of yourself in the midst of a party?"

She exhaled through her nostrils, nearly blowing out the candle. "If that were the case, then I'd give you the blame for infecting me with your tendencies."

That made him grin. "I would readily take the blame if it were mine," he said, surprised at how much he liked the idea of having as great an influence on her behavior as she was on his. "Yet we both know you fled the parlor when your attempts at flirtation were successful."

"Perhaps I'm searching for reading material to better understand the topics of the widow Pearce's luncheon conversation."

Her blue eyes sparkled with amusement, as if she doubted his ability to know anything about her in the short time of their acquaintance. After spending days with her occupying his thoughts, he'd catalogued every mannerism, every *tell*, that gave her away.

He also knew the difference in her blushes now, the subtle alterations in color that told him if she was nervous, embarrassed, or *curious*.

At the moment, the soft peach tint to her cheeks and the steadiness of her gaze told him it was the last. The knowledge should have warned him away, for her own good as well as for his, yet the opposite happened. He took another step toward her.

She pretended to return her attention to the shelves. Raven ringlets spilled over her forehead, no doubt, in an effort to conceal her brow, though he couldn't fathom why. It was one of the things he liked best about her. *One of the things?* There was another sobering thought. If that was only one, then there had to be scores of others.

Her gown was of a simple design, a high-wasted confection in blue silk with cap sleeves. Fine stitches of silver-embroidered ivy followed the neckline down to the enticing handfuls of her breasts. On anyone else, such a gown might be considered plain, but her form needed no enhancement. Her slender body curved in all the right places and made his palms itch with the desire to mold and caress her flesh.

He leaned in to whisper. "The truth of why you fled the parlor is, you're unsure of yourself and what's expected of you. You detest being uncertain."

She turned sharply. "How could you—" She broke off when she noted his close proximity. He feigned innocence, pretending to read the titles with her. "I'm certain no one enjoys the prospect of finding oneself at another's mercy." The haughtiness of her tone quickly turned to a husky breath.

His gaze dipped to her mouth. "I don't know, Miss Wakefield. In my limited experience, being in a darkened study a week ago—at the mercy of a professed thief, mind you—was quite liberating. Seduction can be tiresome work. All that plotting and wooing..." He let out an exhausted sigh before a grin tugged at the corners of his mouth. "I must say it was a nice alteration."

The candle trembled in her hand. "There was no thievery involved, if you recall."

Oh, he *recalled*. Far too much. Every blessed moment of that night and every moment since. "The becoming blush on your cheeks belies your bold tongue, my dear." He chuckled and lifted his hand to snare the curl teasing the shell of her ear.

Miss Wakefield's lips parted, and her eyes closed as if in anticipation for his touch. Then, at the very last moment, she took a step back. Her eyes flashed open, her pupils still wide with desire. "I take back what I'd said before about having no proof of your prowess for flirting. You are quite skilled. My embarrassment and curiosity are constant rivals. It leads me to wonder how you became the man I see before me."

"The usual manner." He shrugged absently, letting his hand fall to his side as he propped a shoulder against the bookcase. He enjoyed their play. Again, *far* too much. So it was probably for the best that he allowed her to steer the conversation onto another path.

"Why is it that you do not have a wife and heir and profess to desire neither? It goes against all the lessons young women are taught. We are educated and refined for the purpose of convincing gentlemen that we would not only make good wives but mothers to their children—children who will inherit the title and resume the entire process for generations to come."

He smiled easily, amused by her effort to unsettle him. "Not all men want the same thing, Miss Wakefield. Some enjoy the freedom of their pursuits."

"For a time, of course. Some men even enjoy those pursuits after marriage," she said, undeterred from her topic, even when another blush threatened to undermine the aloof pretense she'd adopted.

"And you wouldn't mind if your husband continued his own"—he took a step toward her—"*pursuits* after marriage?"

She held her ground and brushed the curls from her forehead. "If I should be lucky enough to find love and respect in my marriage, then I would expect fidelity, of course."

Her brow was exposed, sending another surge of lust through him. She had no idea how much time he'd spent fantasizing about the tempting arch. How he'd imagined her with her brow arched in a carnal challenge to pleasure her for endless hours.

"*Find* love?" he asked, shifting ever closer. "Do you not already possess it for your Mr. Clairmore?"

At that, her gaze turned wintry. The color of her gown brought out the striations in her irises, inviting him to notice the different hues threaded together, captivating him. "Surely, the answer to that question could be of no interest to you. I am, after all, a marriage-minded woman."

"More's the pity." If only she set her determination on a prize worth winning. Like what? Him? To become his mistress? No. That was no prize. Such a life wasn't good enough for her and would only lead Venus into heartache. She deserved more than that. More than someone like him.

When she made a move to exit, he reached out and snatched her hand.

"I find this conversation tiresome," she said, staying a step apart from him, though without any effort to free herself.

He felt his mood slide into darkness, but it did not dissuade his desire for her. Quite the opposite. In fact, knowing that Eve had invited Montwood solely for sake of flirting openly with Merribeth, he suddenly felt an overwhelming urge to bolt the library door and take her against the bookcases. Claim her. Leave his mark on her.

"I came to dictate your second lesson."

"I do not think—"

"Your smile," he interrupted and watched her flinch.

"What about it?"

He moved a half step closer. "You cannot hide it." It would be easy to pull her into his arms, yet somehow he managed restraint. "For every time you do, you'll owe me one kiss. And not the borrowed kind either. These, I will keep."

Her soft fragrance rose from the heated flesh of her throat, where he saw a single bead of perspiration make a slow journey downward toward the valley above her collarbone. His nostrils flared as he inhaled deeper. The desire to taste her shuddered through him.

"You ask too much of me."

"Perhaps." Bane affected a shrug, all the while feeling the heated rise of his pulse and the weakening of his control. He hadn't planned this. Then again, he hadn't retracted the challenge either. In fact, anticipation nearly consumed him. The desire to claim her, to make her his, thundered through his veins—*his soul*—heedless of right or wrong. "You are determined to be successful in your quest, are you not?"

"Of course." Merribeth lifted her gaze and stared at him intently, as if searching for honorable intentions or promises for the future.

She would never find those things in him.

He accepted her plain statement as her acquiescence. "While you're flirting with all the other gentlemen, know that I will be watching." Through her glove, he stroked the edge of her finger that curled over the brass lamp handle. "Waiting. Counting my winnings."

A frisson of awareness trampled through Merribeth. Not because she was alone with Bane in the library, but because she realized she had no desire to flee. She glanced down from his eyes to his mouth.

"*All* the other gentlemen?" she mocked. "First of all, Colonel Hamersley is too old. Sir Colin is too quiet—I would never know if he was returning my flirting. And you must know that I detest Archer." Though she didn't know why, she felt the need to clarify her part of this strange bargain. "So the only one I'm likely to flirt with is Montwood."

And perhaps, try to make Bane jealous.

"*He* was about to lose an arm," Bane said, his voice dark with warning, like stampeding horses carrying the cavalry into battle. A thrill shot through her.

"Because you envy his skill on the piano? Or because he was aiding my quest to renew Mr. Clairmore's affections?"

She felt it important to say the words aloud for herself, though Bane didn't seem to appreciate the reminder of her main goal.

Silver heat flared in his gaze like a shaft of lightning. He snatched the candle from her and set it on the shelf behind him with enough force to extinguish the flame. He took hold of her, curling his hands beneath the ruffled cuff of her sleeves. The heat from his palms seared her flesh. "Because you're mine."

"*Yours?*" she mocked, but even as she said it, she felt her body go weak. Any part of her that might have resisted such a blatantly primitive claim now only heeded the call of the pagan drummer.

"*Mine.*" He ground out the word as if something had snapped in him for a moment, revealing a hardness she hadn't seen before. He pulled her close, crushing her breasts against the hardness of his chest. "*My* pupil until the end of the party," he corrected, expelling a deep breath as if she'd yanked the air from his lungs.

Her lips parted.

He shook his head, silencing any argument from her, and lowered his mouth. "Now, pay your lesson master the forfeits you owe for tonight."

He didn't wait for her to give the kiss. Instead, he took one.

Then, he took another. His mouth, body and the power he emanated made it impossible to resist.

She tilted her head, entreating his tongue to plunder past her lips and delve inside. The contact—the sweet shock of tongue against tongue—stole the air from her lungs. A low moan escaped her. He groaned in response. The vibration tickled her palate and teased the soft lining of her cheeks into giving up more moisture. She swallowed, tasting his essence in return and drawing him deeper into her mouth.

He pulled her closer. One hand slid to her nape and the other skimmed down her spine to the curve of her back. Her legs clashed against his. She shifted to get closer still and felt his hand slide possessively lower, over the swell of flesh of her derriere as he lifted her, settling her against the hardness of his thigh. Startled by a throbbing sensation where her body met his, she inhaled sharply.

Bane didn't release her or ease the potency of his kiss. Instead, he deepened it even further. Percussive music played within her, accelerating until it was all she felt. A need, primal and desperate, came over her as she lifted her hands to circle his neck. She arched against him. His fingers dug into her flesh as he lifted her, dragging her up along the hard, male ridge of his body.

She'd never been kissed like this before. William's had always been simple and chaste. They'd never lasted long enough for her to get a taste of him or draw his exhalation into her nostrils.

With Bane, the kiss felt as if he were leaving his mark on her. Claiming her.

His tongue was roughly textured and hot, flavored with the wine they drank at dinner, the coffee afterward, and a deeper essence her body identified as exotically male. *Him.*

She was certain not every man tasted this way…or kissed this way. It felt as if each pull from his lips captured strands of her soul, leaving a void behind that only his breath could fill.

Her body arched against his again—a purely primitive offering, a pagan sacrifice.

Bane turned his head, pressing his cheek against hers, his breathing hard and heavy in her ear. "Venus, you're going to kill me."

It took a moment for the name to breech the heavy cloud of desire and find her brain. *Venus?* From anyone else's lips, she would have taken it as an insult. But from Bane, it sounded like the sweetest endearment.

She nuzzled his neck, pressing her lips above the line of his cravat. "One more. We are not even. I'm certain I took one back to keep for myself."

He groaned but ended on a wry laugh. "Only one?" His hands gripped her hips for a moment longer before he set her on her feet. Then he reached up to untangle her hands from behind his neck and took a step back.

"Must you stop?" Her body was still humming, throbbing, restless. All her senses were alert and too aware. Every breath was filled with his scent. She felt tingly all over, as if her body had fallen asleep only to awaken painfully. Rubbing against him was the only way to ease the ache. The taste of his kiss lingered on her tongue like the very last sip of coffee. She felt deprived and anxious. She couldn't possibly go on like this.

"Yes." He scrubbed a hand down his face and made a point not to look at her. "The servants' stairs that lead to your bedchamber are too near and my sanity too far gone."

At that, she blushed, suddenly aware of the consequences—should he have been a lesser man. She lifted her fingers to her lips. They felt heated and swollen, the skin surrounding them tender and likely red. He'd left his mark. "Perhaps your sanity and mine have both fled." *Because I would give anything to return to your embrace.*

His gaze dropped to where her fingertips touched her lips. "Do not expect an apology."

"I wouldn't ask."

"Good." He nodded, studying her with an intensity that made her feel as if he were reliving their kiss all over again. "I took less than I wanted. Believe me, I could still find ways for you to earn an apology from me. Ways that would change your fate and not for the better."

Her sanity was truly gone and any remnant of maidenly honor with it, because…She wanted him to show her.

Apparently reading it in her expression, he shook his head. "Good night, Miss Wakefield. Please lock your bedchamber door when you retire. And bolt your window too, instead of leaving it open as you did last night." He brushed the backs of his fingers down her cheek. "Best not tempt fate."

CHAPTER ELEVEN

Bane knew it wasn't fate being tempted but him.

He thanked the last thread of his control for his ability to walk away from her. Especially when the entire fabric of his being had wanted to take her and claim her, no matter the consequences. Somehow, he'd managed to leave her, escape to his room for a fresh waistcoat, and then return to the parlor. The room, however, seemed empty without her in it.

If his frayed nerves were exposed, no one seemed to notice. Their attention was riveted on Hamersley as he boasted about the stag he'd brought down. Bane listened with half an ear, while the rest of him chided himself for his foolishness. One thing was certain; he needed to avoid Miss Wakefield for the remainder of the night. For that matter, he should probably avoid her tomorrow and the next day as well. Perhaps he should avoid her forever—it could take that long for him to regain all of his control.

Still, he must adhere to the terms of his bargain with dear *Auntie* Eve. He couldn't risk losing Gypsy or the information that would grant him another victory over his grandfather.

In fact, losing in any way wasn't an option. On occasion, he'd allowed others to win but only to his ultimate advantage. This wasn't one of those occasions.

He *needed* to win. The entire purpose of his life hinged on this victory, and he wasn't about to allow one marriage-minded virgin to tempt him into forgetting that—no matter how tempted he was.

Still, he wasn't certain how he'd manage to keep his distance, to keep from recalling the sound of her moan and the feel of her body arching against him.

Bane scrubbed a hand over his face, trying to wipe the memory from his mind. When he looked up, he caught Eve's steady gaze. And then the slow spread of a knowing smile.

He bristled, the sensation of pinpricks stinging the back of his neck. In that instant, he realized that he'd underestimated her. She was playing to win, only—for the first time—he didn't think she cared a fig about winning Gypsy. He even wondered if this was about Amberdeen's pursuit of her land. A voice in the back of his mind whispered to him that she had another purpose. A darker purpose. What it could be, he didn't know. And he *always* knew.

That part unsettled him most of all.

He was slipping. He'd allowed himself to be distracted, pulled away from his own purpose. He'd missed something. Obviously, he needed to steer clear of distraction so that he could figure out what Eve was hiding.

Hamersley's booming voice drew his attention again. "With a single round, and down he fell. It took four grooms-men to hoist the carcass." His chest puffed with obvious pride. "I cleared a place of honor above my mantle for those antlers."

Inspiration struck. "A hunting party. Now there's an idea," Bane said, as if it had been the colonel's suggestion. "We could leave at first light."

Eve frowned. They both knew that separating the men from the women for a day was skirting close to breaking their bargain. Before she could voice her objection, he made sure to assert that the women were also included.

Hamersley chimed in with his agreement. Montwood quickly added his, as did Sir Colin. It seemed the men were all as eager as he to leave the confines of the manor. However, once Archer slurred his interest in shooting anything that moved, any possibility of the women wanting to take part died a quick death.

Bane grinned at his aunt over this small victory. Whatever her game, there was no way he would let her win.

In the morning, before the first threads of dawn wove through the edge of the horizon, Bane saddled his Warmblood stallion, Ares. Believing it was the only place he would find rest and freedom from temptation, he'd spent the night in the stables. However, time had dragged on, suspended. In each moment that passed, he thought about going to her.

One thing was certain: he couldn't trust himself to sleep in the manor for the remainder of the party. He didn't even trust himself to walk into the kitchen for coffee this morning, because he knew it would only lead to more thoughts of her. Dangerous thoughts of forbidden kisses and servants' stairways.

For now, he needed distance and a good deal of it too.

With Ares beneath him, he rode across the land toward Amberdeen's estate in the north. According to the maps, since their party would be shooting on Amberdeen's land, Bane thought it was only right to invite him along.

Moreover, if he could convince Amberdeen to join the party afterward, Bane would have the added bonus of annoying Eve to the ends of the earth. It would serve her right. After all, she'd invited Montwood for the purpose of flirting with Merribeth. *His* Venus.

Mine, the voice said again. That same voice he'd heard last night. The same voice that he'd thought had been guiding him throughout his entire life—the same one that had kept him alive in battle, that had helped him make his fortune, that had kept him on the path of revenge…and now?

He doubted the voice he'd come to trust had ever existed at all.

Most likely, what he'd thought was instinct actually had been his own selfish desires. Because surely his instinct wouldn't lead him to Merribeth. Instinct wouldn't tell him that she was *his* to kiss, *his* to claim. Instinct wouldn't tell him to take her virginity as well as any hope she had of a future.

True instinct—without selfish intent—would push her away. And keep her far away. The problem was, he craved more than her kisses and the promised heat of her body. He liked talking to her, teasing her. She spoke to him plainly, honestly, and didn't hide her motivation or try to deceive him with her wiles. Because of that, he trusted her—which was a substantial feat, as he hadn't trusted anyone in a very long time.

Bane exhaled, long and slow. Those thoughts were dangerous and unsettling.

Up ahead, he saw a figure, mounted on a dapple gray stallion. He instantly recognized it as Lord Amberdeen. When he drew closer, they exchanged a companionable greeting.

"What brings you to these woods so early, Knightswold?" Amberdeen handed his carbine to a waiting groom.

With a nod, Bane noted the two pheasants hanging on the side of his saddle. "It appears we have the same idea this morning. In fact, I came to ask permission as well as invite you to join a hunting party."

Amberdeen gave a wry smile. "Something tells me your aunt will not be among the riders."

"I should think you'd find relief that she did not have a loaded weapon while in your vicinity," Bane said with a laugh. Amberdeen was a good sort. Far too good for the likes of Eve, but there was no accounting for taste.

"Quite so." Amberdeen turned then and gave quick instructions to his groom to have the house ready a luncheon. He insisted on being the host, even when Bane told him it was unnecessary.

A short while later, they were riding back toward Eve's estate for the others. Bane saw this as a perfect opportunity to settle, once and for all, at least one of the questions in regard to his wager. "My aunt tells me that you would like a foal from Gypsy."

Amberdeen's brow lifted in surprise. "What man among our set wouldn't covet such a trophy? If I did make the comment, it was merely in passing. If I'd any real designs, I'd have come to you directly."

"As I suspected," Bane mused. When Amberdeen gave him a questioning look, he went on. "She believes a foal would settle the land dispute between the two of you."

Amberdeen looked ahead, as if he could see through the stone façade of the estate to pinpoint the exact location of its mistress. "She knows very well that there is only one *acceptable* proposal to settle matters."

Now that Bane had that puzzle answered, some of the pressure surrounding him lightened. He could breathe easier. A morning mist hovered over the grass, resembling the steam rising from his stallion's nostrils. He was starting to feel better. More like himself. Riding always helped him clear his head and focus his thoughts. He knew what was important. *Revenge.*

The only reason he was here at all was because of the bargain he'd made with Eve. She had information for him. Information to exact his revenge was the only thing he wanted. There was no room for Venus in his life. She was a distraction he should avoid.

If only he could.

Chapter Twelve

By the time Merribeth was brave enough to walk down to the breakfast room and chance another encounter with Bane, she learned the men would be hunting all day. Her shoulders sagged in relief. At least she wouldn't have to face him today.

Of course, that wouldn't keep her from thinking about that blistering kiss. Or about William and how guilty she felt, because she hadn't thought of him at all until this moment.

Why had she never felt this dithery with William? He'd certainly never caused her such turmoil that she'd questioned nearly everything she knew about herself.

She supposed it was because William was perfect for her. Everyone said so. He fit into her life nicely without causing any uneasy stirrings.

Kissing Bane had made her feel positively wild, filling her with primitive notions—like wanting to keep him in the library and press her lips to every pulse point on his body, craving to learn the beat of *his* drum. Even as that thought kept her riveted, she still wanted more. More of the sound of his voice and the way it stampeded through her entire body. More of his wry wit and teasing banter. More of his dark warnings about servants' stairs and losing one's sanity over a kiss. And more of those, too.

He unsettled her. Made the secret places inside her churn and throb. Since they'd first met, he'd never left her with a moment's peace.

So then why did she crave to see him again and continue to feel this way?

It made no sense. Yet now, she suspected she knew what William had meant when he'd told her that he felt violently toward Miss Codington.

She pondered that for a moment as she placed a crumpet on her plate and then took a seat beside her aunt at the glossed maple table. Bleary light filtered in through the mist hovering outside the broad windows, casting gray shadows within the breakfast room.

Sophie eyed her over the tarnished rims of her glasses, concern evident in the furrowing of her brow. "You didn't sleep." She reached over and patted Merribeth's hand before she nudged the jam caddy in front of her plate. "Don't worry so. We'll get him back. There's still time."

Him. Her aunt meant *William*, of course. This was all for William. She'd given him the last five years of her life, only to have him leave her reputation in tatters. And that was before she'd done anything to deserve it.

Oh dear. But now she'd kissed a rake—*twice*—and all to regain William's affections. She kissed another man. Not only that, but she wanted to do it again.

In the very least, she should feel guilty.

"Doesn't this seem strange, Sophie? That I'm here, learning to flirt with other men so that I can regain William's affections."

Her aunt's gaze turned thoughtful and distant, the way it did when she'd learned something new from one of her journals. "I admit, I was skeptical when Eve first announced this plan. It seemed the opposite of what a young woman with her reputation hanging by a thread would normally do."

Merribeth blanched. "How sweetly put."

Sophie blinked and focused on her. A small smile lifted her features, making her look years younger. "That, right there, is the reason I went along with it. Ever since that night at Lady Amherst's, I've noticed a change in you, in your demeanor, in the little things you say. It reminds me of a journal article I read, involving the trials that a boy must go through in order to be considered a man in his tribe. First, he must venture out alone to hunt and kill an animal. Then he must consume either the blood or the heart. Finally, he must skin the animal and wear the pelt at a ritual ceremony."

Merribeth swallowed down a rise of bile in her throat and pushed her plate away, no longer able to look at the raspberry jam atop her crumpet. "I don't see how that pertains to me."

"This entire ordeal is your trial—your effort to become accepted by your tribe."

Her tribe—the *ton*. The notion was disheartening. "Then why do I feel more like the hunted animal than the boy?"

"At first, perhaps," Sophie said with a nod, pursing her lips. "But once you were challenged, you switched places. You picked up the spear, as it were, and decided to take control of your own fate."

Best not tempt fate. A shiver raced through her at the memory of Bane's final words to her last night. "And the animal I must kill? What *is* that, exactly?"

Sophie turned back to her breakfast. "That is for you to figure out."

This still didn't answer her question. By deciding to go along with Eve's plan, she'd essentially picked up a symbolic spear with the intent of slaying a nameless, faceless beast. Yet the beast had a face, didn't it? Wasn't William the beast she needed to slay—*marry*—in order to belong to her tribe?

The idea didn't help abate the queasiness of her stomach. "I think I'd like to explore more of the house this morning. Would you care to join me?"

"Normally, I would love to," Sophie said around a bite of ham, "but Lady Archer and I are going into the village shortly to speak with Reverend Sandleland. Would you like to join us? I'm sure there's plenty of room in the carriage."

Merribeth stood and considered her options. Though she had loved needlework, now, each time she picked up a needle and thread, all she could see was her wedding dress and the uncertainty of her future. All she could see was a life without hope, without children and, most depressingly, without love. Without her needlework to occupy her, or any desire to resume it, she was left with her thoughts as her main occupation. The prospect of going on another quest with Aunt Sophie held even less appeal. "I think I'd rather rummage through the attic and see what old costumes I can find, if any."

Sophie dabbed her mouth with a napkin and grinned, hope lighting her eyes. "I imagine you'll find interesting costumes, as well as needlework that might inspire you."

"Perhaps," Merribeth said absently. Her thoughts were more focused on the question of what she must do to take control of her own fate. She doubted she'd find it in the attic. In fact, the only time she'd felt she'd had any control of her own fate was when she'd lost all control in Bane's arms.

Fool that she was, she hoped to lose control again.

After spending the rest of the morning and the better part of the afternoon in the attic, discovering more gowns and fine needlework than she had ever seen in one place, Merribeth had taken out the silver needle, thread, and handkerchief her friends had given her. However, while lounging on the divan in her room, she hadn't been inspired. The bare scrap of linen had stared back at her, as if waiting for her to pick up the tiny spear that would decide her fate.

She couldn't do it. That feeling of certainty was still out of reach.

Frustrated, she settled down in the library with a book and watched the sun sink below the tree line. The gentlemen had not yet returned from their hunting trip. Her aunt and Lady Archer were resting before dinner. Eve was in the parlor with Cordelia and Daniela.

Merribeth was daydreaming when she heard the scrape of the door along the carpet behind her. Peering around one of the chair's wings, she saw that it was Eve.

"A book instead of needlework in your lap? That is not how I usually see you," Eve said as she stepped into library.

Merribeth remained in her curled-up position. "I blame it on this old chair. I walked past the door and saw it sitting here, all alone." She left out how the memory of Bane's kiss had lured her here.

"I've never liked that chair. The red upholstery has faded to an unattractive orange hue. It's coarse, like a horsehair blanket. And no matter how many times I have the servants air it in the sun, it still smells musty."

"It's quite comfortable." Surprisingly enough, as the cushion was flat and bowed in the center, too.

"Yes," Eve mused, stopping in front of the window to stare out at the rolling hills. "My husband loved that chair."

"Lord Sterling?"

Eve laughed. "No, he hated anything that was older than he was—which wasn't much—but included my legacy." She turned and lifted her hands to encompass everything around her: the house, the lands, and the centuries that had built and protected it.

Having thumbed through the book of the family's history in her lap, Merribeth knew that every one of Eve's ancestors had felt that this place was worth dying for, as if their very lifeblood ran in veins beneath these grounds.

"It was Spencer who loved that chair," Eve continued, turning back to the window, her voice quiet, as if to keep the heartbreak from being heard. "He understood my love for this land better than anyone could. Of course, his father's obsession had a great deal to do with that. Similar to my love for this land, the purity and longevity of the Fennecourt line was what the old marquess prized above all else."

Merribeth puzzled over this. "Is the Fennecourt line prolific, then?"

"Not at all. In fact, Bane will be the last."

Will be. The words left no room for speculation. It was a simple statement of fact.

"When he spoke with my aunt the first night, he seemed rather adamant about never marrying. As the last of his line, one should think the opposite would be true," Merribeth said, trying not to reveal her curiosity.

In profile, with the waning afternoon light behind her, a peculiar smile settled on Eve's face. "Bane would sacrifice everything to ensure that his grandfather's legacy dies with him—an act of ultimate revenge against the man who tried to take everything from him: his parents, his home, his title. And all because his mother had gypsy blood. According to the old marquess, she wasn't pure enough to produce a true heir."

Merribeth cringed, the idea appalling her. It seemed like an archaic belief that she might have read about in one of Sophie's scientific journals. "But he is a true heir. His blood is Fennecourt, of that there can be no question. Otherwise, he wouldn't hold the title."

"Yes, though it took years for him to get it back, once the old marquess had it stripped from him."

Merribeth uncurled her legs and shifted to the edge of the chair, wanting to understand how Bane came to be the man he was. However, she also knew she must keep her interest under guard.

"In the end, I think the real reason behind the old marquess's hatred was vanity," Eve continued without prompting, being uncharacteristically straightforward. "Every time my father-in-law looked at his grandson, he saw nothing of the Fennecourt line—the tawny hair, pale skin, and green eyes. While Bane's stature and physique might have been, and still are, exactly like his father's, his hair, eyes, and even the olive tint to his skin all came from his mother."

His grandfather had hated Bane for something he couldn't control. A grandfather was supposed to love you and dote on you. At least, that was the fond memory Merribeth had of her own. "You implied that Lord Knightswold's grandfather was responsible for his parents' deaths as well."

"It was never proven. Carriage accidents are common enough," Eve said with a flippant gesture, her gaze fixed out the window. "Bane was lucky enough to be thrown from the wreckage before it dashed his parents and their driver over the cliffs."

"Oh!" Merribeth's hand rose to her throat. "He was there when they—"

"A tragedy you both have in common," Eve answered with a nod, and that peculiar smile returned. "He was slightly older than you were. Fourteen, I believe. At that point, he came to live with Spencer and me. Unfortunately, he brought his grandfather's hatred with him." She glanced over her shoulder. "You see, with Bane alive, there was still the matter of the title going to an impure Fennecourt. So the old marquess managed to destroy the church records of the wedding between Bane's parents, and he convinced people Bane was a bastard, which put Spencer in line for the title."

Merribeth gasped, unable to hide her feelings of outrage and the unfairness of it all. "Surely, there had been witnesses at the ceremony, someone who would vouch for his legitimacy."

"Anyone who did found themselves ruined by scandal, put in debtor's prison, or simply disappeared altogether."

She felt sick. How could one man harbor such hatred? "And your husband?"

"When he adamantly spoke up for Bane's legitimacy, Spencer lost his entire inheritance, his lands, and his money. We came to live here, believing distance would settle my father-in-law's quest. It didn't." The cold remnants of a long-standing abhorrence hardened Eve's expression. "Of course, while Bane was off at school and then later, while playing soldier against the French as an enlisted man, Spencer battled to keep my legacy from being stolen by his father as well."

Merribeth took offense at the way Eve had said Bane had been "playing soldier," as if his heroism meant nothing, but she didn't let on that it bothered her. Eve was no doubt bitter about the entire tragic episode, as anyone would be.

"Then, one day, it was all too much for Spencer," Eve said quietly, but there was a razor edge to her voice. "Somehow, he got the idea stuck in his head that if he weren't here—if his father no longer had a target for all his hatred—then it would stop. That my legacy would be saved. So he rode to his father's house and hanged himself in the study." She said the last without expression, as if the ordeal had stripped her of emotion. Or perhaps, because her anguish was buried so deeply that nothing could escape.

Merribeth's heart went out to Eve, only now realizing how little she knew about her aunt's friend. "I imagine seeing your nephew's desire to end his legacy, when you and your ancestors have sacrificed so much for yours, must be difficult to understand."

"Not at all." Eve shook her head. That peculiar smile made another appearance, sending a shiver of warning through

Merribeth. "I see that we are alike, in that the greatest asset to both of us is a single-minded determination to get exactly what we want and to give others *exactly* what they deserve."

She wasn't certain whether being blind to everything outside of one's goal was an asset or a flaw. "I'm not sure I understand."

"Of course you do. Take Mr. Clairmore, for example, and his treatment of you. There are certain events in one's life that can never be forgotten, events that drive a person to do things he or *she* never wanted to be capable of doing, but that offer a sense of peace all the same."

Merribeth frowned, mulling that over. After William's betrayal, did flirting with Bane—*kissing Bane*—offer a sense of peace? Not at all. She was feeling more turmoil inside her now than during those weeks when her reputation was on nearly everyone's lips.

"My father-in-law wasn't deterred by his sons' deaths," Eve continued. "He never stopped trying to reach his goal. He remarried a pretty young girl, before she'd finished her first Season. Yet she was, perhaps, too young. Both she and old Fennecourt's last chance for an heir died in childbed. He followed a year later." Eve punctuated her comment with an absent shrug, moved away from the window, and crossed to the open door. "I suppose it's time I see about dinner. I'm sure the men will be arriving any moment, eager to share their birds with the cook."

Merribeth watched her disappear into the hall. Her mind was at sixes and sevens. Was her single-minded determination to get Mr. Clairmore back at any cost truly like Bane's quest for revenge?

No matter how much she wanted—vehemently and unilaterally—to deny it, she couldn't.

Perhaps it was time to reevaluate her main goal. This whole idea of flirting in order to instill confidence had been Eve's idea all along. And yet...she couldn't possibly regret all of her own actions. Being brave in those moments that normally would have made her turn the other way had been liberating.

Already, she felt changed. She felt it in her skin each time Bane looked at her, as if he knew what had been inside her all along.

Yet if her ultimate goal no longer concerned flirting with him, how could she rationalize seeking him out? Then again, knowing he was so near and for such a short time, how could she possibly stay away?

Chapter Thirteen

Bane stayed in the stables while the other men went inside to enjoy their scotch and brag to the women of their shooting kills. The day still hadn't provided him the respite he needed.

In fact, today's journey had only left him with the desire to return, to be nearer the source of his constant temptation. All day, he'd felt as if he were unraveling, and the only way to set himself to rights was to return and be stitched together again. To follow the others into the house and to find the person who seemed to be holding the other end of his thread.

Instead, he remained in the stables and brushed down the horses. The repetition of smooth, fluid strokes offered another distraction.

Now, he was in Gypsy's stall. Cooing soothing words to her, he brushed her down and rubbed her distended belly. Her time was coming soon. No doubt, the foal would be big, like its sire. The knowledge caused Bane a modicum of worry.

As if hearing his thoughts, the mare lifted her head and gave a snort through her wide nostrils.

"You'll do fine," he said, wishing he were convinced. "When it's time, I'll stay right here with you, and you won't have to be alone. Not for a minute."

She blew her breath against his cheek, nudging him playfully. When he tried to resume his grooming task, she sidestepped and whickered. Looking at her, he noticed that her attention was on the open stall door. Then, with a glance over his shoulder, he caught sight of a retreating slip of gray muslin.

Venus. He felt an immediate tug deep inside. The impulse to go to her and bring her back made the muscles down the length of his legs jump. Yet, at the same time, his sense of self-preservation willed his feet to stay flat to the ground and not to move a single inch. There was so much at stake.

Gypsy nudged his shoulder, hard enough that he took a step forward to regain his balance. He glanced back at her. "Do you want to meet her?"

The silky black mare dipped her head. It might not have been a nod, but he decided it was close enough. While he could deny himself, he could never deny Gypsy.

Looking again at the open stall door, he watched as that gray slip of muslin and the woman within it emerged from the hall.

Miss Wakefield stopped a few feet from him, her fingers knitted before her. She tilted her head to the side. "What was her answer?"

"What makes you think she gave one?" he asked, warning himself that her curiosity was a dangerous entity, one that had the power to make him forget.

Somehow, he managed not to close the distance between them. The strength of his will even allowed him to turn his back on her and resume brushing Gypsy. Then, out of the corner of his eye, he watched Merribeth step further into the stall.

Apparently, fate had not yet finished doling out temptation to him. He steeled himself against it.

"You have a way with her," she said quietly. "When you crooned to her a moment ago, she responded with different sounds, as if you were having a conversation."

"Then you were eavesdropping." The words came out with more censure than he felt. While he'd felt unraveled earlier, now, the closer she stood, the more tightly wound he became. It seemed the only thing his hunting trip had managed to do was to make him want her all the more.

Clenching his teeth, he kept to his task and brushed the pregnant mare with long, fluid strokes from her withers to flank.

"She's beautiful," Merribeth said, ignoring his jibe. "If I draw closer, will I startle her?"

Perhaps she shouldn't worry about the way her presence affected Gypsy but what it did to him instead. Her nearness unsettled him, making his shirt and waistcoat feel tight and itchy. He wanted to relieve the discomfort by removing both items and then invite her to run her cool hands over his feverish flesh.

He blew out a breath as a shudder rambled through him. Gypsy exhaled a quick snort and scratched the ground with her hoof in impatience.

Beside him, Merribeth stilled. "I should go. It's obvious she doesn't want company."

And it was obvious to him that Merribeth wasn't truly talking about Gypsy.

Bane shook his head, even as a grin tugged at the corner of his mouth. He dropped the brush in the pail and turned to face her. "She hasn't been introduced to you yet and isn't certain she can let down her guard."

He held out his hand in offering.

"Is that all it takes?" She slipped her fingers into his palm without hesitation, proving that she trusted his intentions far too much.

He wished she'd hesitated. Perhaps then, he would have been better prepared for swift tightening of the coil inside him. With it came a jolt that shot tracks of heat—as hot as a branding iron—up his arm and over his entire body. "It sometimes takes even less."

Denying his endless list of urges with a force he didn't know he possessed, he pulled her only a single step closer and settled her hand against the length of Gypsy's nose.

His fingers splayed over hers, guiding her touch as he situated her so that she stood in front of him. "Let her snuff you and see that you are here with me. I won't let anything happen." He bent his head, inhaling the soft fragrance of her hair.

"I know you won't," she whispered, her voice low and sure.

Merribeth received a snort and nuzzle from Gypsy. Undeniable approval.

"I can see why you prefer her company to mine and that of the other guests," she said with laugh as the mare's forelock tickled her nose. "You're at peace with her. She's gentle and—"

"And wise," he finished but didn't dare correct her assumption. There was *one* person whose company he preferred. And it was making him insane. "She has excellent taste in people."

Ignoring the compliment, Venus ducked her head and stepped away in order to retrieve the brush. She took up the task he'd abandoned with practiced ease, making him wonder if she kept a horse.

"I had a pony when I was a girl," she said before he could ask. "Like Gypsy, he was dark as a raven's wing but with a blaze of white. He would prance around with his head high, as if he were pony to the king. Because of that, I called him Ravencourt, and together we would ride to the edge of the forest that lined my father's house and search for twinkling fairies at twilight."

Ravencourt. Of course. The name of his father's estate and now his.

Bane nearly laughed aloud, not out of humor but out of incredulity. A laugh aimed at the gods for mocking him, for reminding him of his true purpose, and for tempting him with things that could never be.

Not for him anyway. But they could be for her... with someone else.

"Why are you going to marry a man you do not love?" The question was out before he knew what he was saying. He'd intended to ask why she'd come here to the stables. Instead, he asked her what he'd wanted to know since the first night of the party.

Now, she hesitated before stepping around to the opposite side of Gypsy to continue brushing her. The mare closed her eyes in apparent bliss.

"Love is not necessary for marriage," she said plainly, not bothering to deny his accusation. "Surely, as a member of the *ton* you understand that marriages happen for the sake of certainty—certainty of a legitimate heir, certainty of fortune…"

"Certainty of fidelity?" he mocked, crossing his arms, his irritation returning. "*Your* Mr. Clairmore has already proven untrustworthy on that account." A man completely unworthy of the woman before him.

She pressed her lips together and drew in a breath that flared her nostrils. Her brush strokes punctuated the air. "I've tried to become practical in the recent weeks. Even cynical. I see marriage for what it truly is. Women throughout time have made the decision to marry for the sake of certainty, including my aunt Sophie. Why should I be different?"

Practical and cynical? No! That wasn't her, at all. Venus was romantic and dreamy and full of innocent passion ready to be awakened. Yet she claimed love wasn't necessary for her. He could believe that about anyone else. But not her.

"Why, indeed?" Frustration crawled up his spine, gripping the back of his neck like a vise. He lashed out at the cause. "If you choose to settle for whom you do not love, it can be no concern of mine."

Gypsy whickered and shifted her stance. He knew his raised voice and changing mood was beginning to affect her. Not wanting to cause the mare distress when her time was so near, he gestured for Miss Wakefield to precede him out of the stall.

Without a word, Merribeth came around to his side, dropped the brush into the pail, and walked into the empty stall across the aisle.

He closed the door behind them, glancing down the long row of stalls toward the tack room to see if any groomsmen were hanging about. They weren't, so he followed her and quietly closed them inside.

"You have no cause to be angry," she huffed, glaring at him, her brow arched, her hands on her hips.

Oh, but he was. "Perhaps not," he said, rolling his shoulders in an effort to dislodge this foreign anxiety that had no place in his life. It wouldn't budge. "It isn't your fault. Not everyone witnesses a marriage based on a deep, unshakable love, such as the one my parents possessed. If not for that, they would never have survived their trials. I'm merely pointing out your future trials, as any friend would."

Her gaze softened marginally. "My parents were deeply in love as well. In addition, my aunt and her husband grew into love in the short time they were married. I believe in love, Lord Knightswold, but that isn't what I need."

He scoffed at her sudden use of his title, as if that formality could suddenly erase everything between them. "And the only thing you need is certainty?"

She walked over to the window, he suspected, to avoid looking at him. "At the very core of who I am, there is a ten-year-old girl who watched her father be swept overboard during a storm at sea. That same girl clutched her mother, only to have another wave wrench her from me as well."

Bane stilled, his frustration receding on an exhale. They'd experienced the same horror. No wonder he was so drawn to her.

"That same girl," she continued, her voice so quiet it compelled him closer, "saw her aunt fall to her knees when she learned the news. Then, as she clutched my waist and sobbed, she spoke the words that still haunt me to this day."

Her breath hitched, but she cleared her throat to disguise it. "*What will become of us?*" She looked over her shoulder, her face pale but her gaze strong and steady. "That is why I need certainty more than anything else. Even love."

His heart broke for her *and* for the girl she once was. He hated the idea of her living her life without love, of not having what she deserved. She was too bright and passionate to end up as a cleric's wife. She deserved more. But there was nothing he could do about it.

Even if he offered her an estate and enough money to live whatever life she chose—which he was surprisingly tempted to do—the action would cheapen her in the eyes of society.

She deserved a husband who loved her and children to hold. Nothing he could give.

Without anything else to offer, he walked across the crushed straw at his feet and drew her into his arms. She came without objection, her face nestling perfectly against his shoulder. This felt right, holding her close, his hands rubbing slow circles over her back, even as he felt the dampness of her tears soak through his shirt.

"This may sound trite and meaningless, but if I had the power to change your fate…for the better, I would."

"The sentiment was quite nicely said." She lifted her watery gaze and swiped her fingers across her cheek. "However, we both know differently."

Seeing a tear she missed, he leaned down to kiss it dry. The salty drop dampened his lips. He pressed them together, tasting the essence of her sadness. He wished he could remove the pain from her life just as easily as he had the tear. "We do?"

She nodded. "Eve explained your reasons for not marrying. If it means anything, after what you and your parents and even your uncle suffered, I might be inclined to seek revenge as well."

Stunned, he lifted his head and abruptly dropped his arms from around her. Irritation and anger swept over him at full force, like a racehorse from the starting gate. Eve had overstepped her bounds. "And did my *dear aunt* volunteer the information or answer a question you posed to her?"

Miss Wakefield took a step back, taking her warm softness with her. Affronted, no doubt by his sudden coldness, she put her hands on her hips. "It bothers you that I know your reasons for not marrying?"

Bugger it all, yes. "They are mine, just as your reasons *for* marrying belong to you."

Her eyes went from narrowed slits to opening wide, her brows lifting. "Yet fool that I am, I offered mine to you. I thought if you knew we shared an experience, it would help you—"

"Help *me*?" His temper climbed. How dare she look at him with pity! He was no longer the boy who'd watched his parents' carriage fall off a cliff and smash against the rocks below. He'd buried those scars a long time ago, and he was a different man now. A hardened man, capable of dangerous things. Vengeful things. "Do not imagine for an instant that I require help in taking a bride. If I ever chose that path, I have a title, lands, and wealth to aid me. There is *nothing* you could offer that I do not already possess."

She jerked back as if he'd raised a hand to strike her.

"Clearly, I have wounded your ego by bothering to care for the man behind the *title, lands, and wealth*." Swallowing, she hiked up her chin and straightened her shoulders. "Nevertheless, I will keep this memory with me. I made the mistake of believing we were friends and offered my concern. I won't make that mistake again."

Friends? The word felt like a spike being driven through his chest. When she attempted to walk away from him, he took hold of her arm. "My *friends* stay out of matters that are not their own."

"With this reaction, it is no wonder!" Hardness flashed in her gaze, altering the warm, summer blue to winter. "It is a shame really. Your parents, who loved each other so deeply, likely wanted the same for you. Yet you are so blind in your quest for revenge, and apparently so rich in wealth and friendship, that you cast aside someone who truly cares for *you*"— her voice broke—"for *your* future."

"A future in which you have no stake," he reminded, releasing her. "So what does it matter to you?"

"Matter? To me?" She laughed, the sound high and piercing. "Not a whit, I assure you."

"You are a maddening, nonsensical creature!" He had the urge to take hold of her again, grip her by the shoulders, shake her, or haul her against him and kiss her.

"What does it matter to you?" She stormed out before he could answer.

Matter? To me? Apparently, far too much.

So much, in fact, that it frightened him.

CHAPTER FOURTEEN

The following evening, dinner was an interesting affair. For the first time, they gathered in the dining hall. Twin pendant chandeliers hung down from the fresco-painted ceiling. Above them, angels, like the ones in the foyer, gathered on high, while below, the atmosphere was anything but heavenly.

The party sat along a dark walnut table that extended far enough to seat twice as many, but also was narrow enough for easy conversation with those directly across the richly glossed surface.

Unfortunately for Merribeth, Bane was that person.

She still struggled to calm her anger and hurt over her encounter with him in the stables yesterday, and she attempted to don a mask of cool regard. She'd hoped that after another day of avoiding Bane, it would be easier. It wasn't. There was such a tumultuous mixture of frustration and concern warring within her that part of her wondered if there was any way she could sit across from him without *accidentally* throwing her knife at him.

Odious man!

Yet the rest of her wanted to be back in his arms.

Why did it feel so right in his embrace? It felt as if the outside world no longer existed. Worry and anguish vanished, leaving only the warmth of his body pressed against hers. She wanted to feel that way forever.

Troubling her most of all was his quest for revenge at all cost. What kind of life was that? Didn't he realize his determination to ensure his grandfather didn't win made Bane the one who lost much more?

Having no answer, she focused on making it through dinner. However, an aura of tension seemed to settle around everyone. Of course, it might have to do with the new addition to their party.

Lord Amberdeen arrived only moments before dinner. In the Great Room, Merribeth overheard that yesterday, the gentlemen had been hunting on Amberdeen's property, and so it seemed that an invitation to dinner was a suitable payment. Yet the bad blood between Eve and Amberdeen was palpable.

"This is the finest fowl I've tasted in a long while," Amberdeen commented with a salute of his wine glass toward Eve, at the opposite end of the table. "Had I known you had such an excellent cook, I would have—"

"Tried to claim her as your own as well?" Eve interrupted with a razor-edged sweetness. "No doubt you could produce documents with every *appearance* of legitimacy."

Amberdeen's grin of admiration never faltered. He possessed an aura of control that seemed as much a part of him as the silver threaded through his hair or even the regal set of his features. "It pleases me that you still give me far too much credit."

For an instant, the dining room went eerily quiet. The only sound came from Eve's fingernails tapping against the stem of her glass. Without a word in response, she slowly disconnected her gaze from the unwanted guest and addressed her table partner. "Colonel, you must tell us that fascinating story of your adventure in Egypt."

Conversation resumed, albeit stilted. Because of the undercurrent of tension, at least no one noticed how Merribeth couldn't quite meet Bane's gaze across the table. No one would suspect there was anything between them, other than a casual acquaintance.

If only it felt that way to her too.

When dinner ended, Sophie took her arm and walked with her toward the parlor. Halfway there, she pulled Merribeth into recessed alcove partially hidden beneath the stairs.

"Eve is in a state," Sophie whispered, pushing up her spectacles and worrying the bridge of her nose. "She's furious at her nephew for inviting Lord Amberdeen without her permission. The strangest part is that I know he realizes how much Eve despises her neighbor. This leaves me to wonder if there is a rift between them." She blew out a breath and cautiously glanced over her shoulder. "Just between us, I've always had an inkling that if it weren't for the fact that Amberdeen wants Eve's land, she might actually have liked him. The same goes for Amberdeen. I think the only reason he pursues the land is actually to gain Eve's attention."

Merribeth didn't know which was more interesting—the fact that her aunt was confiding her preoccupations with her, or the fact that she seemed to be playing matchmaker. "Do you believe that is the reason why dinner was so...tense?"

Sophie offered a tentative shrug of her shoulders as she pulled off her spectacles and rubbed the lenses with the corner of her shawl. "But it is peculiar, don't you think, that Lord Knightswold would do such a thing?"

Peculiar? No. An act of revenge? Most definitely.

Merribeth suspected that the only reason he would have done such a thing was to get back at Eve for sharing information about his past. He was a man driven by revenge at any cost.

"Perhaps he merely shares the same inkling as you—that Amberdeen and Eve are well suited," Merribeth said, surprised at how convincing she sounded. She almost believed it herself. "Not only that, but Eve made mention that even with Montwood, we are one gentleman short for an even number at the party."

A sharp gleam lit Sophie's eyes as she replaced her spectacles. "You are right. I hadn't thought of that. Perhaps using that reason—the even number of males to females—would ease Eve's mind. Seeing Amberdeen in a social setting might soften her heart toward him as well."

"Aunt Sophie, are you turning into a matchmaker?"

Ever the bluestocking, Sophie mulled over her response carefully as she pursed her lips. "I'll observe them this evening before I make my decision."

After the gentlemen joined them in the parlor, Montwood set about entertaining everyone with his rambunctious skill on the piano. Lord Amberdeen sat near Sophie, making pleasant conversation on village improvements.

Her aunt continually steered the conversation topic toward Eve's accomplishments, and to his credit, Lord Amberdeen expounded on her virtues. It seemed Sophie was right about the attraction, at least for *one* of the neighbors. Merribeth only hoped that Amberdeen enjoyed a challenge. She highly doubted Eve would easily accept the widower's pursuit.

"I daresay you've heard of our hostess's dilemma," Sophie said to Amberdeen. "We are shy one gentleman for our outing to the village tomorrow. Perhaps you would care to ease her burden?" Yes, her aunt was, indeed, playing matchmaker.

"I should like nothing more," the gentleman responded, staring directly at Eve, who was standing near enough to observe the exchange and let out a growl of incredulity. Merribeth knew a challenge when she saw one. And apparently so did the rest of the party.

Eve also noticed that she'd become the center of attention but then used it to her advantage. Settling a hand over Montwood's shoulder, the music fell away. Then, with an unspoken command, the doors to the hall opened.

"Tonight, I've planned something of a scavenger hunt with a small twist. I wouldn't want to make it too easy, after all. Each of you will be given a key," she said, gesturing to a footman who held a platter of keys with different colored ribbons tied to each end. "Each of these keys leads to a locked door on the main floor of the house. Inside the room that your key opens is a list of items you must find. Find the room. Find the list. Find the items," she continued, ticking off each with a pointed finger. "And the person who returns at the end of the hour with the most will be declared the winner."

Once everyone had taken a key, they were each given a lamp, holding a single taper. Once the tapers were lit, the footmen extinguished the sconces and chandeliers. A scavenger hunt in the dark was a twist indeed.

"One word of warning: if you rush around too fast and your flame goes out, you have lost," Eve concluded, her face cast in eerie shadow, giving her an almost sinister appearance.

Merribeth felt a chill of foreboding. The peculiar smile she'd witnessed earlier had returned. She couldn't help but wonder if there were higher stakes to Eve's game than a mere victory.

Then, right on cue, the clock on the mantle began to chime. Midnight. They had one hour before their return to the parlor.

A slow procession of candles filed out of the room, one by one. In the hall, quiet chatter filled the air with murmurs and soft giggles as pairs of people began to split off in different directions.

With Sophie lagging behind in the parlor, Merribeth decided to go alone. Walking toward the music room, she stopped when she noticed Archer trying his key in the lock as Daniela giggled and held the candle aloft.

Merribeth quickly made the decision to head in the opposite direction.

She was just passing the alcove beneath the stairs when a dark figure moved in front of her. Whoever it was did not hold a taper, casting the stranger in shadow. Then, suddenly, her flame went out with a puff. In the next instant, her lamp was pulled from her grasp. But before she could draw breath enough to gasp in surprise, or even outrage, she felt a familiar hand against her lips, before it dropped lower to curl around her elbow and drag her a few steps deeper into the shadows.

"What could you possibly want?" she hissed, crossing her arms over her chest instead of starting or shrieking in maidenly outrage. Even though she couldn't see him, she knew exactly who it was.

A small laugh rumbled in Lord Knightswold's throat. "How did you know it was me?"

There were many reasons. Because her heart beat differently when he was near. Because her skin tingled and every sense came alive. Because she knew the feel of his hands on her arms as if he'd branded her.

However, she wouldn't tell him any of that. Instead, she chose a bland explanation. "Your scent."

As impossible as it seemed, she heard him grin. In the quiet moment that passed between them, she wondered if her admission wasn't as bland as she thought. She paid close attention to the sounds around her—the quiet scrape of his boots on the floor, muted conversation nearby. Strangely, she didn't see the light from anyone's candle. The moment that thought occurred to her, she heard the soft but unmistakable click of a latch.

"Where are we?" she asked, trying to remember if she'd seen a door nearby when she was standing here with Sophie earlier.

"A concealed closet below the stairs," Bane whispered and moved a step closer. Close enough for his breath to stir the wisps of hair along her temple. "Tell me, what do I smell like?"

She shivered and swallowed simultaneously. Her anger and confusion about him was temporarily put on hold as the realization struck her that they were alone, completely closed off from the others, yet at any moment, they could be discovered. "It isn't one thing. It's more of a mélange of fragrances," she stammered.

He leaned down, drawing in a breath in a way that gave her the sense he was drawing in *her* scent. The inner drumming she thought gone forever suddenly returned, albeit unsteadily, as if not quite recovered from their argument. Merribeth knew she should leave and heed Bane's warning about tempting fate.

"What kinds of things?" From the warmth of his tone, she guessed that he'd also put aside his anger from yesterday.

Closing her eyes, she felt the first percussive beat deep inside and drew in a deep breath of her own. "Freshly cut straw. Sandalwood. Leather. Coffee." Her mouth watered. "The piney scent of horse liniment."

"Ghastly." He rubbed his nose along her temple.

She tilted her head, encouraging him to continue. "Actually, together they make a very pleasant aroma. Uniquely yours."

"Mmm…" was his only response as he moved closer, his lips grazing the shell of her ear.

Oh, that was nice.

At the same time, he ran his finger down the back of her arm, slow and meandering, like a silk shawl slipping off her neck and gliding to the floor. "Your scent isn't as simple as pinpointing different flora and fauna," he offered but hesitated for a moment, as if debating whether or not to continue. His lips traversed upward, nudging her hair aside to drift along her forehead. "It evokes a memory of one spring day, long ago. I was only a lad. My parents and I were climbing the hill behind *Raven*—our Essex estate for a picnic. They had me by the hands, swinging me between them. A warm wind blew through the pear blossoms, ruffling my hair. I remember laughing." He released a shuddered breath. "And that's what you smell like."

She could easily see him, smiling and laughing, with the sun shining on his face and the wind ruffling his coal black hair. *Too* easily.

He was such a private person, always guarding himself as well as his past. And yet he'd shared this memory with her. The fact that she reminded him of such a happy moment in his life made her heart feel as if it were vibrating instead of beating.

In that same instant, all her romantic sensibilities rushed through her, as if they'd been locked in a dungeon all this time. The moment she saw the boy that Bane had been in her mind's eye, she also saw him as a man—eyes closed and face lifted to the sun, smiling—and in that brief, earth-shattering vision, she saw herself standing in his arms.

Oh dear. She felt it when it happened—the precise instant her heart leapt from her own breast, like a horse over a field-stone wall, and landed directly into his. For a moment, she couldn't feel the beating of her own. Only his. And his heart pounded hard and fast enough for both of them.

Unable to help herself, she uncrossed her arms and pressed her empty hand against his chest. Then, because it wasn't enough, she pressed the hand holding the key against him as well.

Uncertainty had plagued her for weeks until now. She didn't know her what her future held. She was unsure of her standing among the *ton*. She'd been trapped in a state of limbo without any hope of escape. Yet now, with a sudden burst of clarity, she became certain of one thing:

She'd fallen in love. Completely and irrevocably. Perhaps, insanely. Because she'd fallen in love with an irredeemable rake and lifelong bachelor, who'd closed himself off from any hope of a future without revenge. Which guaranteed, with absolute certainty, his future had no room for her.

This was the worst moment of her life, and yet, it was also the best. Her sense of certainty had returned at last. But at what cost?

Hating her foolish heart for falling in love at the worst possible time, she lowered her forehead to his chest. Must he always keep her at odds with herself? She hadn't had one iota of peace since they'd met.

As if sensing her plight, he pressed a kiss to the top of her head.

Two short taps sounded on the door. This time, she did start. Her reputation would not merely be in question but *destroyed*, if she were found alone in a closet with Bane.

"It's only Bitters," he crooned softly, using the same reassuring tone he had with Gypsy. "He's going to gather the items for the hunt."

Her lips parted in shock. "You planned this?"

"I wanted to speak with you privately without endangering your reputation."

"And being locked in a closet below the stairs with you will ensure that." She nearly laughed at the absurdity. "You would have done better to simply escort me to my room at the end of the evening." The moment the words were out, she realized the potential hazards of such an act, especially after the kiss they'd shared in the library. If the servants' stairs had been too close, then a mere door would likely be *much* too close. "Then again, this was likely the better option."

"Your blush is lovely, even in the dark," he said, his lips curving into a grin as they grazed her temple. "Now, give me your key."

His fingers trailed down the length of her arm to where her hands were resting against his chest. She slipped the key into his palm and felt him close his fingers around it securely. Then, with her hand still covering his, he lifted it up to his lips for a quick kiss against her knuckles. Her romantic sensibilities fluttered at the gesture. Turning, he opened the door a crack and handed the key to Bitters without a word.

The latch fell into place again before he resumed his place before her. He took both her wrists, lifted her arms so they encircled his neck, and settled his hands at her waist.

This was how he planned to speak to her *without* endangering her reputation?

"I can hear the arching of your brow, Miss Wakefield." As if to prove it, he bent his head and pressed a kiss there. "There is nothing I can do about it. I must hold you this close in order to keep our voices low. A whispered conversation where one's back is constantly bent would likely cause me to require a cane before the end of the night."

He said it with such humorless conviction that she couldn't keep a breathy giggle from escaping. She stayed in his arms. Her heart wouldn't have allowed her to pull back if she'd wanted to. Which she didn't. They were tethered now by strands of misguided emotion and rash judgments.

Sewn together by fine threads of silly romantic notions and no possible future.

Lovely. She wasn't sure if she should cry or sing.

She did neither, trying her best not to reveal this horrendous mawkishness. No wonder William had seemed crazed when he'd told her about his love for Miss Codington. Having experienced love for only a few moments, she was already feeling completely *mad.*

She knew if she managed to convince William to marry her when he arrived for the end of Eve's party, she'd be saving them both from insanity. Only now, the necessity of doing so felt incredibly painful and dishonest.

"This is not what I expected," she sighed, resigned to madness for the time being. "I couldn't even look at you at dinner."

"Forgive me," he whispered, his lips moving from her brow to her temple again, his nose burrowing into the fall of curls.

It was more of an order than a request. She couldn't help but smile at his arrogance. Only he could rail at her for invading his privacy, offer her a glimpse at a precious memory, and then demand her forgiveness, as if her opinion mattered to him.

Perhaps it does, her romantic sensibilities told her. Wanting to believe that voice more than anything, any residual anger she might have had evaporated. "Your temper, it seems, is as quick to recede as it is to ignite."

"Hmm...so it seems," he mused, his lips grazing the shell of her ear once more. His heated breath swirled inside. *Ooh.* "In my own defense, I thought you were conspiring to marry me."

What a lovely idea.

However, just as the thought of having Bane with her like this for the rest of her life started to form, the cynicism and practicality she'd adopted took over. Too quickly, she reminded herself of the certainty of utter despair if she continued to keep her eyes closed to the truth.

"That would be a fruitless endeavor," she said, leveling with herself. "You're not the marrying kind. In fact, you likely keep a mistress in every county from here to France."

His chuckle vibrated through the delicate flesh beneath the corner of her jaw. "It's a wonder I have any time to myself."

She stiffened. That wasn't a denial. Her hands slipped from his shoulders to push against his chest.

He lifted his head and pressed a quick kiss to her lips, another arrogant chuckle rumbling in his throat. "I don't currently keep any mistresses. My assignations are usually of a shorter duration, by way of mutual understanding."

She imagined that he added the last for her benefit, as if he thought her jealous. For now, she didn't let his incorrect assumption deter her from their topic. "So every woman you're…*with* knows from the beginning that you will not marry her?"

"Of course." The slight edge to his voice made him sound mildly offended. "I'm not so callous as to toy with a woman's affections."

She'd guessed as much by his straightforward manner. Like her, Bane seemed to prefer honesty above all else. However, that thought gave her another. "Do they all know why?"

He brushed the curls away from her forehead and traced the shape of her brows with the pad of his thumb. "Other than my aunt, you are the only other woman to know my reasons."

She didn't know why being one of the people who knew about his past tragedies and his plot for revenge caused a light to flutter beneath her breast. Perhaps it was just the way he said it. Or perhaps it was the way his touch made her feel cherished instead of ridiculed. "You're no longer angry that I know?"

"I decided it was only fair," he said, bending his head so that his lips could follow the same path as his thumb. "After all, you've shared your secrets with me. I will keep yours, and I've no doubt you'll keep mine."

"I will," she promised on a breath, feeling her entire being turn liquid. "I only ask one thing in return."

He stilled. His body tensed as if he were suddenly made of armor. Slowly, he lifted his head.

She missed the intimate caress immediately. When he didn't respond, she quickly continued. "Do not be alarmed. It's a simple request to know your given name."

He didn't exactly relax, but some of the tension left him. "No one calls me by my given name. So why would you want to know it?"

Because no one calls you by your given name. Because a woman should have the name of the man she loves in order to whisper it to the heavens in her dreams. Because I love you, and perhaps saying your name will keep my heart from shattering when we part company in eight days. "Because if we ever find ourselves together in a darkened closet, I believe standing this close demands a modicum of familiarity."

The remaining tension left him in an instant, the muscles relaxing beneath her hands. She even heard him smile again.

"That would make our bargain uneven. Not to mention, the likelihood of our meeting again in a darkened closet is remote at best."

Her silly idealistic notions wouldn't allow her to be disappointed. Instead, she held on to an absurd hope that this wouldn't be the last time she'd be in his arms. Somehow, she'd make sure of it. "There is still a week of the party remaining. You might have the need to apologize to me yet again."

"There is always that hope," he said with another chuckle. "All right. I give you leave to call me Simon whenever we might find ourselves in a darkened closet together. *If* you pay me a forfeit for its use."

A forfeit. Mm-m. Rapid staccato beats of the drum rumbled through her at the endless list of possibilities. "I will call you Simon whether I pay a forfeit or not," she said, hoping her voice sounded sure and strong instead of breathy and eager. "And since I do not play at bargaining, it will be the latter."

He tilted up her chin as if he were peering through the darkness and into her gaze. "You do not play at bargaining? You are perhaps the slyest bargainer of all."

A short laugh escaped her. "When you are the one who demands a forfeit? Who promises to keep a tally of each one of my hidden smiles in order to collect a debt? I have demanded nothing in return."

"I know enough to realize that the one who demands nothing, seeks everything."

Her mouth opened on a lie. "I don't want—"

"Know this, Venus," he stopped her, his voice abruptly gruff and cold, even while the arm at her waist snaked around her tightly, pulling her closer. "I can never give you what you want. I could set you up with a house, visit you from time to time, give you money enough for your material needs...But I cannot give you certainty for your future. No husband. No children. And soon enough, you would grow to hate me for robbing you of your dreams."

Pressed flush against him, her breasts flattened to his chest, she could hardly breathe, let alone think. Even so, she made no move to free herself. "For the use of your name, the forfeit I pay is to become your mistress?"

He inhaled sharply, his hand flexing into her lower back. "Not a single woman has ever possessed the option or wanted it. They were all content with what I could offer. You..." He let out a breath, slow and harsh, as if it were pulled from the very center of his being. Then, suddenly, he dropped his hands and took a step apart from her. "You would never be."

Denial was on her lips, along with a plea to be held again in his arms, to accept the terms of this unexpected bargain. But before she could do anything so completely foolhardy, another knock sounded on the door.

Bitters had returned at the precise moment when her romantic sensibilities died a miserable death, and she was left with only cynicism and practicality. Not to mention a bruised heart.

"As always, Lord Knightswold, I appreciate your candor. Now, if you would excuse me, I would like to return to the party."

"One day you will thank me, Miss Wakefield."

"I believe I already have. Now we are even."

CHAPTER FIFTEEN

Standing on the bluff, Bane fed his Warmblood stallion a handful of sweet grass as well as a carrot he'd saved from the day of the picnic. Below him, the others strolled along the pebbled beach as low waves left ribbons of foam along the break.

Invariably, his gaze followed the figure in pale blue muslin. Her head was tilted away from him, but he could still see how the wind whipped the raven tresses that escaped her straw bonnet.

He also noticed how she hadn't looked at him once today. After last night, he'd expected no less.

Bane dragged out a sigh and patted Ares on the neck. "That's a dangerous one there, old boy. Her curiosity and guilelessness could bring a man to his knees. Make him forget what truly matters."

Thanks to Bitters, Bane had avoided a catastrophe of monumental proportion. Though his faithful valet had arrived a moment too late to keep him from all but begging Venus to become his mistress, he had arrived just in time to help him come to his senses. *And* apparently Merribeth had come to hers as well. The knock had been perfectly timed to offer at least one of them the presence of mind to walk away.

"Only my revenge matters," he said, paying no attention to the way the words sounded hollow. Paying no attention to how raw he'd felt last night after everything he'd admitted to her.

The glimpse of her radiant smile distracted him. Even from this distance, he felt the impact of it, felt the sun shining on his face, felt the breeze through his hair. And as impossible as it was, he caught the distinct fragrance of pear blossoms.

When she lifted her fingers to conceal her smile, however, he felt a swift rise of irritation as well as a stirring of desire. That made three today. Adding that number to the tally he kept, she now owed him twelve.

A dozen kisses that he would never demand. Because, after last night, he knew he couldn't trust himself to be alone with her. Something had changed for him, and he didn't like it one bit.

"My ingénue seems to be ripening," Eve said, surprising him with her sudden emergence from the path, a calculating gleam in her eyes.

He knew that denial, no matter how insincere, was the best option. "What ingénue would that be, Auntie?"

Her mouth curled up at the corners in something just short of a grin. "I must say, I was surprised at how quickly she managed to gather her items for the scavenger hunt last night. And with the length of her taper when she returned to the parlor, she must have collected them all in the dark."

Without waiting for a comment, she turned from him to face the beach strollers. "I was also surprised that she chose Montwood as her picnic partner this afternoon for her prize. But they do make a fine pair, do they not? And she could learn so much from him in the ways of flattery. A few well-placed compliments would do our Merribeth a world of good to regain her place, insignificant as it was, among the *ton*."

"Perhaps," he managed to say without gritting his teeth. "Though Montwood is far too foolish a fellow to be left on his own. He seems more interested in sowing his oats—"

"Sounds like someone else I know."

"—rather than spending time with a marriage-minded miss," he continued, ignoring the smug purse of Eve's mouth. "No doubt, there are better ways to tutor without misleading one's pupil into thinking he has an interest in her."

She fiddled with the cuff of her kid gloves. "I might have encouraged him to spend more time than a young man of his interests might, if left to his own devices. For Miss Wakefield's benefit, of course."

"Of course," he said evenly, strands of suspicion weaving through his mind. For a fortune hunter like Montwood to abandon the kettle of heavily dowried chits in London, he must have been promised quite the boon. "You are ever the philanthropist."

A low laugh purred in her throat. "She has little to recommend her. Not a sixpence to her name. No real connections—unless you count her recently married friend, which many seldom do. Although Merribeth is pretty enough, I suppose, if it weren't for her teeth and that unbecoming arched brow of hers," She looked askance at him.

Sensing that she was trying to draw him out, he bit his tongue to remain silent.

"It breaks my heart to think of her losing her beau after so long an attachment," Eve continued. "You should have seen her wedding gown. A stunning work of art. Merribeth has the finest needlework skills. It's a shame I haven't seen her pick up a needle since Mr. Clairmore's betrayal. Anguish must have robbed her of her love for everything else."

He kept his gaze out to sea, even as the others began their trek up the path. "Then you are not confident your ploy will work?"

"Oh, you know me better than that." She laughed. "I enjoy winning too much."

Something about this entire exchange unsettled him. "Usually too much to play by the rules."

She grinned. "Which brings our bargain to mind. Daniela Pearce is very cross. At first, it was because you kept your door locked night and day, and now she seems to have this notion that you are a sadist. Are *you* playing fair?"

"Merely following the rules set to me." He kept the key tucked in his waistcoat pocket at all times, apparently for good reason. He didn't want anyone rifling through his belongings to make a false claim against him either. It didn't seem to matter that he spent nearly every night sleeping above the stables.

Eve pursed her lips in speculation. "That is so unlike you, Bane. I imagined you would have found your way around them by now."

He shrugged. "There is no female companionship worth the loss of Gypsy."

Shielding her eyes against the sun, she stared out at the beach. "I made the mistake of inviting Cordelia. I cannot stand the woman or the way she hangs on the colonel's arm," she said with a pout. "From my understanding, the two of you were close at one time. I thought she might tempt you."

"Married women do not tempt me." This earned him an insincere gasp.

"Bane, you surprise me yet again. No married women. At all?" When he shook his head in response, she pulled a frown. "A rake with principles, I never took you to be so...*boring.*"

His frustration mounted as he watched the party's progression up the winding incline. Ever solicitous, Montwood kept his hand beneath Merribeth's elbow. Bane felt the urge to hurl the lad into the sea. "Perhaps you should stop believing rumors."

"Hmm...perhaps." She absently adjusted the clasp of her earring. He knew toying with her jewelry was one of her *tells*, one of the ways she revealed that she was up to something more than she was willing to let on. Clearly, she was hiding the trump card for the final trick. "Though I should hate to have to hand over the information I've procured—as a matter of my own principles. In the very least, I should punish you for inviting Amberdeen to dinner. Now, you have put Sophie on a matchmaking quest. I don't think I will ever forgive you for any of it." Although the words were said in playful context, they came out with startling severity.

The peculiar tenor in her voice brought to mind the day after his grandfather died. With the softest of whispers, she'd said the same words. "*I don't think I'll ever forgive you for any of it.*" Only, at the time, he thought she was directing her hatred toward his grandfather. Now, he wondered if it had been him all along.

An icy shiver slithered down his spine like a black eel, spreading unpleasant currents through him.

"I should return to check on Gypsy," he said, masking the disquiet he felt. "She was restless this morning." Her time was drawing near.

Eve waved her hand in a careless gesture. "Of course. Go on ahead. I'm sure we'll be right on your heels."

Bane hoped not. He needed a few moments alone to settle his disturbing thoughts.

When this bargain was first proposed, he'd taken it on as a lark. Eve enjoyed playing games to win, and this entire episode could be just another game to her. Besides that, she was family to him. The only family he had left. It felt disloyal to suspect her of anything more than her usual trickery and manipulation. And yet, his growing suspicions told him that the stakes were much higher. He felt the sudden compulsion to be certain.

Mounting Ares, he set off toward the house but waited to spur the gelding faster until he rounded the bend.

Once he arrived, he handed the reins to a groomsman—something he rarely did—and made his way into the house. As it was Sunday and most of the servants were in town, there were no maids milling about.

His steps slowed at the study. For a moment, he wondered if the document Eve possessed might be hidden in plain sight all this time. Yet, knowing Eve's desire for control, he knew she would keep such a prize under lock and key. Perhaps even in her bedchamber.

Taking the stairs two at a time, he soon found himself at her threshold. Another boon for him was her unlocked door, though he locked it behind him once inside.

Crossing the room to the bureau, he was startled by the recognition that it was a companion piece to the one that once had been in his grandfather's study. Strange that she would keep such a reminder here with her every day. It was almost as if she *wanted* hatred to fill her life.

Perhaps Eve was more like him than he realized. The idea gave him pause. Along with it came a sharp sense of certainty. Whatever proof she had of the secret solicitor would be here. And for the first time, he wondered if that's all he would find.

The lid was locked. *Of course.* He expected no less. Quickly, he scanned the room, searching for the key's hiding place, when his gaze landed on a wooden chest atop her vanity table.

He thought of the way she fidgeted with her jewelry, and the answer suddenly seemed obvious to him. Lifting the lid of her jewelry chest, however, he merely saw a tray of rings and earbobs. A tray beneath that revealed bracelets, and beneath that, hair combs. At the very bottom, beneath the last tray, sat a small key.

Wasting no time, he crossed back to the bureau and unlocked it. The surface hosted a messy array of letter paper, a broken quill, half a bottle of ink, and dusting powder. Even though it looked disorderly, he had the distinct impression that the dusting powder had been spilled intentionally, to let Eve know if anything was out of place.

Bane was careful not to disturb the powder or any items as he worked his finger into the half-moon–shaped hole at the back. Remembering the search through his grandfather's bureau for clues regarding the secret solicitor told him there was a latch to release the secret drawer.

It sprang open with a faint click. At that precise moment, he heard the sound of the party opening the door below stairs. Their chatter rose up and gave him a sense of urgency.

Deftly, he slid out the drawer; the corner of a letter appeared. He drew in a breath. In an instant, he saw that it was the correspondence that Mangus had with his sister.

This was it.

A rush of excitement tore through him as he read the letter, confirming it was, indeed, the proof that Eve had promised. A rapid skimming of the words revealed the name of the village. The county of Berkshire wasn't too great a distance from his grandfather's estate.

However, she hadn't kept all the information secret, as she'd told him. At the bottom of the page, in the corner, was a single word that stood out from everything else. It was written in a different hand, with a decidedly feminine flourish.

Bane went still.

Now, the reason behind Eve's bargain and her peculiar behavior became clear. He only wished it hadn't. This was no mere game or lark.

The name said it all: *Clairmore.*

Bane stared down at the page in disbelief. At last, the key to his revenge was within his grasp. He could finally punish the man responsible for burning his parents' marriage records, for their murders, for blackmailing anyone who stood up for his legitimacy, and for ruining his uncle at the cost of his life.

In the back of his mind, he recalled Merribeth mentioning that her Mr. Clairmore's father was a solicitor. Apparently, Clairmore had been the type of man who was willing to do anything for the right price. Or perhaps he shared in Bane's grandfather's obsession with pure bloodlines. Now, it was only a matter of discovering the driving force in order to make the blackguard pay.

He imagined the worst thing that could happen to man like Clairmore. *If the man is just like my grandfather, then having his son marry a woman with gypsy blood would work.*

Unless…

He went cold everywhere. A mixture of triumph and dread battled within him. The solution was almost too easy, as if a banquet of revenge had been laid before him. All he had to do was feast. Then he would have everything he desired.

Everything.

And Merribeth was the key.

CHAPTER SIXTEEN

"William is here!" The door to the bedchamber flew open, and Sophie hurried in, out of breath.

Merribeth bolted upright in bed, heart pounding. "Already?"

She'd been resting in preparation for the long night ahead of her. Her last night here. Her last night with Bane. Now, she felt anything but rested.

Leaving the blank linen handkerchief and silver-threaded needle on the divan, she rose and moved to the window, staring out at the expanse of balconies along the side of the house. For a man who'd offered to make her his mistress, Bane was doing a terrible job of seducing her. In fact, he'd been avoiding her for days.

There were no more clandestine meetings in the library. No encounters in the hall outside her bedchamber door. No more tender embraces in the stable. And certainly no more intimate conversations in the closet.

He was polite enough at dinner, especially when it seemed Eve was determined to seat them together every evening. On the off chance they should find themselves in close proximity in the parlor afterwards, they each inclined their heads by way of greeting but said nothing of consequence.

Bane was no longer warm and flirtatious. In fact, he was cold, and his determination to keep her at a distance was quite evident. He'd made himself perfectly clear: He would take her as his mistress, but she was deluding herself if she thought for a moment that he'd fallen in love with her. Or ever would. She guessed that the recent alteration in his behavior was his way of helping her come to a decision.

Yet she was ashamed to admit that the idea of becoming his mistress ran in a constant stream through her mind. But knowing that she would be giving up any possible future with a husband and perhaps children of her own kept her from actually considering it. Well...*almost.*

These days apart were taking their toll. She didn't know how much longer she could stop herself from approaching him.

"William looks very ill," her aunt said after catching her breath. "My dear, he asked to speak with you directly. I'm sure this can only mean one thing."

Merribeth glanced over her shoulder and met Sophie's gaze. Perhaps William's affection for her *had* only needed time and space. "Do you think he means to propose?" The idea churned inside her stomach like seawater.

"Why else?"

She felt her legs tremble a bit when she stood and walked to the door. "Perhaps he only means to apologize for ruining my reputation." There. That made her feel marginally better.

Sophie shook her head and adjusted her spectacles. "I think not, for he wouldn't be in such a state. It stands to reason that he has suddenly realized he wanted to marry you all along."

Merribeth's legs nearly gave out. It felt as if the room were rocking beneath her like a ship at sea. This was it, then. The moment she'd hoped would come. The moment she now dreaded.

Without another word, she steeled herself and made her way downstairs.

Everything her aunt had said was true. William looked quite changed—his cheeks ruddy, his eyes solemn but clear, his pale hair swept back from his forehead as if he'd ridden against the wind for miles. Aside from that day in the garden, he'd always been perfectly composed. She could see he was struggling with it now and realized he would never let down his guard completely with her. And she would never want him to.

He bowed to her in greeting. "It's good to see you, Merr."

"And you," she said in all sincerity. His face was nearly as familiar as her own. There was a sense of comfort in that. But the parlor was not the place to hold their conversation, especially with Daniela Pearce, Sir Colin, and Lady Cordelia eagerly watching their exchange. "Would you care to walk the grounds?"

He gave her a smile that was more relief than happiness and inclined his head. "I'd love nothing more."

Outside, the air was pleasantly warm, with a slight breeze that brought the scent of fresh straw to her. Her gaze naturally drifted to the stables, where she saw groomsmen using pitchforks to toss tangles of golden stalks through an open door. A movement from within drew her attention as well. *Bane.*

The moment she saw him, her pulse quickened. However, the beats felt hollow against her wrists and throat.

She missed him. A lonely ache resided in her breast, and she knew instinctively that he was the only one to ease the pain of it. She'd enjoyed their unlikely friendship from the beginning. Now, the certainty of living without it for the rest of her life made her feel empty.

These days apart from him had seemed to drag on and on. Yet each night in her dreams they went by too quickly. Because each night in her dreams, she imagined herself with him.

Of course, she tried to stop dreaming of him, of how it would be if she gave herself to him, agreeing to become his mistress for whatever duration.

She wanted to dream of her life with William, instead— the small house in the village, the children they could have, the certainty of having him back in her life the way it had been since her parents had died.

Yet no matter how hard she tried, the image wouldn't form in her mind. William's was not the face she saw when she closed her eyes.

Pathetic, she knew. Apparently, her romantic sensibilities had completely taken over. She was a new spectacle on display of *Wallflower Specimens and Doomed Romantic Notions*.

William released a heavy sigh, drawing her attention back to him. For a moment, she'd forgotten he was walking beside her. He had his face tipped up to the sky, but his features were drawn as if in agony, as if a great weight were pressing down upon him.

"William, are you unwell?" she asked, her hand automatically reaching out to rest against his forearm.

He stopped and scrubbed his eyes. "I don't know how to go about this, so I'll just come right out and say it." He blew out another agonized breath before he met her gaze. "I've abused our friendship abominably, Merr. It took some time before I realized it, but when I did, I knew there was only one thing that would set matters aright and that's...marriage."

The air left her body in a sudden whoosh. "*Our* marriage?" she asked, just to be sure. She didn't want another misunderstanding.

He breathed out again, his brow furrowed. "Yes. You and I will marry. We'll have a house in the village. Or perhaps, we'll find a new place, and I, a new parish, where I can finish my instruction and leave...all else behind me." His voice shook with those last few words, leaving her to wonder at its cause.

A strong suspicion crept into her mind. "What about Miss Codington? I thought you'd planned to marry her and continue to be cleric beneath her father at the parish in Fernbough."

He closed his eyes and turned from her so that she couldn't see his expression. "She has changed her mind."

Ah. So that's what this was. William was hers again, but only by default. "Why?"

"Her reason made no sense to me." His shoulders sagged as he lowered his head. "She said that her father had decided against it shortly after he'd received a letter. Within it, she said, were things that brought *my* father's character into question. My father is highly respected and revered. I knew that whatever slander she'd learned could not be true. When I told my father, he suggested that Miss Codington was most likely casting off blame for her own fickle mind and that she was no longer worthy of the Clairmore name."

Once again, Merribeth's gaze wandered toward the stables to see the man who stood inside the shadows. Bane wore buff-colored riding breeches with only his waistcoat and shirtsleeves, rolled up to the elbow. He didn't stand around waiting for the groomsmen to finish their task but grabbed a pitchfork of his own. Even though he didn't acknowledge her presence, she knew he'd seen her. Against her will, she was drawn to him.

"My father has many high-ranking friends, one of whom knows the Archbishop of Canterbury," William said, turning to face her. He drew in a breath that seemed to fortify him, an instant before he dropped to one knee. "We can be married directly."

Her hand flew to her mouth, whether to hide her gasp or a sudden sob, she wasn't sure. All she knew was that a sense of certainty returned to her. It was swift as a storm at sea. As devastating as a wave crashing over the bow.

Without a doubt, she knew she couldn't marry him.

They had been friends too long. Although he'd hurt her by making a declaration of love for another woman, deep down she wanted him to be happy. She wanted him to be with the woman who made him insane with love.

At that thought, her gaze drifted toward the stables. Bane turned his back and disappeared into the shadows.

It suddenly occurred to her that a life filled with certainty, whether it was spending her years with Mr. Clairmore or with Aunt Sophie, was no life at all without love.

"Oh, William," she said with a sigh born of self-loathing for having wanted this exact outcome—well, perhaps she would have preferred to be his first choice, solely for the sake of her ego. "We have been friends for a very long time. And as your friend, I cannot deceive you. You see…I do not love you."

From deep within the stable, Bane saw Miss Wakefield striding toward him. However, the last thing he wanted at this moment was to speak to her. He felt wounded, betrayed, and confused—the last because he had no business feeling the first two. She wasn't his. She would never be his.

Never. He'd made his decision. No matter what Clairmore's father had done, he could not use her in any way to exact his revenge.

"There is something I want to tell you," she said, ignoring the fact that he was making every attempt to appear too busy for conversation.

With his grip on the pitchfork handle, he searched for a pile of straw to stab. He didn't want to hear about the return of Clairmore's affections. "Ah, yes. Many felicitations on your upcoming nuptials."

"You *were* watching, then." She set her hands on her hips as if something he'd said had angered her. Or perhaps it was his own anger spilling over and infecting her. Neither mattered. Not anymore.

"I saw enough to know that soon you will have your singular desire—*the certainty of your future.* Isn't that the secret for a happy marriage?"

Now, she crossed her arms beneath her breasts and arched that wicked brow at him. She looked utterly magnificent and he wanted—*oh,* how he wanted.

"It is more than you've offered."

Torturing himself, he let his gaze roam over her face, absorbing every detail, memorizing the exact shade of blue in her eyes, every striation. "You forget; I am a man solely driven by revenge," he declared, mocking himself as well. "That is my singular desire. Nothing else matters."

"I don't believe that."

He scoffed and pressed the tines deep into the dirt at his feet. "Do you know what I did to my grandfather's estate when he died?" Not waiting for her response, he continued. "For the price of one horse, I allowed my mother's people to loot and set fire to it."

She didn't gasp, or start, or even stare at him in horror, as she was supposed to. *Damn it all,* her gaze softened.

"Gypsy is that horse, isn't she? That's why she means so much to you." Merribeth lowered her voice and took a step toward him. "I understand. But I need you to understand something too, before we part ways and never see each other again."

"The moment cannot come soon enough." His statement lacked the necessary vehemence for conviction. He sounded more like a petulant child who'd had his most precious object stolen from him.

Nonetheless, she ignored him and continued. "By not marrying, you're not only ending the Fennecourt line but your mother's as well. Don't you see how you're letting him win after all?"

No. She was wrong. She simply didn't understand the whole truth the way he did.

"Because of him, my mother is not alive to care whether or not she has grandchildren. Both of my parents were robbed of a future of any kind—*certain* or not," he mocked, and this time with enough spite to see her flinch. "I owe it to them to see their murderer pay the ultimate price."

Venus still didn't give up. She took yet another step closer, her arms uncrossing as her hands lifted in a beseeching gesture. "Though I didn't know your parents, I'm certain they loved you. They would have wanted you to spend your life surrounded by the people who bring you joy, not cut off out of misguided justice for a man who's no longer alive to feel the punishment you're inflicting."

Rage rose within him. How dare she tell him what his parents would have thought?

Yet even as heated waves scoured his veins and tightened around his throat like a noose, he hated even more that she was getting to him. Her words blistered his skin like hot shards from a blacksmith's hammer. More than anything, he wanted to silence her. He wanted to forget everything she'd ever said. Wipe her memory from the threads of his soul.

But she was inside him now, tangled up in the jumble of knots that formed his entire being. It had all started with that damned kiss she'd borrowed. He wished he could give it back. Take her in his arms, crush her mouth to his, and kiss her until every fiber of her was dragged from him.

"Tell me this," she continued, daring to step closer. "If he is still able to feel your wrath, then what makes you think your parents aren't able to feel sorrow for how empty your life has become?"

He clenched his fists and dug the toes of his boots into the ground at his feet. He didn't trust himself to keep the distance between them. What made it worse was knowing how readily she'd once welcomed his embrace.

"Go, Miss Wakefield. Leave before you become my next victim." He had to make her understand somehow. She didn't realize how the idea of taking her, here and now, tempted him. If he did, he could finally have the one woman he craved with more passion than he ever remembered feeling. If he gave into Eve's way of thinking and sullied Merribeth with his gypsy blood before she returned to Clairmore, he could have his *ultimate* revenge.

The last thought sickened him but kept him apart from her. For the first time since his quest for revenge began, he was starting to have a conscience. He was starting to feel something more powerful than loathing. And that scared him most of all.

"There is a way to have everything—revenge and happiness," she whispered, her gaze locked on his as if she'd never been surer of anything else in her life. "You could marry."

The breath he drew was so harsh and bittersweet that it nearly choked him. "You don't know what you're saying. That would defeat the purpose."

"No. You said so yourself. Your revenge is about not letting your grandfather's blood live on. You could marry a woman who loved you enough to understand." Her cheeks flushed with the most exquisite color, like the barest blush inside the petal of a flower. "I'm sure you know ways to guard against having children, or else you'd already have failed in your quest."

"It wouldn't work, and we both know it. After a year or even two, you—*she*," he corrected, "would want a babe in her arms. I would be the vilest scum ever to walk the earth if I withheld anything from…*her*."

Her eyes filled suddenly, wrenching a new pain from his chest. He reached out to touch the tear on her cheek until he saw his hands were covered in filth. With a sigh that he felt to the very core of his soul, he dropped them.

Down a few stalls, a groomsman appeared and cleared his throat. "It's time, my lord."

Bane nodded before he turned back to Merribeth. "I must go. I'll offer my farewells to you now, Miss Wakefield." He studied her once more, committing every lash to memory. "I've a feeling Gypsy's time won't be easy, so I will not see you at the ball this evening. In fact, I'll likely be gone at first light tomorrow as well. Just know that my only wish is for you to have a long and happy life."

Another tear spilled down her cheek, this one nearly bringing him to his knees. "If this is our last good-bye, then your wish is more of a curse." She swiped at it and drew in a staggered breath before she turned away. "However, I shall wish the same for you, Lord Knightswold. And that every happiness life can afford is yours only to request."

A curse, indeed, Bane thought, for he understood suddenly that the only happiness he'd ever known had just walked out of his life.

CHAPTER SEVENTEEN

"I hate to admit it, but I'm surprised Eve's plan worked after all," Sophie said as they stood together near the punch table in the ballroom. "Lady Amherst is even here, all abuzz over the renewal of Mr. Clairmore's intentions. She is taking full credit for it, reminding everyone how her steadfast support kept you in society and therefore in William's admiration."

Both Merribeth and her aunt knew the truth. She would not marry him. However, since he knew that two failed engagements would not look good on him, William had asked her to pretend they were engaged for the remainder of the party. Perhaps he even believed she'd change her mind. Merribeth didn't mind having his company, whatever his reasons.

"I'm just as baffled over the success of the scheme as you are."

As Eve predicted, being seen with William had given Merribeth's reputation a much-needed boost. She even danced with him for the first set, with all appearances of an understanding between them. Soon, word would spread that Mr. Clairmore was the type of young man who didn't know his own mind, and her place in her tribe would be restored. Even though she wouldn't marry him, Merribeth could now live with Aunt Sophie without sullying her by association.

"I expected her to be more triumphant," Sophie mused, staring down into her amber punch. "Instead, she seems quite upset about something. Earlier, I caught her murmuring that she refused to fail. Yet when I asked her, she looked startled and told me I was hearing things."

"Odd. I've never known you to hear things," Merribeth added and then gave her aunt a sly grin. "Of course you *read* about strange things all the time."

Sophie offered a small grin in response. "I don't suppose there's any use in worrying over it now. Shall we take a turn and soak in the splendor of the ballroom one last time?"

Setting down their cups, they walked together.

For someone as reputedly destitute as Lady Eve Sterling, she certainly spared no expense for the ball. Serving girls from the village had been hired to help with the cleaning and kitchen work and temporary groomsmen to help with the carriages lined up outside. The number of Eve's guests had tripled in the course of a single day, and each one was offered a room in the massive estate—a fact that was very peculiar to Merribeth. If all those rooms were finished, then why had she been given one so distant from Sophie?

It was a puzzle she wasn't likely to have answered before she left.

The grand ballroom was alight with scores of candle flames, all winking through crystal teardrops hanging from the chandeliers. Nearly a full orchestra played in the minstrels' gallery, filling the chamber with a score of sweeping music.

"I was surprised to learn that Lord Montwood had gone already," Merribeth said, her gaze skimming the dancers. He hadn't said his good-byes, either, which made her wonder about the haste of his departure.

Sophie adjusted her spectacles and looked askance at a new guest, Lord Coburn. Standing with Daniela Pearce, the two looked to be on very affectionate terms. "It is my understanding that he's in quite deep with a certain new arrival."

Merribeth nodded in understanding. "Although, one would think a person as well schooled on scandal as our hostess could have prevented their meeting by not inviting Lord Coburn."

Her aunt frowned. "That thought occurred to me as well."

When they neared Lord Amberdeen and the colonel, deep in conversation, they ceased their exchange. As they passed, what Merribeth overheard caused her heart to stop.

"Knightswold had the right of it," Amberdeen said with a nod. "Breeding his mare with Rhamnous would have made a fine racehorse."

"A shame," Colonel Hamersley said on a deep exhale. "The foal had promising bloodlines. Now, it seems neither it nor the mother will survive."

Merribeth covered her mouth and bit back a sob.

Gypsy made a sound of distress as her labor pains grew stronger. Everything seemed to happen at once. The birthing sac protruded but with only a single hoof. The other hoof was locked inside. The mare stood, walked around the stall, and lay down again, looking to Bane for help. Even though this was her first birth, she knew something was wrong too.

Bane went to help her. The timing was crucial. He needed to unlock the elbow joint and pull it free. Reaching in, he discovered the situation was far worse than he imagined. The foal's head was turned as well. It was trapped inside, battering against the pubic bones with each contraction. It would take a miracle to save them both.

If he lost them, he would have nothing. Nothing but his quest for revenge—revenge that was cold and ruthless and could never ease the ache he felt inside. Revenge would never challenge him with summer blue eyes and the wicked arch of a dark brow.

There was only one person who'd offered him anything close to the contentment he'd felt when his parents were still alive.

Only with her, it was so much more. With her, he felt the sun on his face, no matter the hour of the day. The darkness he wore as a cloak around him had fallen to shreds. He couldn't sew it back together if he'd wanted to. He was forever changed.

Forever.

A tremor ran though him. Could he truly value revenge more than her?

... shadow ...

CHAPTER EIGHTEEN

The ball ended on a final swell of music that flowed in
through Merribeth's open window. The steady murmur of
voices told her that many guests were still milling along the
corridors.

All she could think of was Bane. After learning that Gypsy
wasn't expected to make it through the night, she knew his
heart would be breaking. Gypsy was much more than a horse.
She was a symbol for all that he'd lost, all that had been stolen
from him, and more. To him, she was like family.

No matter how things had been left between them earlier,
she couldn't let Bane believe he was all alone. And she was
willing to risk her recently renewed reputation to make sure
he knew someone cared.

Without changing out of her gown, she opened the window to her balcony and climbed out. The full moon crested
over the treetops, bathing this side of the manor in pale, silvery light. While her path wasn't hindered by shadows, the
gap between their balconies and the distance to the ground

turned her stomach weak and watery. As luck would have it, his window was left open.

Be brave. Those words had become her mantra. She repeated them again and again as she climbed over the wide railing. Holding on with hands that had gone icy with fear, she reached out with her slippered foot to the rim of Bane's balcony. In truth, it was no more than a step away from hers, *if* she were on the ground and walking at a normal pace. However, since she was so high up, the distance seemed more like a wide gulf.

Merribeth wasn't about to turn back. This was too important—not only for tonight but for the rest of her life.

She didn't want to leave the party tomorrow morning with anything unsaid. Bane deserved to know, in the very least, that someone cared for him. Someone was willing to share the burden of his pain. Someone loved him.

And tonight she would tell him. No matter what it cost her.

Emboldened by her decision, she pushed off from her own railing and launched herself at his. Before she knew it, she scrambled up over the side and was taking in a great lungful of air as if she'd scaled the manor.

No sooner had she slipped into his room than she heard a key in the lock of Bane's door. She held her breath and stood perfectly still in the space between the open window and the bed.

When he walked in, he turned to face the door immediately, setting the key inside the lock. Not wanting to startle him with the sound of her voice, she continued to wait, air locked up tight in her lungs, burning to get out.

For a moment, he merely stood there, pressing his forehead against the door as he let out a ragged exhale. His loss over Gypsy must be breaking him into pieces. She longed to comfort him, to ease his pain, and help him forget, even if only for a night.

Then, he lifted his head and walked in the opposite direction, toward his dressing room. He didn't bother lighting a candle. The moon was bright enough for her to watch his progress. However, once inside, he was cloaked in shadow.

Unable to see him any longer, she could only listen. The simple fact that she was here, alone with Bane, struck her with a sudden sense of clarity. She could hear her own pulse, the beats rushing so close together that it sounded as if she stood beside a waterfall. Somehow, above the din, she heard the rustling of clothes. Waistcoat and shirt, she imagined, were removed hastily and dropped to the floor.

She swallowed. Surely, now was the time to announce her presence. Still, her voice did not come.

The splashing sound of water as it poured from pitcher to bowl drew her attention next and kept her mind stirring. More splashing followed. Her pulse pounded in her ears in a terrible rush now. She felt dizzy and realized belatedly that she needed to release the breath she'd been holding and draw fresh air into her lungs. When she did, the sounds died away. At any moment, he would leave the dressing room and see her.

Again, she told herself to be brave. This was what she wanted, after all. She was prepared to sacrifice her future for the man she loved. Instinctively, she knew he would be the only man she'd ever love. There would never be another who pulled at her soul and filled her heart.

Bane stepped out of the dressing room, glancing down at the sash of the banyan he tied around his waist. She caught a glimpse of flesh and a dusting of coal black hair before he drew it closed. Her eyes were still on the banyan, curious and seeking, when he stopped abruptly.

"What are you—how did you—"

Merribeth's gaze jerked up to meet his, heat flooding her cheeks. "The window."

Moonlight illuminated his features. Something akin to anger flashed in the depths of his gaze as he looked to the window and across the distance to balcony.

"That was foolish and reckless," he hissed, clenching his teeth. "You could have slipped, fallen to your"—he clenched his fists and moved a step closer, as if he meant to shake her, but then stopped. "No one would have found you until morning."

"Chastising me does not alter the fact that I am here, standing before you, unharmed. Would you care to rail at me some more?"

His gaze darted from hers to the place above, where her brow arched in challenge. Suddenly, his anger receded, replaced by a different kind of heat in his eyes. She'd seen that look before.

"You should leave. Before it's too late. Before a maid or anyone realizes you're missing."

"I'm not leaving." She held her ground, hoping her words would keep him from noticing how she trembled.

"Damn it, Merribeth." He raked a hand through his damp hair. "The house is full of the very people who recently claimed your reputation was in question. You're putting yourself at risk on the eve that your engagement to Clairmore has repaired the damage."

"I cannot control the fact that they make assumptions that are not true."

Something stirred in his gaze. Since she'd never witnessed it before, she couldn't guess what it was, but it almost seemed both pained and tender. "You're not engaged? But I saw—"

"After scolding you for poisoning yourself against the idea of finding true love and happiness, how could I, in good conscience, sentence Mr. Clairmore to the same fate? As you so aptly pointed out, I do not love him."

All she'd ever wanted was a sense of certainty, of knowing what her life would be like, day after day. If her parents had known they would be married a paltry dozen years only to die tragically, would they have given up the chance of being together in order to live a longer, more miserable existence with someone else?

Her heart knew the answer.

Bane's broad chest rose and fell with his breaths. He took a step toward her but then stopped. "Even so, you should leave. With you here, I cannot trust myself."

She smiled. "Then I shall trust you enough for the both of us."

A visible shudder rolled over him, tensing the cords of his neck. "If you heard about Gypsy, and that is why you are here…" He broke off, studying her reaction. Her expression must have given him the answer because he continued. "Then I must tell you that both she and the foal will live."

Relief flooded her, making her heart feel light and airy. "That's wonderful news."

That sense of clarity returned again. Suddenly, she knew she was willing to sacrifice any hope of a certain future, just to spend one night with him. She took a step toward him. Then, because that wasn't enough, because it seemed like she'd waited her entire life to find a place in his arms, she closed the distance.

Her hands trembled as she reached out and laid them against the hard expanse of his chest. His heart beat fast beneath her palms. Bane didn't move. He stared down at her, searching her gaze.

"I know why I am here. I believe you do as well." Her hands slid up over the silk banyan, following the line of his throat to his jaw and up until her fingertips reached the silken strands of coal black hair at his temples. They were cool and damp in contrast to the heat emanating from his scalp. She watched as his lids grew heavy.

"This will change your fate." His hands settled on her waist. For a moment, she believed he was going to set her apart from him and send her away. She stepped even closer, pressing her body against his, feeling the warmth pouring from his body. He was solid and unmoving. "This will change *everything.*"

Undeterred, she refused to retreat. "You need me."

"*Venus,*" he rasped in a sound that was part growl and part agony. Something inside him must have shifted, because in the next moment, he crushed his mouth to hers.

The kiss was fierce and raw and full of the passion that had sparked the first moment they'd met. Yet this was more than mere passion. It was something greater, something desperate, and they both felt it. She reveled in the feel of his mouth on hers, as if her whole life were in this kiss. Every hope and dream she'd ever had was now here, with him. She would give him anything, everything.

Her hands left his hair to clutch his shoulders. She needed to be closer. She needed to dive into his skin, to find the home where her heart resided.

More insistent and demanding, her pulse pounded out the beat of the pagan drum. She rose up on tiptoe, prepared to crawl up his body. As if sensing this, he lifted her against him with one hand cupping the flesh of her derriere and the other at her nape as he deepened the kiss.

In three strides, they were to the bed.

They fell together in a tangle of eager mouths and limbs. The wait had been too long. An eternity had passed since they'd first met. As if to confirm he felt the same way, he lifted her so that she could feel the deliciously hard ridge of him. She parted her thighs, and he pressed his weight against her. She would have cried out his name in ecstasy if her mouth had been free. Instead, a moan rose from her throat and into his.

His mouth moved from her lips to her cheek and then to the shell of her ear. His breath stirred a hot, erotic mix of sensations. Her fingertips dug into his shoulders as she arched off the mattress. "Lie still, I beg of you. I cannot be gentle if you continue."

"Then don't be gentle," she said, her voice nothing more than a rasp of passion. Unable to help herself, she rubbed against him. "I need you too much. I ache for you. The pain is deep inside of me. I'm overwhelmed. I feel like I could die from it any moment. *Please, Simon.*"

He swore and took her mouth again, hard and hungry. His hand left her nape, drifting down to the hidden fastenings of her gown, making quick work of them. In less time than it took her to draw a breath, he tugged the front of her gown loose. He lifted away from her just long enough to pull her gown and petticoat over her head together. She helped him by raising her arms. Her stays went next, followed by her chemise. She still wore her stockings, though somewhere along the way she'd lost her slippers. But she didn't take too much time worrying about them as she caught the look in his eyes.

Heat and hunger were there but also tenderness. Her heart gave a funny flip when she noticed how he trembled as he reached for her.

Even though his hand had yet to touch her flesh, she tingled with a combination of awareness and longing. Her breasts plumped beneath his ardent gaze. Her nipples hardened in anticipation, the dusky center coming to an aching peak. He drew his hand away without touching her, and she nearly cried. But then, he lowered his mouth instead, and a cry tore from her throat all the same.

Her hands clutched his head, knitting her fingers through his hair as the burning wetness of his kiss drew her deeper into her mouth. Lifting her from the mattress, he feasted on one breast and then the other, like a man half starved for the taste of her. He shifted his hold. His thigh pressed between hers, making the ache inside more intense. Throbbing, pulsing, the familiar beat took over, urging her to rock her hips against his thigh as he suckled her flesh.

Then abruptly, her body spasmed in quick unsyncopated jerks. She held on to him as an unfamiliar wave of contentment washed through her, dowsing the overwhelming ache in cool bliss. "Simon," she whispered in awe. "What was that?"

"The beginning, my love," he answered with a tender kiss. "Only the beginning."

Trying to catch her breath, she felt her lips curl into a smile. "I like the beginning."

Bane chuckled, though his voice sounded strained. He tilted her chin up, making sure she met his gaze for his next words. "Then remember this feeling, and trust that I will bring it back to you."

"Of course." She trusted him with her heart and everything she possessed. Her fingertips ran over his scalp, threading through his silken hair, cherishing this moment with him and feeling cherished in return.

He lifted away from her and rose up to his knees to remove his robe.

Beneath it, he wore nothing. In the moonlight, he was bared to her greedy gaze. She sucked in a breath. He was magnificent, all sinew and muscle, from the breadth of his shoulders to the narrowness of his waist. And though her body wanted to draw in another breath at the sight of his thick, jutting flesh, she couldn't seem to breathe. But she did the next best thing…she reached out and touched him.

He jerked as if she'd hurt him, and his hand closed around her wrist, stopping her. Lifting her gaze to his, she saw something rawer than passion, fiercer than desire. It was longing. And it made her heart soar. He released her, but she had the sense that he would allow her only so much freedom to explore.

She touched him again, tentatively. His flesh was like velvet, so smooth she couldn't help but brush her fingers down the length of him. Bane groaned in response but did not stop her. A bead of dew at the very tip caught a shaft of moonlight, making her curious. Lifting up on her elbows, she studied him closely, noting the dusky color of his engorged flesh, the veins that ran the considerable length of him, the thatch of thick coal black hair at the base. Her fingertips explored all of him, eliciting more groans from his throat and making that part of him twitch and follow her touch. The bead of dew swelled, drawing her complete attention. She touched it, feeling the slick silken texture of it between her fingers.

Curious, she went to touch him again only to have him stop her. She looked up and saw his eyes turn dark with passion. Now, there was only the barest ring of silver around his pupil. The tendons of his neck strained against his flesh as he breathed hard and heavy through his nostrils. "No more, my love. I need to have you. Now."

Though his words were said with some urgency, he gently took her hand in his, threading their fingers together as he lowered his body over hers. She felt the heat of him instantly, felt her legs tremble as that hard ridge pressed between them. He kissed her tenderly, his lips brushing back and forth over hers. She let out a breath she didn't know she'd been holding and felt her body relax. Strange, she wasn't even aware of being nervous until the feeling was already gone.

Still holding her hand, Bane stroked the sensitive flesh of her palm with the pad of his thumb. Even though he stroked her hand, she felt it somewhere else.

Oh. Her lips parted on a sigh of wonder. The tip of his tongue swept in to taste her. She opened for him, tilting her head to take him deeper. At the sound of his groan, the ache flared back to life. A swift torrent of flames burned deep inside her, begging for that cool rush of ecstasy.

Merribeth squeezed his hand. Restless again, she rubbed against him, hips arching. The coarse hair on his chest teased her nipples, making them ache as well. He shifted lower, nudging her thighs apart with his. She gasped when she felt that jutting part of him press against her, against the insistent throbbing, as if he alone knew how to ease the ache.

Proving it, he rocked his hips, sliding his length against her. She squeezed his hand tighter, wanting more, begging for it as his name tore from her throat. He obliged with another slow, torturous slide. It only made the throbbing more insistent.

She craved that sensation of bliss, but the ache only grew and grew. He wasn't pressing hard enough. Instinctively, she lifted her knees to anchor the heels of her feet into the mattress.

Bane made a sound of approval and rewarded her with a deep, drugging kiss. He shifted again until she felt his thickness prod the opening of her body. Thousands of sensations flooded her. When he moved his hips, she could feel his heat inside her. He stretched her—her body welcoming him and yet feeling invaded at the same time. As if sensing this, he withdrew.

The second time he edged inside, the stretch began to feel pleasant. The nuances left her hungry. The ache had shifted. It lay deeper now, at her core, and she was impatient to have him at the source. "More," she said, arching against him. "I want more of you." Her soul demanded it. She wanted all of him.

He groaned. "Soon, my love. I want to give you pleasure again."

He pushed slightly deeper. Her body resisted. Closing around him caused a sweet tug against her throbbing flesh. *Oh, that was nice.* And because he seemed to know the wants of her body better than she did, he withdrew and pushed inside again, making her want more still.

He kept this up, with shallow thrusts, building her need, making her moan. She felt close to the precipice. Then suddenly, like before, her hips jerked and arched. The first wave of bliss crashed. He drove deeper, tearing her, stretching her, filling her. "Ah!"

He held still, his body flush against hers, his breath heavy against her cheek. He was giving her time, she realized, to take an accounting. Her body clenched around him in quick syncopation with her pulse. That part felt nice. However, she was also aware of pain, of feeling too full and slightly bruised. It was sort of the same pain as when she bumped her knee into a low table, albeit in a completely different place. Whenever that happened, she rubbed her hand over the injury to stop the painful stinging. She wondered if the same method would apply.

"Again," she said but closed her eyes in case she was wrong.

"Beautiful but demanding." He chuckled, though it too sounded pained as he brushed his lips over hers. "Allow me a moment, my love. You feel extraordinarily warm and snug, and I am nearly over the edge."

She blinked up at him and saw his grimace. "*Oh.*" The word left her on a breath.

"Precisely." His features softened as he gazed at her. Then he drew up the hands that were still entwined and turned her wrist to press a kiss there. Lifting her arm, he settled it over her head and pressed another kiss to her Wakefield brow, lingering. His kiss drifted down over each eyelid, the crests of her cheeks, the tip of her nose, both corners of her mouth, and then finally settled firmly in place, drawing a sigh of pure pleasure from her.

He moved within her slowly, the pain forgotten moment by moment. As his kiss deepened, so did his thrusts, gliding inside her with a delicious friction that made her match his movements. With her captive hand, she squeezed him, and with her free hand, she clung to him.

His free hand slipped beneath her, settling into the curve of her lower back. He lifted her hips from the mattress, driving into her with even more speed and urgency as if they were racing toward a summit.

She felt it too, the need to reach it together. Her body tingled in a way that she now identified as the instant before ecstasy washed through her. Yet this time it was building more and more, as if something bigger were about to happen. This was new to her, so she couldn't be sure. All she knew was that she trusted Bane. She loved him with her heart, her soul, and now her body. She was *his* as much as he was *hers* in that moment—

His name left her lips on a sob of sheer rapture. He must have felt it too, for he shouted a wordless oath as he thrust hard once—twice—three times, before stilling.

Bane pressed his forehead against hers, their labored breaths merging as one. The sweat of his brow felt cool against her fevered skin. He kissed her again, and in that moment, she felt cherished. It was magic and more than she could have ever dreamed. She was right to fall in love with Bane. This was perfect.

And yet, it couldn't last. Not for him, at least. For her, though, this would be the single brightest moment in her life. A sudden sting of tears pricked the corners of her eyes. Before she could control it, her vision turned watery as she gazed up at him.

"Tears of Venus," he whispered, pressing a kiss to the corner of each eye. "I will drink them in and take away your pain."

"They're not from pain."

He did as he said he would and kissed her until her tears were gone. "Then what?"

From love, she would have said if she'd remembered to be brave. "I don't know."

He smiled down at her with such tenderness that she felt he must know the truth, but he didn't call her on it. "Then I'm certain I don't know either." He shifted, leaving her body to lie beside her. Drawing her into his arms, he settled her head against his shoulder. "Perhaps if we lay here a while, we'll find the answer."

The hair on his chest tickled her lips, and so she pressed them against his flesh before she lifted her face. "I should be going."

"There's no rush." He kissed her brow. "We have hours before dawn."

And because she wanted to cling to this moment for as long as she dared, she didn't argue.

CHAPTER NINETEEN

Merribeth awoke in her own bed. Alone.

In the early hours of the morning, Bane had removed a storm shutter from his window and placed it across the space between their balconies. Then, he'd picked her up and carried her to her room. Following her inside, he'd built a fire in the hearth to take away the chill in the air. Before he left, he'd kissed her with such tender affection that it was almost too easy for her to imagine that he loved her too.

While she knew nothing could come of it, not with his mind set on revenge, at the same time she couldn't deny how extraordinarily contented she'd felt. She even laughed when he'd reached the window and then turned back to cross the room to her, in order to kiss her again and tell her that there was something he wanted to discuss with her later this morning.

She agreed, knowing with certainty that he would ask her to become his mistress. Even though their arrangement would only be for a time, she would accept. If she had mere days to love him, she would cherish every single one of them.

At breakfast, she felt ravenous but couldn't manage a single bite. Her stomach was too fluttery as her eager gaze kept darting toward the door, waiting for a glimpse of him.

He never came. Too soon, her aunt had their things packed, prepared to get an early start on their long journey to Berkshire.

Merribeth didn't want to leave without saying good-bye or giving Bane her address. She hoped he would call on her. Then, as luck would have it, he descended the stairs, just as she'd decided to leave a note for him.

His gaze collided with hers, never disconnecting for a single step. It was impossible to conceal her joy at the sight of him. Her heart fluttered with gentle tugs, as if theirs were tied together with invisible thread. Had she breathed at all?

He looked handsome in his slate blue coat and buff riding breeches, with his Hessians polished to a regal shine—which was far different from their usual scuffed state, as he spent most of his time at the stables. He even wore a gleaming silver pendant in the folds of his cravat, as if he'd dressed for a very special purpose.

The thread tugged harder on her heart as her mind filled with anticipation. Did he plan on asking her to become his mistress now, before she left?

His gaze dipped lower for an instant and then returned to hers. A grin slowly lifted the corners of his mouth. It was only then that she noticed she'd pressed her hand against her heart. If she weren't blushing already, she was now, and then even more when he lifted his hand and pressed it to his own heart, as if he were similarly affected.

"Good morning, Miss Wakefield," he said softly when he reached the bottom of the stairs. "Your blush is particularly enchanting this morning."

She smiled and this time did not conceal the gap behind her fingertips. She doubted she ever would again. "I have no idea what you mean, Lord Knightswold."

"What a delight," Eve said, suddenly appearing from the direction of the alcove beneath the stairs. "Just the people I'd longed to see."

Their hostess appeared to be in very high spirits. However, something about her smile sent a frisson of warning through Merribeth. The only other times she'd seen Eve's face take on such a look of triumph was when she'd been plotting.

She came forward and took Merribeth by the hand. "You were not thinking of leaving without saying good-bye, were you?"

In the same moment, Sophie reappeared in the doorway, after having directed the placement of their trunks to the driver. "Of course not," her aunt answered. "You knew I'd wanted to get an early start. I was just about to seek you out and give you our thanks for our lovely diversion. The party was positively splendid and quite successful."

"I couldn't agree more." Eve smiled in that peculiar way that unsettled Merribeth. "Come into the parlor for a moment. I have something of great importance to discuss with you, and it cannot wait until our next visit."

Merribeth looked to Bane as Eve pulled her along. His set features did not put her at ease. "Auntie, surely nothing can be so important as to delay them."

"Never fear. I want you to be part of this discussion as well." Though the words were spoken as a request, they sounded far more like a demand.

Even Sophie wore a worried frown when Eve closed the parlor doors. "What's this?"

Eve gave a flippant gesture, as if this was nothing of consequence. "You know how much I enjoy to gamble. So I just had to tell you of my latest conquest."

"Of course, but surely another time would be more appropriate." Sophie looked to the clock on the mantle. "After all, I don't see what this has to do with—"

"With you?" Eve finished for Sophie. "Not you directly, no. Mostly the wager involves Bane and I, wouldn't you say, dear nephew?"

"A wager which I lost and you won, so let's leave it at that," Bane said, his voice low and ominous. "You have everything you want now. There can be nothing else."

He'd lost another wager? This was news to Merribeth. Curious, she looked at him, wondering what it could be this time. Though she expected it to be something as trivial as before, when he'd confessed to losing a bet to keep his friends.

"Oh, but that isn't quite true." Eve placed her arm over Merribeth's shoulders and gave her a quick hug before she moved to the center of the room. "The only one among us who's lost something monumental is our dear Miss Wakefield."

In an instant, Merribeth went cold. Her lips parted. *Surely Eve can't be referring to…to…last night.* Her gaze flew to Bane for reassurance.

His casual air was absent. There was no quick smile. No easy flirtation. Instead, he was hard and closed off, his mouth set in a grim line.

"Eve. Let. It. Go. You've won. There's nothing more to say."

A wager. Eve won. The words were starting to sink in but slowly, like the thaw after a harsh winter.

"Not to worry. She already knows how much revenge means to you. How it's the driving force behind everything you do." Eve lifted her hand and tapped her finger against her lips. "Hmm...I just wonder if she realizes her part. I mean, once you found out Clairmore was the name of the solicitor responsible for all those *dirty deeds* of your grandfather's—"

Merribeth gasped. William's father? *No.*

"I'm surprised you managed to wait an entire week before you made an example of her. I'm sure the young Mr. Clairmore will be devastated once he discovers the truth. You with your gypsy blood and all, tainting what's his. And speaking of blood, my maid made an interesting discovery just a moment ago. Imagine my surprise when—"

"I cut myself before I left the stables last night," Bane interrupted. "I was too exhausted to tend it. Bitters bandaged me this morning."

Merribeth felt so cold. Everything—every single, life-altering moment—had all been about revenge?

Eve tsked. "How very surprising, Bane. You're not usually so careless." She tilted her head and toyed with the blood red stones she wore in each ear. "In the future, you should probably take note of the order in which a woman keeps her jewelry trays when you're searching for clues to complete your revenge."

Merribeth kept her gaze on Bane, trying to understand, hoping to see that Eve was wrong.

He stared at his aunt, fury igniting the silver depths of his gaze. "This isn't the place to discuss the matter," he growled.

But his response confirmed the terrible accusation at his feet. For Merribeth, every last hope she possessed died. She'd sacrificed everything for one precious moment with him, only to realize that she meant nothing to him. Nothing more than a means to an end. Nothing more than a tool for his revenge.

Worse than losing the chance of spending any kind of future with him, certain or otherwise, her heart and soul were just ripped from her body. They fell into a great void, tearing away from the fibers that had once held them within her, plucking free of each vein like broken threads.

Sophie crossed the room to Eve and slapped her across the cheek. Hard enough to leave a red mark in its wake. "You are despicable. I thought you'd changed."

"We can never change who we really are," Eve spat, clutching her cheek. A bright sort of madness lit her gaze. "Scholar that you are, you should have known better. You should have questioned why I'd taken such an interest in helping your niece have her Seasons."

"I took you at your word, that you'd wanted to make amends." Sophie's voice went quiet and broke at the end. "Now, I see you'd planned this all along."

Eve didn't deny it. "Since I first learned Mr. Clairmore's name."

Merribeth's hand went to her throat, sure that her heart had stopped beating. There was no answering thump of her pulse. Her fingers were like icicles. Her head spun in a dizzying circle. The plush Persian carpet at her feet seemed to stretch before her, elongating the room to where Bane stood. She felt her knees buckle. Sophie cried out in alarm. But it wasn't her aunt's arms she fell into. It was Bane's.

He lifted her, his face a convincing mask of concern.

She tried to push him away, but she lacked strength. "You never wanted anyone to love you. I see that now. I was a fool."

"You're wrong," she heard him say, but whatever words might have followed, died away as she slipped into blackness.

Bane took Merribeth and escorted Sophie into the carriage, wanting them free of the spectacle and out of harm's way. Or at least, out of further harm.

He laid Merribeth on the seat, her head resting on her aunt's lap. She was breathing steadily as if asleep, yet it was a nightmare, not peaceful slumber, that had claimed her.

Pain like he'd never known burned inside his chest, wrenching his heart into tight, brittle pieces. He wished he knew what to say, if there were words enough to make this better. But there weren't. No words could heal what he'd done to her. This was his fault. He'd brought this upon her.

"I never wished for this. She deserves better. She deserves…everything." Everything he could never give. For a fleeting moment when he'd awoken this morning, he'd imagined having an entirely different conversation with Merribeth. A very important one.

But that dream was too brief and just as swiftly gone.

"She'll be fine," Mrs. Leander said, stroking her niece's cheek. "After all, she's survived worse. In the end, we still have each other."

Without another word, he took one final look at Merribeth and quietly closed the carriage door. The driver set off for Berkshire, leaving nothing more than dust in his wake.

Making love to Merribeth had been more glorious, more profound, than he'd ever thought possible. In those precious moments, he'd had a glimpse of the rest of his life. It was full of smiles—hidden or not—and the wicked arch of the finest brow he'd ever kissed. He'd even imagined children, laughing and riding ponies at twilight to catch fairies. He'd never wanted anything as much as he'd wanted that dream to come true.

But now, that dream turned to dust, kicked up in the wake of her retreating carriage. He knew she would never forgive him.

Bane stared the length of the driveway until each particle settled.

His heart hardened once again. Forged with a new purpose, as he strode back into the manor.

Eve was sitting in the parlor, the papers of their agreement on the wine table beside her. He couldn't believe he'd been so blind. How could he have not seen that her quest for revenge was equal to, if not greater than, his? The only thing was, she wanted revenge against *him*, not his grandfather. All this time, and he'd never realized.

"So, you've gained your revenge at long last. Does it taste sweet, Lady Sterling?"

"Of course," she said with all appearances of being smug. Yet there was a distinct edge of pain lingering in the corners of her eyes. "I have finally bested the man responsible for taking everything from me."

"That was my grandfather—"

"No," she snapped. "It was you. Always you. If you'd never been born, if Spencer hadn't tried so hard to protect you, none of it would've happened." Her eyes widened for a moment as if even she was appalled at her reasoning. Before she continued, her breath hitched. "I almost lost *everything*. Don't you see? Centuries of my family's blood has been spilled to protect this land. Even Spencer's blood."

He opened his mouth to argue but closed it just as quickly. There was no victor here, no matter what he could say. They'd all lost something—someone—dear. And he was about to lose more.

Reaching out, he swiped up the contract between them and threw it in the fireplace where low embers suddenly flared to life. He wanted no record of what he'd done, not for his sake but for Merribeth's. No one at the party must know that she'd selflessly given everything to a man who was unworthy of her.

"You're not honoring you're part of the bargain? I should have expected as much from a Fennecourt." Eve stood and set her claws into his forearm, as if to draw him away from the fire. "Or perhaps it's your mother's gypsy blood that makes you more like a thief. I want what's mine."

A month ago, he would have shot a man for such slander. But he was no longer that person. Now, he looked at her with pity. She was grasping, he knew, searching for a way to inflict more pain. He let her words slice into him, hoping the overwhelming emptiness he felt would turn to anger.

Unfortunately, it didn't.

He strode over to the secretaire in the corner of the room and lifted a sheet of parchment from beneath a polished bronze paperweight. The quill he dipped into the ink wasn't sharp, but it would do the job. As a matter of finality, he signed his full name and title with a flourish.

"The price of my wager." He held out the document. "Gypsy is yours, along with her foal."

Without a word, she snatched it, her brow furrowing as she read it over and over again.

"That is the last you'll ever receive from me," he said as he walked toward the door. "As of this moment, we are no longer family. We are no longer friends. I will not recognize you in a crowd or accept any invitation of yours. You are nothing to me now."

And with that final promise, he bowed and left.

He only wished he'd realized the cost of revenge before it was too late.

Chapter Twenty

"And so it's done," Merribeth said, setting down her tea-cup and saucer on the low table in the Weatherstone's parlor. "I've sold my wedding gown to Forester's"—she could not bear to see it on display at Haversham's—"and I'll begin work as a seamstress once I return to Berkshire after the ball at Hawthorne Manor. All in all, Aunt Sophie and I will manage nicely."

The past two days in London had been a blur. Merribeth was exhausted and drained, but she couldn't let herself stop for a moment. She needed to keep going so she wouldn't fall apart.

Penelope and Emma exchanged a look that Merribeth was only too eager to ignore. Commenting would only bring more questions that she didn't want to answer. What happened between her and Lord Knightswold would stay hidden in the darkest cupboards of her mind and would, one day, become a long forgotten memory.

At least, that's what she told herself. Though it was impossible to believe. Deep down, she knew she'd never forget loving him. She knew she'd never be the same again.

Mercifully, word of her scandalous behavior had never reached town. If she still possessed any misguided romantic notions, she might have imagined that it was because Bane had done something to protect her. Yet no matter how she once saw him, she had to keep reminding herself that he was not the heroic kind. He lived for one thing only. Revenge.

Merribeth picked up her tea again instead of her needlework. After having forgotten the handkerchief in her room at Eve's estate, she'd hoped if she brought a new project, something fresh, that she'd be more inclined to rediscover her love for it. But like the tea in her cup, she merely tolerated it.

"I must say, the plan we all feared doomed worked in the end. Mr. Clairmore proposed," Emma said. "Even though you turned him down, perhaps there is something to Lady Sterling's way of thinking after all."

No, Eve's way of thinking had doomed Merribeth from the start. "I believe the success of it was due to his broken heart when Miss Codington refused him, more than for his desire to marry *me*."

"You mustn't think that," Penelope interjected. "You and Mr. Clairmore had been friends for so long. I'm certain he was fond of you."

Merribeth had pondered this over the past few days as well. "We were never friends as you were with Mr. Weatherstone, or how Emma was with Lord Rathburn. The only true connection we had was our proximity to one another." She set her tea down again. "We were both of a same age, living in a small village. Neither of us had common interests. Our conversations were a matter of cordiality and expectation. I merely realized it too late."

The truth was, she'd only realized it because of what she'd had with Bane—the conversations, the banter, the undeniable pull to be near him, the instant spark she never had with William.

At the time, she knew it was exactly what she'd been searching for all along. Of course, now she knew even that was a fabrication. Sadly, she was still trying to convince herself that none of it was true for him.

It would take time. Perhaps a great deal of it. She could easily see herself an old doddering woman, still half believing he'd cared for her, had even loved her, if only for a moment in time.

She felt herself perilously close to tears and searched for a new topic of conversation. "Where's Delaney? I thought she'd be here by now, bringing a whirlwind with her." She needed a dose of her friend's vibrancy right now.

Penelope and Emma exchanged another look.

"We didn't want to worry you," Penelope said in her soothing manner. She sat forward slightly, as much as her slightly rounded belly would allow.

"Her leaving was sudden. As ever, our Delaney is impulsive," Emma added with fondness. "So when she came to me three days ago and asked if I had a place for her to escape for a time, I offered her Rathburn's hunting box in Scotland."

It was true that their friend was impulsive, but she'd never run away before. "Does her father know? Her sister?"

Emma pulled the corner of her mouth between her teeth. "Here, I must admit to a slight deception. I allowed her to inform her family that she was staying with us but merely leaving ahead of us. The truth is, we do not plan to go until we travel with the Weatherstones toward the country estate for Penelope's confinement."

"The doctor said that I am in good health, and there is no rush for me to leave before Mr. Weatherstone's business matters are settled," Penelope said, her worried look mirroring Emma's and likely Merribeth's as well. "We aren't leaving until the end of the month."

"But is she all right, do you think?" Merribeth asked, searching her mind for the answers it seemed none of them possessed. "Indeed, I have no engagements. I could go to her."

"I'm sure that would be lovely, but..." Emma leaned in to whisper. "She expressed a desire for complete solitude. I cannot help but leap to the conclusion that this involves a matter of the heart."

Penelope nodded in agreement, worrying the loose threads of her latest needlework project. "If *the incident* didn't send her into hiding, I don't believe anything other than a dire matter of the heart could. She must be in love."

"In love!" Merribeth gasped. "I was only away a fortnight. How could it happen so"—she coughed, nearly choking on her own words as they tripped past her tongue—"quickly?"

Yet hadn't it been the same for her? She'd fallen in love with Bane in mere moments, or so it seemed.

"The truth is, we've no idea."

They all sighed in unison. "As ever, Delaney is our mystery."

"Oh, how I wish we could all be present for the ball tonight. With so many gone from town, I fear Rathburn and I will be known for giving the dullest parties. Quite the opposite from our predecessors."

"Are you looking to cause a scandal then, Emma?" Penelope asked with a laugh.

"Of course not. You know I'd never hear the end of it if from the dowager," Emma said, though she sounded far from outraged. "Well…perhaps just a small smidge of a scandal, just to prove myself."

"Then I suppose it will be left to Merribeth and I to do something entirely scandalous," Penelope said with a conspiring grin. "What do you say? Shall we put your flirting prowess to the test?"

Merribeth swallowed and prayed her cheeks did not go pale. She'd had her fill of scandal.

CHAPTER TWENTY-ONE

No doubt, the gypsy Marquess of Knightswold was about to cause the scandal of the Season. Even though he wasn't invited to the Hawthorne Manor Ball, he'd be damned if he let them keep him out.

"See here! What's this about?" Viscount Rathburn called to his head butler, slamming the door to his study. "If you think for one minute I'll let anything go wrong tonight, when this ball means the world to my wife, then you—" His speech ended abruptly the instant he saw Bane across the room, seated in a high-backed chair, with two footmen on either side of him, acting as guards. "What are *you* doing here?"

The last time he'd seen Rathburn, Bane had been trying to seduce Rathburn's wife, then Emma Danvers. It had been another scheme of Eve's, with which Bane had only gone along to rankle his old friend. In the end, he'd proven that Rathburn was of a jealous nature. Not only that, but the man wasn't inclined to forgive easily.

"I'm not here to cause trouble," Bane lied smoothly. *Old habits and all that.* "I came to offer my sincerest apologies and to wish you and your lovely bride many felicitations."

Rathburn clenched his jaw, not inclined to gullibility, or so it seemed. "There are no tables here this night and therefore no unlucky sod for you to finagle into ruin."

"In my own defense, all those unlucky sods deserved what they had coming."

Rathburn squinted. "Have you been drinking?"

Bane wished he had. "Care to smell my breath? Examine my pockets? Search my horse?"

At the mention of his horse, Rathburn's interest appeared to rise. "I heard a rumor at Tattersalls the other day, concerning your prized broodmare. Is it true?"

Bane gave a noncommittal shrug.

Rathburn eyed him shrewdly but gave the signal to his footmen and butler to leave them. "I never thought I'd hear of the day when you lost a wager over a horse, and a prized one at that."

Bane stood, admitting nothing as his old friend walked over to the sideboard and withdrew two short cut-crystal glasses from the cabinet. Then, he proceeded to pour a finger of scotch into each.

As if recalling Bane's preference for the finely aged whiskey, Rathburn handed one to him, speculation still lingering in his gaze. "Since you've never lost without intending to, I have to wonder what you gained in its stead."

"Wisdom, my friend." He lifted his glass in a toast and downed the amber liquor in one swallow. It burned all the way down, setting fire to the anxiety churning inside him. "The meaning of life."

This earned him a smirk and another splash of scotch in his glass. "Do tell."

This time, Bane butted his glass against Rathburn's before he downed the contents. He needed the fortification. "I assumed you already knew. After all, you have it here."

Rathburn looked around him. "The manor?"

"Somewhat, but no," Bane said, not intending to sound cryptic. "You rebuilt this place in order to make it a home once again. However, in order to make it a home, you needed Miss Danvers—er—that is to say, Lady Rathburn."

Instant fury filled Rathburn's gaze as he stalked toward Bane. "She's not yours, and she'll never be. Get...out!"

Bane raised his hands in surrender. "Of course she's yours. There is no question. I only meant that you have found your counterpart, as she has found hers. Together, you've unearthed the wisdom of the ages. That is all." Carefully, he set down his glass on the desk. "I only came to wish you well."

He walked toward the door, knowing full well that Rathburn would stop him before he turned the knob.

"Wait."

Bane grinned.

Emma and Rathburn's ball at Hawthorne Manor signaled the last event of the Season for those who were still in town. It also signaled the last social event for Merribeth.

Her future would host no more London Seasons and not simply because she lacked the money or a sponsor, now that

Eve had revealed her true purpose. Merribeth had connections enough with her friends to be invited to gatherings, dinners, and parties…But the truth was, she had no intention of marrying. Ever.

She walked down the stairs from one of the rooms in which Emma had settled her and Sophie for the previous few days and entered the lavishly decorated ballroom.

Emma was beside her in an instant, her nerves showing in the way she chewed on the corner of her mouth. "It's too much, isn't it? I know it is. The dowager demanded that garlands be draped over each window and doorway, while my mother insisted that columns of white silk by the garden doors would give the illusion of more light. Earlier I thought it looked pleasing, yet now I worry that it looks like I'm trying too hard and that I don't really deserve to be Rathburn's viscountess."

Merribeth squeezed Emma's hand. "It's lovely. Do not doubt yourself. I can see your own touches in the way the room is bright and cheerful without being ostentatious. You chose the flowers in the garland, did you not?" When she received a small nod, she continued. "The colors complement the wallpaper perfectly. I feel as if I'm in a living painting, as if beautiful art and magic were housed together here. It appears very much as if you've made Hawthorne Manor your own."

Emma beamed and hugged her. "Don't say another word, for if you do I shall cry. And if I cry…"

A small laugh escaped Merribeth as they stood apart. "Yes, Rathburn would not be pleased."

"He's positively fierce at times," Emma said with a sigh, the light from the chandeliers sparkling in her dark eyes. "And I love him all the more for it."

"Speaking of your husband, I thought he would be standing here." However, it was early yet and the guests had only started to arrive.

"And here I shall stay, from this point forth," Rathburn said as he stepped up behind them. In a familiar gesture, he settled his hand at the small of Emma's back and pressed a kiss to her temple. "I was momentarily detained."

"Oh?"

He offered a shake of his head, as if the matter were of no consequence. "The arrival of an unexpected guest."

"But not unwelcome, I hope."

Merribeth went utterly still at the sound of that familiar voice and watched as the man who plagued her dreams slowly emerged from the shadows behind Rathburn.

Simon.

The heart she thought dead these past days suddenly leaped beneath her breast like an eager puppy. She pressed the flat of her hand over the hard thumping, as if she could force it to quiet.

"Lord Knightswold. What a pleasant surprise," Emma said with a degree of astonishment before she held out her hand.

Bane bowed over it. "I've done little to deserve your gracious welcome, but I accept it nonetheless."

She withdrew her hand and tucked it securely into her husband's. "I see you've mended fences."

"More like, we've come to an understanding," Rathburn said with a smirk before he directed his attention to Merribeth. "Miss Wakefield, I should like to introduce you to the Marquess of Knightswold."

Bane took a step closer. His gaze drifted to the hand she had not offered him, the hand that was still concealing her heart.

Emma noticed too. "Merribeth," she said in a quiet voice, "are you unwell?"

She lowered her hand and swallowed down the rise of misguided longing before she answered. "We've met."

"Yes, though I would like to pretend for a moment that you are meeting me for the first time as a changed man."

She felt the twitch of her Wakefield brow. "I hardly think a man who spent his life in a singular pursuit could change so quickly."

Bane winced, and only then did she hear the bitterness in her own voice and was ashamed. Yet she did not apologize.

"If that man had good reason, he would," Bane said quietly, taking a step closer. "However, I am not without flaws in my character still. Perhaps I merely abandoned one obsession in favor of another."

Seeing him here, standing within arm's reach, made her ache all over. She felt lightheaded as well, but her heart was taking up far too much space, leaving her lungs no room to fill with air. "I'm certain obsessions of any kind are unhealthy."

He grinned. "And I'm glad your certainty has returned." Before she was aware of his intent, he reached out and took her hand. "May I have this dance?"

She started and tried to pull free, but it was no use. "The musicians are merely tuning their instruments."

Steely determination flashed in his gaze. He took her hand and placed it firmly in the crook of his arm as he strode to the middle of the ballroom. Once there, he lifted her free hand to his shoulder and settled his at her waist. "While I would love nothing more than to lock you in a room where we can speak privately, this is my only option at present. I cannot wait another moment."

Pulling her in close, he drew her into a slow, meandering waltz with the discordant threads of violin and cello merging into a dreamlike sound. Of course, she could walk away at any moment, leaving him there alone on the vacant floor, but the truth was, she wanted to be in his arms. Just once more.

"I tried to stay away from you," he began and then clarified. "After I learned Clairmore's name, I felt as if my world were split into two pieces. One part wanted revenge against his father, while the other wanted you."

Her eyes suddenly filled, remembering exactly what he'd decided. "In the end, you appeased both halves."

"I know it seems that way, but I came here so that you would know the truth." Still holding her waist and moving in slow turns, he reached into his superfine coat and withdrew a handkerchief. He quickly dabbed it at the corners of her eyes before he pressed it between their hands.

"It happened when Gypsy and her foal were struggling to live," he continued. "In those tenuous moments, I realized that I was fighting for something I'd never appreciated. *A life*. For years, my sole purpose was revenge and making sure that I died as the last Fennecourt. I lived only thinking about my death."

"Which is no life at all," she whispered, unable to tear herself away from him. He held her captive with no more than a beseeching look, and she granted him pardon until he said what he came to say.

"As I learned," he agreed, his voice tender. "You came along and challenged my beliefs, turning them around until I saw past my own stubborn resolve. What you said about my mother, and how I was punishing her as well as my grand-father, struck me to the core. But I only felt the enormity of it when the foal drew her first breath." He breathed in too and then smiled at her, effectively stopping her heart. "I'd wanted to tell you right away.

"Even though it was the middle of the night, I went to your room. I raised my hand to knock before I had the presence of mind to realize I was behaving like a madman." He chuckled. "So I went to my room, prepared to wait until morning to speak with you. Yet when I left my dressing room, I found you, standing in the moonlight, your hair spilling down your shoulders, your gown white as an angel's wing. I thought you were a dream at first or that I truly had gone mad."

Now it was her turn to take a breath. Somewhere in the last few turns, her tears had dried, and her heart had started again. Merribeth was reliving it all over again, feeling nervous and shy, as if they were standing alone in his chamber instead of the middle of the ballroom.

"I should have confessed the whole truth—not only of Clairmore's unexpected involvement but also the war that had plagued me for days. However, I feared that telling you all the dark paths my mind had taken would make you hate me, and I couldn't bear it." He held her gaze. Something raw and tender flared like a silver flame in their depths. "And when you boldly declared your refusal to leave, I knew in that moment that I had a choice to make. I could either begin the rest of my life, or I could turn you away and die with the knowledge that I'd let the only woman I'd ever love slip away."

"You…" Her voice trembled with suppressed emotion. She shook her head, unable to speak the words, unable to hope, for fear of dying if her every wish never came true. "My head is spinning."

He stopped dancing, his expression grave as he took both her hands in his. "Instead, I tried to show you without words how much you mean to me."

He only wants a mistress, the voice of practicality said. *He'll set you up in a house and visit you for a time. Is that truly enough?*

She pulled back a step and looked toward the door. Emma and Rathburn were watching. Beside them stood Penelope and Ethan, and all of them were looking on with worry and speculation. A dozen or more other guests had arrived as well, and each one watched the spectacle. Her friends didn't know what to make of this. Penelope clutched Emma's hand, and it was clear that they would come to Merribeth's aid if she gave the slightest signal.

"You have something of mine, Miss Wakefield."

Turning back to him, her mind worked slowly. She blinked and looked down at her hands. His handkerchief was clutched in her grasp.

When she offered it to him, however, he shook his head. "No, that is yours. I found it on the divan in your room after you'd left," he said simply, yet there was a searing intensity in his gaze now.

She remembered leaving it there, untended, unable to put forth a single stitch.

"You have something *else* of mine, Miss Wakefield," he amended. "I believe you meant to borrow it and return it directly, but you never did return…my heart. It's been in your possession since our first meeting."

She drew in a staggered breath, daring to hope.

"Though without a heart, one might wonder how I came to be here, standing before you right now," he went on, making her heard spin again. "Do you wonder, Miss Wakefield?"

When she nodded, he grinned and placed her hand over his chest.

"There is a heart in here, but it is not mine. You see, I believe you made a dire mistake our first meeting. When you meant to return mine, instead you gave me yours. Doesn't it beat strangely beneath my breast?"

She searched his gaze, trying desperately not to hope until she was certain. "I should like to have it back."

"Hmm…I thought you might say that," he mused. "Perhaps we could strike a bargain instead. I would suggest an even exchange, but your heart is worth far more than mine. If I gave it up, I would need something of greater value than my own poor excuse for a heart in return."

At that, her brow arched in disapproval. "I do not play at bargaining."

"Then allow me to make another proposal." He lifted her hand to brush a kiss across her knuckles. "I'll keep your heart with me—and you will keep mine—but I'll offer you that handkerchief in exchange."

She felt her brows knit. "You said the handkerchief was mine already."

"Perhaps you should examine it to make certain," he said, his chest rising and falling now with each breath.

Perplexed, she opened her hand and spread the handkerchief over her palm.

The sight of the silver thread stole her breath.

What he'd said was true. This was her handkerchief, the same one her friends had given her. Only now, instead of seeing the length of thread and silver needle tucked safely inside as she'd left it, Bane had used it for his purpose.

Two words were embroidered in the center, the letters malformed and bedraggled. Still, she couldn't recall ever seeing a finer piece of needlework.

Marry me.

When she lifted her gaze, he dropped to one knee. There was a collective gasp around them. Somewhere in the back of her mind, she knew Emma was pleased. No one would ever think of leaving town before the Hawthorne Manor Ball next Season.

"If there were an ounce of poetry in my blood, I could tell you how irrevocably you've changed my life and brought new purpose," he said as he withdrew a ring from his waistcoat pocket.

From the corner of her eye, a cluster of diamonds winked in the candlelight, but she could only look at him and their future in the iridescent shimmer of his gaze.

"Marry me," he said, his voice hoarse. "Share your life with me. Teach our children to ride ponies at twilight in search of fairies."

This time, Merribeth didn't have to tell herself to be brave. She knew the answer with complete certainty.

"Yes."

EPILOGUE

Bane read the note from the messenger before setting off for the stables at Ravencourt. In the distance, his new white mare, Lucina, dipped her head over the fence rail. According to the stories his mother had told him when he was a boy, that was a good omen. The full moon that would be in the sky tonight was also good, but he didn't need any superstition to tell him that. He felt it deep down in the fibers of his soul.

The past year had been a wonder, transforming his life in unimaginable ways. He never thought he could be so happy. He knew he didn't deserve to be, but if he said those words aloud, his beautiful Venus would arch her magnificent, fearsome brow.

Smiling again, as he found himself doing nearly every hour of every day, his gaze settled on his wife. His heart swelled. In these moments, he wondered if one could die from overwhelming bliss. However, he didn't spend much time thinking about it. He spent most of the time thinking about life. His life. Hers. And the arrival due any day now.

Merribeth petted their new pony behind the ears, earning a snuff of approval. At the same time, she rubbed a hand in circles over her well-rounded form, concentrating on one area in particular.

"Perhaps you shouldn't be so far from the house," he said, already used to this strange surge of protectiveness that had arisen in him the moment she became *his*. Stepping up behind her, he placed his hand over hers and pressed a kiss to the curve of her neck.

She leaned back against him with a sigh of contentment. "I was restless. Our son is already like his father, never leaving me a moment's peace."

Her teasing laugh always turned the steady plodding of his heart into a fast gallop. He was certain he'd never loved her more. Then again, he'd said the same thing yesterday, and the day before that.

"Or perhaps our *daughter* is merely anxious to see her pony."

"I still cannot believe you bought our child a pony before *he's* even been born." She turned in his arms and gave him a playful peck on his chin. They had a wager between them.

When he felt her swollen belly tighten beneath his hand and heard her sharp intake of breath, he had the suspicion that it wouldn't be long until they were certain. "How long have you been feeling…restless?"

"Since last night." She blushed, even as her brow lifted. "Shortly after your declaration for knowing the perfect way to help me sleep."

He chuckled and lowered his mouth to hers. "It certainly helped *me* sleep."

The kiss lingered as she pressed close to him, her fingers threading through his hair. He nearly moaned from the rapture of so many pleasures at once. Then, before he could tilt her head and give her another taste of what they'd shared hours ago, he felt her body tense again. Her fingers gripped his hair, and she let out a slow breath against his lips.

Her gaze held his as she lowered her hands to his shoulders. "Perhaps I shouldn't be so far from the house."

A frisson of fear and excitement coursed through him at the same time. It took every ounce of strength he possessed to give the appearance of calm confidence, as if the birth of his first child—the start of their family—happened every day. "Would you like me to carry you?"

She gave him a look of bewilderment and then studied him for a moment before she laughed. "Why, Lord Knightswold, I do believe I can see every card you're holding." Her mockery quieted when she slipped her arm beneath his. "You needn't worry so. Aunt Sophie worked with a midwife for a short time. Besides, she's read every possible scientific journal on the topic, going back to the Druids."

When he nodded, they began walking toward the house. Even though she leaned into him and rested her head on his shoulder, he felt as if she were the one holding him upright.

"Not to mention, both Penelope and Emma have been through this. Their carriages should arrive shortly…unless the messenger brought news that they'd be delayed."

"No, the missive was about another matter." He wondered if he should tell her now or wait.

She lifted her face expectantly. Those cerulean eyes speared through the heart of him every time.

"It was from Lord Amberdeen. Do you still want me to tell you?" He could deny her nothing.

Her pace slowed, and her hand returned to the underside of her womb as she blew out a slow, steady breath. "I should like the distraction. Even if the news is in regard to Eve, you need not be afraid it will upset me."

He slipped his hand around her waist, securing her against him. "Are you certain?"

"While I'd never consider naming our child after her," she smirked, "neither do I hold a grudge against her. If it weren't for her scheme, I might never have met you. And I would have gone on with my life, never knowing about love, never feeling those frantic beats of my heart whenever you're near, never experiencing what it feels like to be cherished and full of such joy that there are moments when I cannot breathe for how happy I am."

He tilted her chin up, his gaze locking with hers. "Remember this feeling during the next few hours—when you'll likely curse me to the heavens—and know that I will give it back to you."

"Of that, I have no doubt," she said, her smile radiant.

Her complete trust never ceased to amaze him and humble him. For that reason, and scores of others, he kissed her again before they resumed their path to the house. "According to the note, Lady Eve Sterling will soon be Lady Amberdeen. Strangely enough, even knowing the worst of her character, he still wanted her."

"Then I am pleased for Lord Amberdeen. Though I daresay, she will have a hard time manipulating him," Merribeth said after a moment. "However, she did end up reuniting

Mr. Clairmore with Miss Codington, so her heart can't be completely black. Right?"

"Ever the romantic," he said, pressing a kiss to her temple. "There was one other letter attached, which puzzles me. It bore a name and address of a gentleman I've never heard of. Perhaps you're familiar with a Sir Herman Wrigglesworth."

Merribeth pursed her lips in contemplation, and then a slow smile spread. "Was this letter addressed to Sophie?"

"As a matter of fact, it was."

"Then I believe it is Eve's way of righting the wrongs in her life."

He highly doubted it, but he refused to let on, especially when his wife stopped once again and gripped his arm tightly. This time, she did not release a breath, and he knew her pain was more intense.

After a moment, she eased her grip and resumed walking. Wanting to distract her, he brought up the subject of the guests that were due to arrive. "We have rooms prepared for Lord and Lady Rathburn and the Weatherstones. Their sons will share the nursery. I thought that when you said *all* your friends had made a pact to be present for the births of each one of your children, that all your friends would be arriving. But you said nothing of—"

"Delaney?" His Venus laughed. "Well, that's a completely different story."

ACKNOWLEDGMENTS

This book, this series, and these characters never would have seen the light of day if not for Chelsey and the incredible Avon Romance/HarperCollins family. Thank you so much for giving me this opportunity.

Thank you to my family and friends for your support and for sharing my excitement.

And most of all, I thank God for everything. Always.

Can't wait for the next Wallflower Wedding?
Keep reading for an excerpt from
Vivienne Lorret's

DARING MISS DANVERS

Available now from Avon Impulse.

Then continue on for a sneak peek from

FINDING MISS MCFARLAND

Coming August 2014 from Avon Impulse.

An Excerpt from

DARING MISS DANVERS

Oliver Goswick, Viscount Rathburn, needs money, but only marriage to a proper miss will release his inheritance. There's just one solution: a mock courtship with a trusted friend. Miss Emma Danvers knows nothing good can come of Rathburn's scheme. Still, entranced by the inexplicable hammering he causes in her heart, she agrees to play his betrothed despite her heart's warning: it's all fun and games…until someone falls in love!

"Shall we shake hands to seal our bargain?"

Not wanting to appear as if she lacked confidence, Emma thrust out her hand and straightened her shoulders.

Rathburn chuckled, the sound low enough and near enough that she could feel it vibrating in her ears more than she could hear it. His amused gaze teased her before it traveled down her neck, over the curve of her shoulder and down the length of her arm. He took her gloveless hand. His flesh was warm and callused in places that made it impossible to ignore the unapologetic maleness of him.

She should have known this couldn't be a simple handshake, not with him. He wasn't like anyone else. So, why should this be any different?

He looked down at their joined hands, turning hers this way and that, seeing the contrast no doubt. His was large and tanned, his nails clean but short, leaving the very tips of his fingers exposed. Hers was small and slender, her skin creamy, her nails delicately rounded as was proper. Yet, when she looked at her hand covered by his, she felt anything but proper.

She tried to pull away, but he kept it and moved a step closer.

"I know a better way," he murmured and before she knew his intention, he tilted up her chin and bent his head.

His mouth brushed hers in a very brief kiss. So brief, in fact, she almost didn't get a sense that it had occurred at all. *Almost.*

However, she did get an impression of his lips. They were warm and softer than they appeared, but that was not to say they were soft. No, they were the perfect combination of softness while remaining firm. In addition, the flavor he left behind was intriguing. Not sweet like liquor or salty like toothpowder, but something in between, something... spicy. Pleasantly herbaceous, like a combination of pepper and rosemary with a mysterious flavor underneath that reminded her... *of the first sip of steaming chocolate on a chilly morning.* The flavor of it warmed her through. She licked her lips to be certain, but made the mistake of looking up at him.

He was staring at her lips, his brow furrowed.

The fireflies vanished from his eyes as his dark pupils expanded. The fingers that were curled beneath her chin spread out and stole around to the base of her neck. He lowered his head again, but this time he did not simply brush his lips over hers. Instead, he tasted her, flicking his tongue over the same path hers had taken.

A small, foreign sound purred in her throat. This wasn't supposed to be happening. Kissing Rathburn was wrong on so many levels. They weren't truly engaged. In fact, they were acquaintances only through her brother. They could barely stand each other. The door to the study was closed—*highly improper.* Her parents or one of the servants could walk in any minute. She should be pushing him away, not encouraging him by parting her lips and allowing his tongue entrance. She should not curl her hands over his shoulders, or discover that there was no padding in his coat. And she most definitely should not be on the verge of leaning into him—

There was a knock at the door. They split apart with a sudden jump, but the sound had come from the hall. Someone was at the front of the house.

She looked at Rathburn, watching the buttons of his waistcoat move up and down as he caught his breath. When he looked away from the door and back to her, she could see the dampness of their kiss on his lips. *Her kiss.*

He grinned and waggled his brows as if they were two criminals who'd made a lucky escape. "Not quite as buttoned-up as I thought." He licked his lips, ignoring her look of disapproval. "Mmm…jasmine tea. And sweet, too. I would have thought you'd prefer a more sedate China black with lemon. Then again, I never would have thought such a proper miss would have such a lush, tempting mouth either."

She pressed her lips together to blot away the remains of their kiss. "Have you no shame? It's bad enough that it happened. Must you speak of it?"

He chuckled and stroked the pad of his thumb over his bottom lip as his gaze dipped, again, to her mouth. "You're right, of course. This will have to be our secret. After all, what would happen if my grandmother discovered that beneath a façade of modesty and decorum lived a warm-blooded temptress with the taste of sweet jasmine on her lips?"

An Excerpt from

Finding Miss McFarland

*After a calamitous debut, Delaney McFarland is
determined to find a husband—no matter what that
proud, arrogant Griffin Croft thinks. Griffin usually avoids
disaster and women who invite it. Yet with a fiery beauty
like Miss McFarland, courting trouble is undoubtedly
more fun than playing it safe.*

"Do you have spies informing you on my whereabouts at all
times or only for social gatherings?"

Miss McFarland followed Griffin for only a moment
before she pursed those pink lips and smoothed the front of
her cream gown, embroidered with rows of spring green ivy.
"I do what I must to avoid being seen at the same function
with you. Until recently, I imagined we shared this unspoken
agreement," she said.

"Rumormongers rarely remember innocent bystanders."

She scoffed. "How nice for you."

"Yes, and until recently, I was under the impression that I came and went of my own accord. That my decisions were mine alone. Instead, I learn that every choice I make falls beneath your scrutiny. Shall I quiz you on how I take my tea? Or if my valet prefers to tie my cravat into a barrel knot or horse collar?"

"I do not know, nor do I care, how you take your tea, Mr. Croft," she said, and he clenched his teeth to keep from asking her to say it once more. "However, since I am somewhat of an expert on fashion, I'd say that the elegant fall of the mail coach knot you're wearing this evening suits the structure of your face. The sapphire pin could make one imagine that your eyes are blue—"

"But you know differently."

Her cheeks went pink before she drew in a breath and settled her hand over her middle. Before he could stop the thought, he wondered if she was experiencing the *fluttering* his sister had mentioned.

"You are determined to be disagreeable. I have made my attempts at civility, but now I am quite through with you. If you'll excuse me..." She started forward to leave.

He blocked her path, unable to forget what he'd heard when he first arrived. "I cannot let you go without a dire warning for your own benefit."

"If this is in regards to what you overheard when you were eavesdropping on a private matter, I won't hear it."

He doubted she would listen to him, even if he meant to warn her about a great hole in the earth directly in her path, but his conscience demanded he speak the words nonetheless.

"Montwood is a desperate man, and you have put yourself in his power."

Her eyes flashed. "That is where you are wrong. I am the one with the fortune, ergo, the one with the power."

How little she knew of men. "And what of your reputation?"

Her laugh did little to amuse him. "What I have of my reputation will remain unscathed. After all, he is not interested in my person. He only needs my fortune. In addition, as a third son, he does not require an heir. Therefore, our living apart should not cause a problem with his family. And should he need *companionship*, he is free to do so elsewhere, as long as he's discreet."

"You sell yourself so easily, believing you're worth nothing more than your father's account ledger," he growled, his temper getting the better of him. "If you were my sister, I'd lock you in a convent for the rest of your days."

Miss McFarland stepped forward and pressed the tip of her manicured finger in between the buttons of his waistcoat. "I am *not* your sister, Mr. Croft. And thank the heavens for that gift too. I can barely stand to be in the same room with you. You make it impossible to breathe, let alone think. Neither my lungs nor my stomach recalls how to function. Not only that, but you cause this terrible crackling sensation beneath my skin, and it feels like I'm about to catch fire." Her lips parted and her small bosom rose and fell with each breath. "I do believe I loathe you to the very core of your being, Mr. Croft."

Somewhere between the first *Mis-ter Croft* and the last, he'd lost all sense.

Because in the very next moment, he gripped her shoulders, hauled her against him, and crushed his mouth to hers.

ABOUT THE AUTHOR

VIVIENNE LORRET loves romance novels, her pink laptop, her husband, and her two teenage sons (not necessarily in that order…but there are days). Transforming copious amounts of tea into words, she is the author of Avon Impulse's "Tempting Mr. Weatherstone" and the Wallflower Wedding series. For more on her upcoming novels, visit her at www.vivlorret.net.

Visit www.AuthorTracker.com for exclusive information on your favorite HarperCollins authors.